Greenberg walked with Jane to her car. She sensed that he wanted to say something to her. When she put her hand on the door handle, he finally spoke.

"Your nanny, Marlene . . . Did she get along with Gil?"

She frowned slightly. "Until they broke up, you mean. I really don't know. Why do you ask?"

"He's a violent man. A violent man with a wild, wicked temper. I wanted you to know exactly what kind of character we're dealing with here."

"You mean . . . Oh my God . . ." Jane's jaw dropped, and a violent shiver shook her. "You don't mean he might have *killed* Marlene!"

"I didn't say that. But we owe it to the girl to track her down as quickly as possible. You should follow every lead you've got. Keep us posted on anything that might help us. And as I said, we'll ask some questions, see what we can find out."

Jane was lost in a terrible mist of fear, as if reality had just been pulled out from under her. She got into her car, started it, and waved to Detective Greenberg as she glided out of the station parking lot, now uniformly dark with rain.

Marlene and Gil had quarreled violently, according to Helen. Whose idea had it been to break up, Marlene's or Gil's? If it had been Marlene's idea, could it have been because she'd been seeing another man? That would have maddened the hot-tempered Gil. Had his fury built until he was driven to punish her for abandoning him?

The branches of the trees looming over Packer Road whipped and swayed in the rising wind, as if trying to convey a terrible message to Jane. . . .

Books by Evan Marshall

MISSING MARLENE
HANGING HANNAH

Published by Kensington Publishing Corp.

MISSING MARLENE

Evan Marshall

Kensington Books
KENSINGTON PUBLISHING CORP.
http://www.kensingtonbooks.com

KENSINGTON BOOKS are published by

Kensington Publishing Corp.
850 Third Avenue
New York, NY 10022

First Kensington Harcover Printing: June, 1999
First Kensington Paperback Printing: May, 2000
10 9 8 7 6 5 4 3 2

Printed in the United States of America

To Martha

ACKNOWLEDGMENTS

Special thanks to my editor, John Scognamiglio, as insightful and supportive an editor as any writer could wish for; and to my agent, Maureen Walters of Curtis Brown, Ltd., an agent's agent in every sense.

Everyone sees you as you appear to be,
few realize what you really are.

—Niccolò Machiavelli
The Prince

One

"So get rid of the dog," Jane said, drumming her pen on the desk. She checked her watch: 3:07. She'd been on the phone with Rosemary Davis for at least forty-five minutes, and the conversation showed no sign of ending soon.

"But he's an integral part of the book," Rosemary whined.

Jane's patience had run out. "Rosemary, look. This is the only offer we have, and they're only interested in publishing the book if you'll deep-six the dog. It's up to you. Do you want the deal or not?"

There was a long silence. Then Jane heard Rosemary slowly draw in her breath. "I'll have to think about it," Rosemary said, calmer now. "Can I get back to you?"

"Of course. Sure. Let me know."

As Jane put the phone down, Daniel appeared in the doorway. He looked concerned. "Line two. It's the secretary at Nick's school."

Nick's school? Nick and Marlene should have been home by now. Jane picked up the phone. "Jane Stuart."

"Mrs. Stuart, this is Mrs. Glenn at Hillmont. Are you aware that Nicholas is still here?"

"Still there? Didn't Marlene come?"

"Well, obviously not."

"Has she called you?"

"No."

"All right, I'll be right there." Jane hung up, shaking her head.

"Is Nick all right?" Daniel asked.

"He's fine." She grabbed her coat, purse, and briefcase. "But Marlene's not going to be. I don't know if I'll be back today."

She hurried out the back door of the office to her car, drove through the alley to Center Street, and followed it around three sides of the village green, whose towering oaks blazed scarlet and gold against a cloudless October sky. At the far end of the green she turned onto Packer Road, which would ultimately take her to Nick's school across Shady Hills.

Within a few moments she had reached the railroad crossing. A police car blocked the tracks. She recognized the officer in the car as Jimmy Mooney, whose parents had owned the butcher shop on the green before they retired to Arizona. Jimmy got out of his car and sauntered over to Jane's car. She rolled down her window.

"Afternoon, Mrs. Stuart. Afraid you can't cross. Train derailed."

"When?"

"About six this morning."

"How did it happen?"

"Kids, probably, putting junk on the rails. Nobody hurt. The repair vehicles are still using the tracks. You'll need to take the other way around."

With a weary sigh, Jane nodded and turned the car around.

At three-forty-five, a full hour after dismissal, she walked into the school office. Nick sat at a small table near the door. He wore his puffy blue down coat and was coloring. He looked up, his dark brown eyes bright with anger.

"Mo-o-o-om . . ."

Across the office, laconic Mrs. Glenn sat at her desk, coat buttoned, purse before her. As soon as she saw Jane, she rose to leave.

"I'm so sorry," Jane said. "I don't know what happened to Marlene."

"It's okay," Mrs. Glenn said dryly, and trotted out.

Jane and Nick followed her.

"Mom, what the hell happened?"

"Watch your mouth, please."

"Where's Marlene?"

She shrugged. "Your guess is as good as mine."

They drove home in silence along roads that twisted through the wooded hills for which the northern New Jersey village had been named. Finally they started up their street, Lilac Way, the car's tires crunching through a thick carpet of fallen leaves. As they crested the hill just before their house, Nick sat up straight. "Mom, look."

Through the break in the six-foot holly hedge that surrounded the house, Jane could see the old dark blue Corolla that Marlene used sitting in the driveway.

Jane parked behind the Corolla, and she and Nick walked up the flagstone path to the front door of the chocolate brown chalet-style house. As soon as she unlocked it, Nick burst past her to the family room. The TV roared to life. This was what she had been keeping him from.

"Marlene!" Jane called from the foyer.

No answer.

She hurried upstairs and along the narrow hall to Marlene's room at the end. The door was closed. She knocked, opened the door, and drew in her breath sharply.

The room was empty. The bed was made, the lamp and the Hümmel figurines on the dresser were neatly arranged, and Marlene's belongings were gone—the jumble of makeup and jewelry on the night table, the ever-present heap of dirty clothes on the floor. Jane opened the closet. It was bare of all but the hangers.

She hurried downstairs to the kitchen. If Marlene had written a note, she would have left it there. But the counters were bare.

Jane sat on one of the counter stools, trying to control her rage. To leave without a word! Not that Jane wasn't secretly relieved. Marlene was a terrible nanny.

Trouble was, she was also the daughter of Jane's oldest friend.

Jane had known Ivy Benson, Marlene's mother, since Jane and Ivy were roommates at the University of Detroit eighteen years before. It was Ivy who had proposed Marlene as Nick's nanny. That was two months ago, in

August. Tina, who'd taken care of Nick for three years, since he was six, had left suddenly to care for her dying mother.

When Jane told Ivy of her predicament, Ivy suggested Marlene. Marlene had graduated from high school the year before. She had been offered a scholarship by a college to study acting, but at the last minute she had changed her mind and refused to go. Instead she was hanging out with a tough crowd in Detroit, where she and Ivy lived.

Jane questioned the wisdom of hiring friends. Moreover, she hadn't seen Marlene in twelve years. On the two occasions that Jane had visited Ivy in Detroit, Marlene had been in Fort Lauderdale visiting her father, Ira, whom Ivy had divorced when Marlene was two.

But Ivy begged Jane. Marlene needed this opportunity. Who better to care for Nick than the daughter of his mother's oldest friend?

Reluctantly Jane agreed, and from the day Marlene arrived in New Jersey, Jane knew she'd made a mistake. Marlene was far too self-involved to be charged with the welfare of another person—though it occurred to Jane that if she looked like Marlene, she might be self-involved, too. Marlene had grown into an exquisite beauty, with a petite yet voluptuous figure; silky, waist-length silver-blond hair; and a delicate patrician face set with startling indigo eyes and a pouting, sensuously downturned mouth.

Marlene performed her duties, but without interest or enthusiasm, apparently living for the evenings, when she would go out and return long after Jane and Nick had gone to bed.

Jane had decided that Nick deserved better. She would give Marlene a decent trial period—say, three months—then tell Ivy it just wasn't working out.

But now Marlene had solved the problem herself—though to leave without notice was inexcusable.

Ivy would have to know. She would still be at the insurance agency where she worked as a secretary. Jane punched out the number, full of self-righteous outrage.

Ivy answered on the first ring. "Basford Insurance. Ivy Benson speaking. How may I help you?"

"Ivy, it's Jane."

"Jane, hi." Ivy's tone was guarded. "Is everything all right?"

"Marlene's gone."

"*Gone?* What do you mean?" Ivy lowered her voice, undoubtedly to avoid being overhead by her cubicle neighbors.

"She never picked Nick up at school today. When we got home she was gone. Took all her stuff. I'm damn disgusted."

"Jane, there's got to be some mistake. Marlene wouldn't just leave. She loved it there."

"Obviously she didn't. Did she say anything to you about leaving?"

"No."

"Well, I guess there's nothing to be done about it. I'll have to find someone new right away, which I don't appreciate, I can tell you. She could have at least given me some notice. I'd have expected *that* from a stranger."

"Jane, listen. I'm sure Marlene will call one of us and clear this all up. Have you talked to any of her friends?"

"Ivy, Marlene never mentioned any of her friends. She kept her social life completely separate."

"What about Zena? She'll know where Marlene is. Maybe Marlene is even with her."

"Who the hell is Zena?"

"Zena Harmon, Marlene's best friend from here in Detroit. Marlene must have mentioned *her*."

"No."

"Zena grew up around the corner from us. She and Marlene have been friends since they were little girls. They both went east at the same time."

"And where is this Zena?"

"New York City. She's studying fashion design at FIT. That's the Fashion Institute of Technology."

"I know what it is, Ivy. Have you got Zena's number?"

"No, I'll get it from her parents. Don't worry, Jane. We'll find Marlene and make her go back to you."

"I don't want her back, Ivy."

"What do you mean, you don't want her back? It's her *job*. It's her *responsibility*."

"Tell me about it. But she's no good at it. I . . . didn't know how to tell you."

"Well, you haven't given her much of a chance, have you? She's only been there two months."

"I knew it the day she arrived. She's got an attitude. She's . . . sullen. Sometimes I'd call her, and she wouldn't even answer."

"That doesn't sound like her. She must not have been happy. Though she certainly said she was."

"Because that's what you wanted to hear."

There was a brief silence. "I'll get Zena's number. You're right—Marlene owed you at least some notice. I'm sorry." There was muffled speaking; Ivy must have had the phone pressed to her chest. She came back on. "I have to go. I'll call you." She hung up.

Jane checked her watch. Four-thirty. Better think about dinner.

She called Giorgio's, the Italian place down in the village that delivered, and ordered a sausage pizza, Nick's favorite. Then she called Nannies Unlimited, the agency through which she'd found Tina. Pia Graven, the owner, remembered Jane and said she had several excellent candidates. She promised to set up some interviews immediately.

Nick wandered into the kitchen and stopped at the dishes of food and water he'd set out that morning for Winky, the five-year-old cat that was the light of his life. He stared down at the dishes on their garish red-and-blue vinyl Spider Man place mat, a puzzled frown on his face. Jane noticed that the dishes were nearly full.

"Mom, have you seen Winky?"

"No, honey, I haven't. I'm sure she's around here somewhere."

"She isn't. I looked."

That was all Jane needed—for Nick to lose his nanny *and* his cat on the same day.

"Do you think she's outside?" he asked.

"No, of course not. You know she's not allowed outside." Too many neighborhood pets had vanished in the dark woods or been found mauled by wild animals to let Winky venture out of her pampered abode. "She'll turn up."

Nick thought for a moment, then gave a reluctant nod. "I'm hungry."

"Pizza's coming."

"Yes! Mom, is Marlene coming back?"

"No, honey, she's not." *Not even if she wants to.*

"That's good. I hate her."

"You hate her! You never told me that."

"Why would I? What would you have done about it?"

She stared at him, feeling a rush of guilt at having ignored his needs for Ivy and Marlene's sake. Nick mattered more than anyone. He was all she had now. She grabbed him and hugged him tight.

"Ouch! Mom, cut it out!" He squirmed, scrunching up his face. He looked so much like Kenneth when he did that. She felt the lonely shiver that had become so familiar since Kenneth's death two years ago. Would the feeling ever go away?

Reluctantly, she let Nick go. "Come on," she said, "let's go watch for the pizza man."

At that moment they heard a scratching sound and stopped. It was coming from the back hall. Nick ran ahead of Jane through the kitchen. When they reached the hall, a loud plaintive meow came from behind the door to the garage. Nick threw open the door.

"Winky!"

The small tortoiseshell cat bounded into the house, glared at them, and let out an angry yowl.

Nick scooped her into his arms. "Winky, you bad, bad girl, what were you doing out there?" He slid a suspicious glance at Jane. "Mom, did you let her out when you went to work this morning? She must have been out there all day!"

Jane was always careful not to let Winky out when she opened the door to the garage, though she supposed it was possible the cat had slipped past her.

"If I did," Jane said solemnly, "I'm terribly sorry." She patted Winky's mottled orange-and-black head. "Sorry, Wink."

Suddenly Winky leaped from Nick's arms, raced across the kitchen, and disappeared down the stairs to the basement, where her litter box resided.

"Oh, poor Winky!" Nick wailed.

The doorbell rang.

"Pizza man," Jane sang out, grateful for the distraction, and they hurried to the front door.

Two

At nine-thirty the next morning Jane stumbled into the office, her arms overflowing with the manuscripts she'd read the night before. Daniel sat at his desk against the far wall, engrossed in a single manuscript perfectly centered on his otherwise empty desk.

He looked especially handsome today in a starched white shirt, which contrasted nicely with his coffee-colored skin, and a narrow maroon tie. His navy blue blazer hung on the back of his chair. Dear Daniel, always so professional. He was one of the most honorable people Jane knew, a young man she felt lucky to call her friend. If she'd been ten years younger, she'd have been jealous of his fiancée, Laura. Oh, hell, Jane *was* jealous of Laura.

Jane dropped the manuscripts on the credenza, where submissions waited to be rejected. She glanced out the window. Across Center Street on the village green, falling leaves swirled around the white Victorian bandstand. A toddler chased the flying bits of color while his white-uniformed nanny looked on.

Jane crossed to the closet, hung up her coat, and pushed the sliding door a little too hard. It shut with a bang. She dropped into the armchair facing Daniel's desk. "Mail yet?"

He nodded. "Opened, sorted, and on your desk."

"Any checks?"

"Just one small one. The signing advance on Marilyn McKenna's Regency romance."

Jane wrinkled her nose. The commission on that check wouldn't even cover a week's expenses. She felt that stab of fear that had visited her so often since Kenneth's death, when his clients had offered their condolences and decamped to the William Morris Agency and International Creative Management and the other super agencies. Leaving Jane with what had previously been gravy: her roster of about thirty writers of genre fiction—mysteries, romances, horror novels, and the like. Not that Jane didn't make money selling their books. Most of these writers wrote two or three books a year, earning handsome if not extravagant livings from their advances and royalties. But none of Jane's clients was at the level that Kenneth's had been.

She gave Daniel a benign smile. "What else interesting?"

Grinning mischievously, he opened a drawer of his desk, whipped out a cover flat—the cover of a paperback not yet bound onto the book—and held it aloft for inspection.

It was for a historical romance Jane had handled. *Sunset*

Splendor, read the swirling gold-foiled title at the top, and at the bottom swirled the author's name, *Rhonda Redmond*. In between, against a purple-and-gold prairie sunset, an impressively muscled man lay naked on the ground while a voluptuous woman, equally naked, sat astride him, her head thrown back in ecstasy, her mass of fire-colored hair hanging straight down behind her. All that saved the painting from being all-out pornography was a spray of roses in the foreground, their delicate peach and yellow petals strategically positioned.

"Subtle," Jane said dryly.

"I thought you'd appreciate it."

"Wait till Bertha sees it," Jane said, referring to the author by her real name—Bertha Stumpf.

"She has. She called this morning. She loves it." With a chuckle Daniel dropped the cover back into the drawer.

"I don't think I can take any more mail," Jane said. "Any calls?"

Abruptly Daniel's face turned serious, uneasy. From the same drawer he removed a pink message slip.

"Let me guess," Jane said. "Roger called."

"He's still furious. He wants to know what Arliss said."

Jane stared bleakly into the middle distance.

The continuing problem of Roger Haines, her biggest client. . . .

She and Roger had met, of all places, at Kenneth's funeral. Jane, standing on the steps of Shady Hills's St. John's Episcopal Church after the service, greeting mourners, had found herself face-to-face with this distinguished-looking man in his late forties who explained that when Kenneth had been an editor, he had bought

Roger's first novel. Roger had always admired Kenneth tremendously, he told Jane, offered his sympathy, and left.

Six months later he called Jane and asked if she would meet with him. He had left his agent, he said, and was looking for new representation. He wondered if Jane would be interested. Jane felt insecure at the prospect of handling books without cleavers or cleavage on their covers, but she met with him nonetheless. They agreed to work together. She found him charming—self-effacing yet stinging when he chose to be.

She also found him extremely attractive—a feeling she suppressed as long as she could. After a year she could suppress it no longer. It was a feeling she knew Roger shared. One afternoon he invited her to his apartment on the Upper West Side of Manhattan to discuss a new manuscript. By page six they were locked in a devouring kiss. They made love, and if Roger wasn't Kenneth, he was special in his own way, tender and kind.

But then Jane pulled back. It wasn't right, it was too soon, he *wasn't* Kenneth. She needed more time, she told Roger, and he said he understood, he would wait.

In the meantime, they remained close, working to build his career.

Then the quality of his work started to fall. *A Better Place,* his tenth novel, was not his best work, and both Jane and Millennium House, his publisher, told him so. But Millennium accepted the book, hoping it was an anomaly.

It wasn't. Roger then gave Jane the manuscript of a new novel, something he'd kept a secret until he was finished. He had called it *In the Name of the Mother*. It was, he said, his finest work yet.

After Jane read it, she was sure that either Roger had lost his mind or she had. So she gave the manuscript to Daniel, whose judgment she trusted even more than her own. Daniel was unequivocal. "This," he pronounced, "is garbage."

How to tell Roger? Jane stalled as long as she could, until Roger demanded to know what she thought. So she made an appointment to meet with him and, at this time yesterday, arrived at her office resolved to tell him the truth.

The trouble was, she'd left the manuscript, on which she'd written her many comments, at home. Freudian, no doubt. Roger was due in the office within the hour. Daniel, always eager to help, drove to Jane's house to retrieve it, while Jane waited for Roger.

By the time Roger arrived, Daniel had returned from Jane's house with the manuscript, and Jane had it ready on her desk. But when she began to talk about it, Roger cut her off. He was clearly agitated; she could tell he'd been drinking. They could discuss the manuscript later, he said. He had more urgent business.

There had been no advertisement in Sunday's *New York Times Book Review* section for *A Better Place*. He was incensed. He reminded Jane that Millennium had promised them a "big push" for this book. So far they hadn't given it even a gentle shove. Roger demanded that Jane force the publisher to make good.

After Roger left, Jane phoned his editor, Arliss Krauss, who with characteristic bluntness informed Jane that *A*

Better Place was dying in the stores and that Millennium had no intention of throwing good money after bad by promoting it. Or by publishing Roger again.

Jane had hung up in shock, confounded as to how to break this devastating news to poor Roger.

Motionless behind his desk, Daniel was watching her. "So . . . what *did* Arliss say?"

"The book's dead. The returns are already flooding in. They'll probably get back more copies than they shipped."

Daniel looked outraged. "Well, they haven't *done* much for it. I thought they planned a big—"

"Push, that's right, a big push. Forget it. Not after they got those low advance orders. But you haven't heard the worst of it. They're dropping Roger."

Daniel just stared. The phone rang, and he shook himself from his amazement and answered it. "Jane Stuart Literary Agency. . . . Oh, yes, Roger. . . . Yes, she's just come in. Let me see if she's free." He pressed hold and raised his thin brows in inquiry.

Jane regarded him briefly, then sighed. "All right." She took the receiver. " 'Morning, Roger," she said with forced cheerfulness.

"Did you speak to Arliss?" Roger's gravelly tones were anything but cheerful.

"Yes. It's not good."

"What did she say?"

"Can you come in? We need to talk."

"Not today, no. I have an appointment in New York." He sounded irritated. "Don't be coy, Jane. Just tell me."

"No, I want to see you. How about breakfast tomorrow?"

"All right, fine. Meet me at Whipped Cream at ten."

She handed the receiver back to Daniel.

"Is he going to rewrite the book?" he asked, obviously already thinking ahead to the process of finding Roger a new publisher.

"He will if he wants a career. . . . This is the last thing I need right now."

"Did you find Marlene?"

"Sure didn't. She's gone."

"*Gone?*"

"Yup. Flown the coop. Without even a 'Dear Jane' letter."

"But why?"

"Guess she disliked us as much as we disliked her. I can't ask her, 'cause I don't know where she is."

"How did she leave?"

"Good question. The car she used was in the driveway. So she either called a cab or got a ride."

"To where?"

"No idea. Her mother thinks she's with a friend from Detroit who came out here at the same time Marlene did. Girl named Zena. She's in New York."

"So you think someone gave Marlene a ride to Zena's?"

"Maybe. Maybe Zena herself. We don't know."

"Did you call Zena?"

"Not yet. Ivy's getting her number."

"How do you know Marlene isn't with someone else?"

"I don't. Trouble is, I don't know any of her friends.

She never talked about them. I don't even know where she went all those late nights."

Daniel gave her a funny look. She knew what he was thinking: Jane should have made it her business to know what Marlene was up to, where she went. And he was right. Jane had owed the girl at least that. After all, Marlene was the daughter of Jane's oldest friend, Jane's responsibility.

"She hung out at the Roadside Tavern," Daniel said.

She looked at him, nonplussed. "How the hell do you know that?"

"She told me."

"When?"

"At your party."

Three weeks ago Jane had thrown a party to celebrate the publication of *A Better Place*. Her home had been the perfect venue for the party, because three weeks earlier Roger had moved from his New York apartment to a rented bungalow Jane had been only too happy to find for him in Shady Hills, only half a mile from her house.

Roger said he had fallen in love with the village during his visits to Jane's office. He told Jane the peace and quiet would help his writing. And since Shady Hills was only twenty-five miles due west of New York, he could still pop into the city whenever he had to.

Jane went all out for the party. She had it catered by Special Occasions, the people a few doors down the street from her office. She invited Arliss, of course, and Bill Parent, Arliss's editor in chief, and various others at Millennium who had been involved in the book's publication. Just for fun, she invited Audrey and Elliott Fairchild from across the street. And, of course, Daniel and Laura were there.

So was Marlene. Jane had considered asking her to help with the party, but then had thought better of it. Everything had to be perfect. So Marlene had mingled as a guest.

"The Roadside Tavern?" Jane said.

Daniel nodded. "On Highland Road."

"I know where it is." It was the worst kind of sleazy low-life dump.

"I figured you knew," Daniel said.

"No." Jane put a hand to her forehead and shook her head. "But I should have."

Three

At ten the next morning Jane sat at her usual table in the back left corner of Whipped Cream, the coffee shop across the green from her office.

Jane loved it here. It was just a little storefront shop, but its walls were of old used brick, and in the fall and winter a fire always roared in the fireplace that occupied most of the wall near where she sat. Jane's friend Ginny had brought Jane's usual coffee and apple-raisin muffin, and Jane sipped and munched as she made notes on a proposal for a romance novel by one of her clients.

This late in the morning most of the tables were empty. At the other back corner a young woman with frizzy black hair, whom Jane had seen here before, sat reading the *Wall Street Journal* while feeding chunks of muffin to her little girl in the stroller beside her.

Ginny appeared with the coffeepot. "Heat you up?"

"Mm, thanks," Jane said. The coffee made a satisfying gurgling sound as Ginny refilled her mug. Ginny surveyed the shop with its one other customer, then cast a surreptitious glance behind the counter. Charlie, the shop's often-grouchy owner, was nowhere in sight.

"He's still at the post office," Ginny said softly. "Mind company for a minute?"

"No, I'd love it," Jane said, grateful for the distraction. Ginny grabbed a mug for herself from the counter, filled it with coffee, and plunked down opposite Jane.

Jane was awfully fond of Ginny. They were both members of the same knitting club, which met every other Tuesday night, and occasionally they went to movies or shopping together. The light of Ginny's life was Rob, a struggling silver-jewelry designer who was never as romantically demonstrative as Ginny would have liked. Often she and Jane discussed their relationships: Ginny confiding her uncertainty about a future with Rob, Jane confiding her wish to take her relationship with Roger to the next level. Ginny, ever brutally honest, made no secret of her dislike for Roger, whom she called an insincere opportunist. Jane felt her assessment was completely wrong, and they agreed to disagree.

"Roger meeting you?" Ginny asked.

Jane stared at her in surprise. "How'd you know?"

Ginny gave a little shrug. "The way you're acting. Kind of expectantly nervous."

Jane laughed. "That about describes it. I am nervous. We're having major trouble with his publisher."

"And he thinks it's all your fault, right?" Ginny shook her head slightly in indignation, her dark curls shaking.

"Well . . . yes, partly," Jane admitted. "The agent often

gets blamed for what the publisher does—or doesn't do," she added ruefully.

Ginny said nothing, clearly restraining herself.

"I know you don't like Roger, Ginny, but I do, and I want to help him. Even if I didn't ... care for him, I'd still want to help him as his agent."

"I know, I know," Ginny said, and sipped her coffee. "Let's talk about someone else. How's that adorable little nine-year-old of yours?"

Jane smiled. "Nick's fine. But—I forgot to tell you—Marlene left us on Monday."

Ginny's eyes grew large. "Left you? Why?"

"I don't know yet. She must not have liked the job. Tonight I'm going to drive up to a place where she hung out, try to find someone who knew her."

"What place?"

"The Roadside Tavern."

Ginny grimaced. "Nice crowd she hung out with. Wear your black leather and studs."

"Ginny," Charlie growled. She jumped. Charlie, barely five feet tall, glared at them over the top of the high counter.

"Back to work," Ginny whispered, and poured more coffee into Jane's mug.

Alone again, Jane returned her attention to the proposal but soon realized she could no longer concentrate and put it back in her briefcase. She dreaded this meeting with Roger. He was so sensitive behind his facade of urbane cynicism. This news would crush him.

How would Kenneth have handled this? That had always been a little joke between Jane and Kenneth—

how would he handle it? But the fact was, Kenneth always *did* know how to handle a difficult situation, always sailed through with a minimum of ruffled feathers.

He was her mentor in the truest old-fashioned sense of the word. At twenty-two, fresh from the University of Detroit with a B.A. in English and a head full of romantic notions about book publishing, she landed a job at Silver and Payne, one of New York City's oldest and most prestigious literary agencies. She would be assistant to Kenneth Stuart, former editor's editor, now one of the city's hottest agents. During their five years together, Kenneth taught Jane more than she ever imagined about being a literary agent and about publishing in general.

It was during their fifth year together that Kenneth (never "Ken," he'd told her from the start) encouraged Jane to take on clients of her own. It was also at this time that Jane and Kenneth became lovers. He called her his tall auburn-haired beauty. She moved into his apartment.

For Jane, living with Kenneth was a natural step. She'd been in love with him since the day she started working for him, because he was, quite simply, the most wonderful human being she had ever met: a truly generous man, innocent in his brilliance, totally devoid of pretension.

Leaving Silver and Payne with Kenneth when he started his own literary agency was an equally natural step for Jane. They set up shop in an office Kenneth rented on West Forty-third Street. Every one of Kenneth's clients left Silver and Payne to go with Kenneth. Jane's own client list grew.

A year later they married. One month before their first anniversary, Jane discovered she was pregnant. They were overjoyed. "Kids need grass and trees," Kenneth pronounced, and they embarked on a series of weekend explorations of Connecticut, Westchester, and northern New Jersey, searching for The Perfect Town. That was how they found Shady Hills, six square miles of woods and rolling hills in northern New Jersey's Morris County.

Hidden among the village's oaks and maples and pines sat snug Tudor, Colonial, and Victorian homes, many occupied by urban transplants like Kenneth and Jane. In the center of this pastoral haven lay the village green, its centerpiece an ornate white bandstand nestled among lilac bushes. The town still used the bandstand on the Fourth of July. Shading the green were massive oaks, among which ran brick footpaths that connected the bandstand to Center Street, which formed three sides of the green. Along Center Street stood gabled Tudor-style shops—the very picture of an English village.

One of these shops, a former real-estate office tucked between a gift shop and an old-fashioned druggist, was for rent.

From that point everything happened quickly. Jane and Kenneth bought the house on Lilac Way, rented the office, and within two months were living and working in Shady Hills.

Jane worried that the agency's image would suffer outside New York City, but Kenneth laughed and said a good agent was a good agent in New York City or in Shady Hills or on the moon. Anyway, the New York commuter train passed right through town, so they could travel easily to the city whenever business demanded—

making them still "New York agents." But any clients who didn't like it could leave. No one did.

Life was good, very good. And when Nicholas was born, Jane, an only child whose parents were both dead, felt her world was complete.

Heaven lasted six years. It ended on the day Kenneth, forty-eight years old, walked out of the Simon & Schuster building on Avenue of the Americas, stepped into the street to hail a cab, and was hit by a produce truck whose twenty-two-year-old driver was tearing into a sandwich and didn't see Kenneth at the curb.

Jane was told Kenneth never felt a thing. She wondered. She always would.

On the morning of the day Kenneth died, Jane had asked him for some advice on a difficult situation involving one of her clients and her publisher. Later, as Kenneth had walked out of the office to catch the New York train, Jane had reminded him about her problem. So handsome in his navy blue suit, he'd turned to her with a dazzling smile and said he'd come up with a brilliant strategy that he'd explain to her when he got back. He was excited that day, like a little boy, because of the deal he expected to make during his meeting at Simon & Schuster.

As it turned out, the editor he met with wasn't ready to make the deal. Later, much later, after Kenneth died, Jane, who had taken over representation of the client Kenneth had hoped to make the deal for, called the editor to follow up. The editor was no longer interested, and it seemed to Jane that the reason was that Kenneth was gone.

That was how it had been with Kenneth. He had the

kind of magical enthusiasm that got editors excited about a project simply because he was.

Kenneth's client eventually left the agency.

As for Kenneth's strategy about her own client, he of course was never able to share it with her. To this day Jane wondered what it was.

Life was funny. Cruel. Or just indifferent. Kenneth would have laughed, and said, "Better get on with getting on, my love," or something like that. And of course she would. Did. She still had Nick. And the agency.

How would Kenneth handle it?

At that moment Roger appeared through the steamy shop window. He waved to Jane and strode in, smiling heartily. He was underdressed, as usual—no overcoat, just a gray tweed sport jacket over black slacks and a cream-colored silk shirt.

He looked very handsome. She remembered the kiss they'd shared as he'd left her party, the softness of his lips against hers, the tickle of his trim mustache. She felt her face flush hotly.

" 'Morning, my dear." He kissed her cheek, then dropped into the chair opposite hers. "Feeling all right?"

"Yes, I'm fine. It's warm in here."

He gave a little nod, glancing back at the fireplace. "And how are things?"

"Hectic till I find a new nanny," she said, though she knew those weren't the things he meant.

He stared at her. "Why? What happened to Marlene?"

"That's right—you don't know. She left Monday."

"Why?"

"I haven't spoken to her, so I can only guess she didn't like the job."

"Why haven't you spoken to her? Where did she go?"

"No idea. She never picked Nick up at school. When we got home she was gone." She was getting tired of telling this story. "Her mother and I are trying to track her down at a friend's place in New York." Ivy still hadn't called with Zena's number.

Roger looked thoughtful, then seemed to shake himself from his reverie. "So! How is my old friend Arliss Krauss?"

Jane looked down at her half-eaten muffin.

"What is it?" he said. "You've *got* to tell me now."

"Roger, it's not good. The book's doing badly. You know they didn't ship as many as they'd hoped to, and the returns are heavy already."

Ginny reappeared with the coffeepot, smiling sweetly. "Coffee, Rog?" she asked, winking at Jane. She knew he hated it when she called him that.

For a moment he didn't seem to hear her, his gaze locked on Jane. Then he looked up distractedly and nodded. Ginny filled a mug for him and hurried off. Roger looked back at Jane. His lips were pressed tightly together, his nostrils slightly flared.

At last he said, "And they refuse to take any responsibility for that, don't they?" Before Jane could respond, he rushed on, "How do they expect the book to do *anything* when they do nothing to promote it? They've pushed me before. Why won't they now?"

"Roger, you know they've never felt this book was as strong as your others ..."

"And therefore decided it wouldn't sell as well, and therefore didn't bother pushing it, and so what we have here is a self-fulfilling prophecy." He leaned forward ominously. "They promised us advertising and promotion on this book, and they will keep that promise. You have to be firm with them."

"It won't do any good, Roger. They've made up their minds. They don't even—" She stopped. She hadn't wanted to tell him like this.

"They don't even what?"

She put down her mug. "They're dropping your option."

"What!"

She nodded.

He sat way back, blew out his breath, and looked down at the floor, clearly mortified. "Oh boy."

Her heart went out to him. "Roger, we have to move forward. There's no point in fighting Millennium about this. They're unmovable. The important thing is to start showing your new book right away, find you a new publisher. The sooner the better."

"You mean before the other publishers find out how badly this book is selling?"

She gave a tiny nod.

He laughed at her. "Don't be naive. They can find out all they want to know right now."

"Maybe, but you've had too many successes for another publisher to turn you away because of one flop. I know I can place the new book ... but you've got to rewrite it."

His gaze snapped to her. "I can't believe you're harping

on that again," he said, his voice rising. The young mother glanced over, then looked quickly away.

He was stubborn—a quality Jane hated in anyone. She forced herself to stay calm.

"I'm 'harping' on it, as you put it, because if you don't rewrite it, you won't sell it. It's as simple as that."

"Are you saying you won't submit the book as it is?"

"Is that what you're asking me to do?"

He shut his mouth tightly, took another deep breath. "Let's put aside the manuscript for the moment. I'm still not willing to give up on *A Better Place* as easily as you seem to be. I am asking you, as my agent, to meet with Arliss and that cretin she reports to, and demand that they advertise the book and set up the promotion they promised. I'd come to the meeting, but I'd wring Arliss's neck. Besides, it's what I pay *you* for. Tell them we'll sue for breach of contract."

"Roger, it's not *in* your contract."

Abruptly he stood, startling her. She stared up at him. "Do—your—job," he said, and walked out.

Jane sat very still, watching him pass the shop window. How dared he! The muleheaded fool.

But could she really blame him? *He* had written *A Better Place*, not she. Why *should* he throw it away so easily? She felt a pang of conscience. Had she fought hard enough? Certainly anything she could do to improve the book's sales would help Roger's future.

Lost in thought, she took her check to the register.

Daniel looked up apprehensively when Jane came in. "What happened?" he asked.

"I told him," Jane said, dragging herself past Daniel's desk and into her office. He got up and followed her in.

Jane tossed her coat on the credenza and fell into her chair.

"Told him what, exactly?" Daniel asked, sitting in her visitor's chair.

"That Millennium is finished with him. That they've written off *A Better Place.*"

Daniel winced. "How did he take it?"

"Badly." She looked down at her hands, spread flat on her desk. "My heart goes out to him—it really does. To find out not only that his publishers have given up on his just-published book but also that they want him to go away.... It's a terrible blow to his ego."

"Which is considerable."

She glared at him defensively. "When you're as talented as Roger is, you're allowed to have a big ego."

Daniel, his mouth tactfully shut, glanced at Roger's new manuscript, sitting at the corner of Jane's desk.

"So it needs some reworking," she conceded.

"Reworking!"

"All right, rewriting. I think he'll come around about that. But he's right—first we have to deal with the problem at hand. Millennium." She picked up the phone.

"Should I leave?" Daniel asked.

"No, no, stay." She punched out Arliss Krauss's direct number.

The call was answered by Arliss's officious young assistant, Roberto.

"Ah, hello, Mrs. Stuart," he said in his velvet tones. "What can we do for you today?"

"I want to talk to Arliss. Tell her it's urgent."

"Uh ... Arliss is—"

"Is she in?"

"Yes, but—"

"It's *urgent!*"

"Hold, please."

A moment later Arliss came on. "Jane, what's going on?" she asked impatiently.

"Arliss, I've just come from a meeting with Roger Haines."

"Oh."

"You have no right to sound so bored, Arliss. Roger is a respected author whose novel you have just published. A novel, I might add, for which you paid a healthy advance. You made Roger and me some promises when we made that deal, and we expect you to keep them."

"Jane," Arliss said on a massive sigh. "Jane, Jane, Jane. We've been all through this. The answer is no. I understand that you have to fight for your client— Do you have him sitting there?"

"No, I most certainly do not."

"Oh. Well, I can't help you. We should never have accepted that manuscript in the first place. We're going to lose a bundle."

"I'm going to have to speak to Bill about this," Jane said. "I want a meeting."

Arliss laughed wearily. "Go ahead. Speak to him. He's the one who decided all this." There was a brief silence. "Why don't you talk to other publishers? Maybe someone will want him—at much smaller money, of course."

"Oh, I intend to talk to other publishers, Arliss. We even have a manuscript."

"Oh yeah? How is it?"

"It . . . needs a little work."

"Mm. Jane, forgive me for saying this, but why don't you do yourself a favor and get rid of this guy?"

Jane felt her face grow hot. "That is highly inappropriate. You're talking about a man whom the critics have called a genius, the new Norman Mailer."

"Yeah, twenty years ago."

Jane was losing it. Her eyes flooded with tears. "A man my husband said was the brightest talent he'd ever seen."

This time the silence was long. At last Arliss said, "I'm sorry, Jane." She sounded truly sympathetic. Jane had never heard Arliss like this. "I wish I could help you . . . with everything. You're a good person and a good agent. You deserve good things. I . . . I'm sorry."

Jane wiped at her eyes, sniffed. "All right," she said quietly. "Good-bye, Arliss."

Daniel was staring down at the floor. Jane returned her gaze to her hands and was aware of him silently leaving the room.

Why was she reacting this way to Roger's misfortune? She knew why. Because she cared for him. She wanted to spare him from pain. For all his gruff urbaneness, he was a sensitive soul, easily wounded. He deserved so much better than the coldhearted treatment meted out by most publishers today. It was her job, as his agent, to protect him. But in this case she simply couldn't. The best thing she could do for him was help him pick up the pieces of his career and move on. He'd listen to her once the shock had worn off.

She slid Roger's manuscript of *In the Name of the Mother* toward her and began idly flipping through its pages, covered with her notes and comments.

Four

That night she drove north on Highland Road, a narrow, unlit ribbon slicing through the woods at the sparsely populated north end of town. Cara Fairchild, Audrey and Elliott's fourteen-year-old daughter, had agreed to baby-sit Nick.

In two days Jane would no longer have to worry about baby-sitters. Pia Graven had been true to her word and sent two prospective nannies to see Jane that afternoon. The first was a wonderfully warm and animated young Trinidadian woman named Florence Price. She had just lost her job as nanny to a little boy in Randolph whose father had been transferred to Chicago. Jane liked Florence immediately, but Jane controlled her impulses and said she'd be in touch soon.

The second applicant reminded Jane uncomfortably of Marlene—a sleekly beautiful young woman named Lillian who showed little interest in Nick and, when Jane asked her if she had any questions, wanted to know how many weeks of vacation she got and whether Jane had a pool.

As soon as Lillian was gone, Jane called Pia for Florence's references. Jane quickly checked them, found them uniformly glowing, called Pia back, and hired Florence. She would start work in two days.

That was a load off Jane's mind. But there was still the matter of Roger. She dreaded telling him she'd been unsuccessful with Arliss. He would go into a rage, throw more accusations. It would be horrible.

She slowed, knowing that the Roadside Tavern was coming up. Then it appeared, a dilapidated flat-roofed building tucked into the pines. At the edge of the nearly full parking lot a faded wooden sign stood on a pair of peeling posts.

Jane parked and got out. Approaching the entrance, she could feel the deep bass thump of music. She opened the door and it hit her in the face—screaming, bouncing Bee Gees disco. But no one was dancing. To her immediate right was the entrance to the bar, every stool occupied, the air thick with cigarette smoke. The bartender, a slight blond man, took his time filling orders, smiling as he traded wisecracks with his customers—all of whom, Jane noticed, were men and women about Marlene's age, late teens, early twenties.

To Jane's left was a larger room filled with small round tables at which sat couples, sometimes four people. At the table nearest Jane a woman with spiked mauve hair and three nose rings gesticulated vigorously as she spoke to a man in tight black leather and studs. Ginny was right!

Jane noticed a waitress coming toward her, a dark-haired woman in a fisherman's knit sweater tucked into baggy jeans. She was frowning slightly.

"Help you?"

"Yes." Jane wished they'd turn down the music. "Yes!" she shouted. "I'm looking for Marlene Benson."

The waitress gave her a funny look. "Marlene? Uh—wait a minute." She crossed the entryway into the bar and disappeared from view. A moment later she reappeared, followed by a hugely obese man of medium height with a silver-gray crew cut and pudgy, childlike features. He wore jeans that tapered at the ankles, giving his bottom half a triangular appearance, and a vast blue-and-white Hawaiian shirt.

"Can I help you?" he asked.

Jane repeated what she'd told the waitress.

"Marlene's not here," he said. "I heard she left town."

"Yes, she's my—" The music really was too much. "Can we go outside for a minute?" Jane yelled.

"Sure." He led her outside, where it was blessedly silent but suddenly biting cold.

"I'm Peter Mann. The owner. Now, you're lookin' for Marlene?"

She nodded. "She worked for me, took care of my son. She did leave, two days ago, but she didn't say where she was going. Her mother and I want to make sure she's okay. I understand she spent a lot of time here."

"Yeah." He considered her for a moment. "There's someone here you oughta talk to."

"Yes?"

"Mm, Helen. She's inside. She and Marlene were always together. Come on, I'll take you to her."

She followed him back inside and into the larger room on the left. It was quieter here, the music not as loud. Squeezing through the maze of tables, Mann led the way to one at the back, at which a young woman in a baggy maroon sweatshirt sat alone.

Jane knew the woman from somewhere. She was big-boned; Jane could tell she was tall. Her face was large and plain, pasty and rather flat, with large brown eyes set a little too far apart. The only makeup she wore was pale coral lipstick, messily applied. She had long dark brown hair pulled into a fat braid that trailed down her back.

As Mann approached her table, the young woman's eyes grew even larger and she frowned, clearly puzzled.

"This lady's lookin' for Marlene," Mann said, indicating Jane. He turned to her. "Didn't get your name."

"Jane Stuart." And to Helen, "Marlene worked for me."

Mann left. Jane pulled out a chair. "Mind if I sit down?"

Helen shook her head. She was still regarding Jane as if she had dropped from the ceiling.

"Were you aware that Marlene left?" Jane asked.

"Yeah." Helen spoke matter-of-factly. She bent for a filthy tan vinyl drawstring bag and took out a pack of Marlboros. "She's my best friend," she said, lighting a cigarette. " 'Course I knew."

"Where is she?"

"That, I don't know." Helen blew smoke that hovered in a dense cloud over the table.

At that moment the waitress appeared. Jane asked for a mineral water.

Helen was still studying Jane. "You know about Gil, right?" she said.

"Gil?" Jane shook her head.

Helen gave a little laugh of incredulity. "That's amazing you don't know him."

"Why?"

"Marlene was going out with him. They met here."

"When?"

"Couple of months ago. Right after she came to town." Early August. "And who is this Gil?"

"Gil Dapero. Marlene was, like, obsessed with him. At first he didn't notice her, but she kept at him—you know, flirting with him. She wanted him really bad, and she wouldn't give up till she got him."

"And did she? Get him, I mean."

"Whoa, yeah. Took about two weeks." Helen dragged on her cigarette, blew smoke, and studied it. "I told her it was a bad idea."

"Why?"

"Gil's dangerous. He's got a wild temper. Some people say he once killed somebody over some money in Newark. A couple of weeks ago a guy came on to Marlene, and Gil hurt him so bad he ended up in the hospital."

Jane's mineral water arrived, and she paid for it. "If she was so obsessed with Gil, why would she leave town?"

" 'Cause they broke up."

"When?"

"Uh . . . four days ago now. Saturday night."

That would have been two days before Marlene left. "How do you know they broke up?"

"Well, like I said, Marlene and I are best friends, so she would have told me, but she didn't have to because they had a huge fight right out there in the parking lot."

"A fight about what?"

"I have no idea. The next day Marlene came to see me at the store where I work—you know the Village Shop on the green?"

Jane nodded. She stopped there occasionally for a newspaper. That was why Helen looked familiar.

"Anyway," Helen went on, "Marlene came in and said she was leaving town." She looked Jane straight in the eye, as if challenging her. "She told me she hated working for you, and she was leaving."

Jane considered this. "I see. And even though you're best friends, she didn't tell you where she was going?"

"No. I just figured she was going home to Detroit. Why don't you check with her mother, see if Marlene's there?"

"I have. She's not."

"Then I don't know. She'll probably call me."

Jane searched in her purse for a piece of paper and a pen and jotted down her home and office phone numbers. "Do me a favor. If Marlene does call you, ask her to call either her mother or me. Then call me and let me know you've heard from her, would you, please?"

Helen took the piece of paper and tucked it in her bag. "Sure."

"Did Marlene ever mention someone by the name of Zena?"

Helen frowned. "Zena? Who's that?"

"Her other best friend," Jane said, and got up to leave. Then she had a thought. "This Gil . . . where can I find him?"

Helen's eyes widened in surprise. "He works at Olympian in Parsippany—that big industrial park next to the Dairy Queen. He's in the warehouse. You gonna go see him?"

Jane nodded.

"Why?" Helen asked, obviously disturbed at this idea.

"To see if he knows where Marlene is, of course," Jane said, as if talking to a moron.

"Well, don't tell him I sent you," Helen said, her gaze piercing. "I told you. He's trouble."

Jane took a last long look at the Roadside Tavern, little more than an oversize shack among the pines, before pulling back onto Highland Road and heading south. So that was where Marlene had spent many of her nights— late nights when Jane and Nick were cozy in their beds.

It was at the Tavern that Marlene had met Gil, a hoodlum—possibly a murderer if Helen's gossip was true— and relentlessly pursued him until he was hers. But then, only four nights ago, Marlene and Gil fought and broke up. The next day, Sunday, Marlene told Helen she was leaving, and Monday Marlene was gone.

Gil, apparently, had been Marlene's only reason for staying in Shady Hills. Marlene had hated working for Jane, Helen had said.

Negotiating a sharp curve in the road, Jane pondered whether she might have missed signs of these feelings in Marlene. The girl had never expressed anger or even unhappiness—had never raised her voice or snapped at Jane or Nick. On the contrary, Marlene's demeanor had virtually always been one of bored nonchalance. Behind that, Jane realized, had lain Marlene's dislike of Jane, and perhaps of Nick, her charge.

Jane wondered if she had given Marlene reason to dislike her. She thought not. But she hadn't given Marlene reason to like her, either. Because the fact was, Jane hadn't liked Marlene, not from the minute she'd laid eyes on the girl walking up the ramp to the gate at Newark Airport. Much as Jane had tried to like this exquisitely lovely creature, the daughter of her oldest friend, Jane had failed. And her dislike, she realized now, must have revealed itself in a cold detachment. Had Jane ever smiled at Marlene, laughed with her? She thought not.

You tend to like people who like you. Jane hadn't given the girl much of a chance—she saw that now—and a guilty sadness washed over her as she reached the end of Highland, turned left onto Packer, and passed the police station, its lights aglow.

And now Marlene was gone. What would she tell her mother about her few months working for Jane? Undoubtedly she would paint Jane in a very bad light.

Jane shrugged. She couldn't help that. She would apologize to Ivy, and even to Marlene herself once she was located. Finding Marlene—that must come first.

Marlene would call Helen, of that Jane was reasonably sure, but she doubted that Helen would keep her promise and call Jane when she heard from Marlene. Helen worked just across the green from Jane's office. Jane would stop in to see her in a few days if Marlene still hadn't called her mother.

Jane turned onto Grange Road, followed it to Lilac Way, and started up the steep dark hill toward home.

Five

Jane pushed scrambled eggs from the frying pan onto a plate, took toast from the toaster, buttered it, and set the plate on the kitchen table in front of Nick. He broke a corner off the toast and passed it surreptitiously to Winky, who sat on the table beside his plate, intently following his every move.

Jane, lost in thought, barely noticed. She stood at the sink and gazed out the window across the narrow backyard that sloped up to dense blue-green pines.

She didn't know Marlene at all; she saw that now. The girl might just as well have lived somewhere else for all Jane really knew about her. Not that Jane had imagined a different private life for Marlene. The truth was, Jane hadn't thought much about Marlene at all, beyond her being an unpleasant young woman and a thoroughly unsuitable nanny.

The phone rang. It was Ivy.

"I wanted to catch you before you left for work."

"I have a phone there, too," Jane said.

"I know, but I have to go to the office soon, and it's hard to talk there. I spoke to Bob and Jill Harmon, Zena's parents. She hasn't called them in over a week. She always calls them once a week. They're getting concerned."

"So why don't they call her?"

"They can't. Zena's never given them her number because her roommate works nights and sleeps days and can't be disturbed by the phone. Zena always calls them when her roommate isn't home."

"Do they have her address?"

"Not her actual address—a post-office box. Zena's afraid the checks they send her will be stolen if they're delivered to her building. Apparently she lives in a bad neighborhood."

"Apparently."

"Anyway, they've written to her at the post-office box, telling her to call them. When they hear from her they'll ask her if Marlene is there; then they'll let me know."

When Jane hung up and turned to the table, Nick was gone and Winky was licking the yolk from his plate.

"Winky! Stop that. Shoo. Shoo."

Winky gave her a resentful look and bounded off the table and into the dining room, where to Jane's distress she leaped up onto the antique mahogany hutch that had belonged to Kenneth's grandmother. Winky then jumped to the hutch's middle shelf and sat down primly between two of Jane's favorite Wedgwood plates.

"Winky ..." Jane said menacingly, approaching the hutch one slow step at a time. If she surprised the cat and grabbed her fast enough, she could prevent any damage.

She had managed to get within a foot of Winky, her arms outstretched, when Nick stomped into the room, struggling with the zipper of his backpack. "Mom, what'd you give me for lunch?"

Winky sprang from between the plates onto the hutch's top shelf, which contained half a dozen of Jane's most cherished photos in silver frames, including her and Kenneth's wedding photo.

"Damn!" Jane said.

"Watch your mouth, please," Nick said.

"Sorry. Honey, can you get her down? She listens to you. I'm afraid she's going to break something."

"Sure, Mom. Winky! Come down!"

Instantly, Winky jumped to the floor, walked over to Nick, and sat obediently at his feet.

Jane shook her head. "Maybe if I get some of that cat repellent and spray it up there . . ."

"Mom! How can you say that? How would you like it if I sprayed mom repellent?"

"You're forgetting one small detail," Jane said. "This is *my house.*"

Or is it? Jane wondered. "Come on." She sighed. "Let's get you to school."

Five minutes later they were heading up Lilac Way. At the top of the hill Jane turned onto Magnolia Lane, which took them past Roger's bungalow. She felt a sick weightlessness in the pit of her stomach as she anticipated Roger's reaction to what she had to tell him.

"So, Mom," Nick said suddenly from the back, "what *did* you pack me for lunch?"

She exhaled gratefully at the distraction. "Peanut butter and Fluff sandwich, no crusts—"

"I told you—I'm sick of peanut butter and Fluff."

"Oh, right. Sorry. Forgot. Never again."

"What else?"

"Cheese sticks, apple, cookies."

"What kind?"

"Keebler."

"How many?"

"Four." She waited for his ruling.

"Okay," he said, then added, "Thanks."

She smiled. He was a good boy; perhaps she would manage to get him raised all right. Alone . . . or perhaps not. And she thought again of Roger.

They were at the bottom of Magnolia now and turning onto Christopher, the school building visible just to the right across the street. Jane pulled into the circular drive and up to the spot where Mrs. DeSalvo, the principal, stood as she did every morning, greeting the children.

Jane rolled down the window on the passenger side and called out, "Hi, Mrs. D!" The older woman smiled sweetly and twiddled her fingers at Jane.

"Bye, Mom," Nick said, struggling to free his backpack from his seat belt. Finally he managed to disentangle himself and threw open his door.

"Bye, honey. Have a great day. I love you," she called. To her gratification, he didn't wince as she saw other children do. She hoped he never would. She waited for him to shut his door, when to her surprise he poked his head back in.

"Mom, don't worry about Marlene."

She just looked at him.

"I know you're nervous about her leaving," he said, "but I don't think you should be. Marlene wasn't so good at taking care of me, but she's real good at taking care of herself."

She smiled in wonder. "What makes you say that?"

He shrugged. "You can just tell. Bye!" He slammed the door and headed up the walk to the building.

Jane pulled around the drive and back onto Christopher, turning left to take the most direct route into town.

Nick was right: You *could* just tell that about Marlene. Beautiful, self-involved Marlene . . .

But that wasn't really the point. Marlene was no doubt fine, but Jane and Ivy needed to know *where* she was just fine. Most likely she was with Zena, her friend in New York. Once Zena's parents reached her, she would tell them Marlene was with her, and that would be that, at least as far as Jane was concerned. What happened after that was between Marlene and her mother.

In the meantime, Jane felt it her responsibility to speak with one more of Marlene's friends—Gil Dapero. She would stop in at the office briefly to drop off some manuscripts for Daniel to return; then she'd drive to Parsippany to see Gil.

Six

Later that morning Jane pulled into the parking lot of the Corcoran Industrial Park in the neighboring town of Parsippany. She switched off the engine and checked her notebook, verifying that she had the right building. She did. It was a warehouse painted in the colors of the American flag: a blue background, a wide red horizontal stripe, and white stars spaced along the red stripe. These were the colors of Olympian, the sporting-goods manufacturer in whose warehouse, according to Helen, Gil Dapero worked.

Jane entered through the only door in the building's side and found herself in a small reception room with painted gray cinder-block walls. An older woman with a shiny brown bouffant sat at a steel desk, typing very fast. "Help you?" she asked without looking up.

"I'd like to see Gil Dapero, please."

"Moment." The woman picked up the phone, punched two numbers, and spoke into the receiver. "Gil Dapero to the office. Gil Dapero to the office." Then she hung up and resumed typing.

Jane studied a display of football helmets on one wall of the reception room. She heard the door open and turned.

Gil Dapero was handsome—she'd give him that. She could imagine him with Marlene. He was of medium height, slim but solidly built, in a skintight white T-shirt and low-slung jeans. His features were even and finely carved, his eyes a startling pale blue-gray, almost silver, fringed with lush black lashes. She noted the fineness of his skin, smooth as a baby's. Wavy black hair swept back from a well-shaped forehead.

He strode into the room, his hands hanging at his sides. Jane noticed his arms, virtually hairless, sinewy, biceps bulging out of the T-shirt's short sleeves. He turned to the woman at the desk. "What is it?"

Without looking up, the woman pointed at Jane. He swiveled to her, his fine brows slightly knitted. He waited.

She came forward. "You're Gil?"

He nodded, wary.

"My name is Jane Stuart. Marlene Benson worked for me."

At the sound of Marlene's name he visibly flinched. "How'd you know I work here?"

"I asked at the Roadside Tavern."

"Asked who?"

Remembering Helen's request for anonymity, Jane shrugged.

"What do you want?" Gil demanded.

"I'm trying to find Marlene. She left on Monday, and I have no idea where she's gone. I understand you and she had a relationship."

He looked her in the eye. "That relationship's over—did you know that?"

"Yes, I had heard you broke up, but that was only two nights before she left."

"I don't know about that—I mean, her leaving. I don't know when she left, or why. All I know is we broke up, and I don't give a damn where she is now."

From out of the corner of her eye Jane saw that the woman at the desk had looked up, finally taking an interest.

Jane said, "Did she ever mention wanting to leave? Wanting to go anywhere? Please, anything you can tell me would be helpful. Her mother and I are worried about her."

He put his hands on his hips in a challenging pose. "She always talked about leaving. She hated working for you. Hated *you*, actually."

People seemed to take great pleasure in telling her this. Hearing it again now, Jane found herself growing alarmed. Why had Marlene so disliked working for her? The only answer Jane could come up with was that she, in her dislike for Marlene, had ignored her, treated her like a nonperson. She felt a sharp pang of remorse.

"I see," she said. "And when she talked about leaving, where did she say she wanted to go? Home to Detroit?"

"No. She wanted to go somewhere with me—that's what she wanted."

"But that's not what you wanted?"

"Not anymore, not after we broke up."

"Did she want to go anywhere in particular with you?"

"No." He seemed to grope for words. "She was a—a dreamer—you know what I mean?"

Jane made no response. She had no idea what he meant. They might have been discussing someone Jane had never met.

"Do you mind if I ask why you and Marlene broke up?" she asked.

He flushed darkly. "Yeah, I do mind. It don't matter. All you need to know is we're finished, and I don't know where she is. I don't want anything more to do with her."

Abruptly he turned and strode back through the door to the warehouse. The door clanged shut behind him.

The woman at the desk was typing again, but Jane could feel the other woman's gaze on her as she went out.

Traffic was heavy on Route 46 because of construction. Two lanes of westbound traffic squeezed down to one; then Jane was crawling past T-shirted men wielding jackhammers. She winced at the noise and rolled her window all the way up, inching along the road.

She forced herself to think about Marlene—really think about her, as a person. That was something Jane hadn't done before. Just who *was* Marlene Benson? Certainly more than just a beautiful girl. A girl with bad judgment, to have become involved with a man like Gil Dapero. It wasn't surprising that Marlene had questionable judgment when it came to relationships, when you considered that from the age of two she'd grown up without a father and with Ivy for a mother. Erratic, hysterical Ivy, the last person Jane would have imagined as a mother—though there had never been any doubt that Ivy loved her only child.

Ira Benson, Marlene's father, had done nothing for the girl beyond flying her down to Fort Lauderdale for two or three weeks every summer and leaving her in the care of his housekeeper while he tended to the rich clients of his law practice. So, basically, Marlene had had no father at all. Nor had Ira helped Ivy out financially—at least, no more than the court had decreed. Ira and Ivy's divorce had been especially violent, and the bitter Ira had done nothing to lift Ivy out of her near squalor, even though it would have helped Marlene, too.

That had left Ivy to fend for herself, bouncing from one secretarial job to another, never staying at any one job for very long because of her basic inability to get along with people. And while Ivy was at work, Marlene was out on the streets of Detroit with what Ivy had described as a "tough crowd." When Marlene graduated from high school and was offered a college scholarship, Ivy, who could never have afforded tuition, had recognized the scholarship as the opportunity of a lifetime. She was crushed when, at the last minute, Marlene refused to go. How much more demoralizing had it been for Ivy to beg Jane to hire Marlene as Nick's nanny?

But Marlene had taken the job. What had she expected to find in Shady Hills? What did she want out of life? Perhaps nothing more than good times drinking with her friends at the Roadside Tavern. Perhaps nothing more than a boyfriend named Gil Dapero. And when she no longer had him, and there were no other reasons to stay, she had taken off.

It was all very sad, Jane thought, finally veering off at the exit for Shady Hills.

Seven

She was fifteen minutes late for lunch with Roger at Eleanor's, one of the few decent restaurants in Shady Hills. Once Hadley's gristmill, it stood beside the Morris River, which ran through the woods about half a mile from the village center. Now the building was a country-elegant combination of rough-hewn wooden beams and the finest china and crystal.

When she arrived at the table, Roger was working on his second Bloody Mary. He always drank like this, though she'd never seen the alcohol affect him much. He rose crisply and kissed her cheek. He looked trim and smart in a black-cashmere turtleneck and gray-tweed slacks.

"Sorry I'm late," she said.

He waved it away. "You're looking very pretty today."

"Why, thank you." She'd tried. She'd worn a new wool suit in a forest green that brought out the green of her eyes and complemented her auburn hair, and she'd added a favorite silk scarf in a vivid mosaic pattern of russet and gold.

"Drink?" Roger asked.

"Just some seltzer, please."

He flagged the waiter and ordered it for her.

"I . . . ah . . . I'm sorry I walked out on you," he said, looking embarrassed.

"That's all right," she said softly. "Let's say no more about it."

He smiled gratefully. "Well." He stroked his mustache with two fingers, a sure sign he was nervous. "How did you fare with Arliss?"

"Not well. It's no use, Roger. They won't budge."

"You mean *she* won't budge. Jane, I told you to go over her head. I want you to *meet* with them."

She shook her head sadly. "Roger, darling, there's no point. They've done all they're going to do for *A Better Place*, and they're not picking up their option. To meet with them now would be—humiliating." She looked into his eyes. "We don't need them. We'll go somewhere even better. But we can't do that unless . . ."

He was watching her, waiting for her next words.

". . . unless you rewrite the new book. It's just not ready to show."

He sat perfectly still. His eyes narrowed to slits. "I can't believe you said that." He looked down at his drink and stayed like that for several moments, motionless. Then he got up, threw his napkin on his chair, and walked out of the restaurant.

She was getting rather tired of being walked out on.

The waiter appeared with her seltzer and a basket of cinnamon rolls. She looked up sharply.

"Will you be ordering lunch, ma'am?"

"Yes. Yes, I will. Bring me a menu, please."

Damn Roger and his childish rudeness. When she was only trying to help him. When she was the only friend he had.

She abhorred his behavior but understood his frustration. He still wanted to fight, whereas she had already decided to retreat.

She'd give him time to think things over, she decided.

Then, grabbing a roll and ripping it in half, she wondered once more how Kenneth would have handled it, and tears sprang to her eyes.

Eight

Since Florence would not arrive until tomorrow, Jane left the office at two-fifteen and picked up Nick at school. He gave her a scrutinizing look as he got into the car.

"Feeling better, Mom?"

She pulled away from the sidewalk and around the drive. "About what?"

"Marlene. Did she call?"

"No. . . . But I'm sure she will soon. It looks as if she's with a friend in New York."

"Oh!" he said, as if that settled that. "Then what's bothering you?"

She frowned. "Who said anything's bothering me?"

"Your eyes are all scrunched up, and you're leaning forward and holding the steering wheel supertight."

Immediately she forced herself to relax, leaned back against the seat, and eased her grip on the wheel. "It's some work stuff."

"What work stuff?"

"Well, Roger's publisher isn't treating him very nicely. I've been trying to get them to do some things they don't want to do. Roger's very upset."

"And you're upset because you love Roger?"

A laugh exploded from her. "Love Roger! Nicholas Stuart, what on earth are you talking about?"

"He kisses you sometimes. I've seen it."

"Oh, really? When?"

"At your party, when he was leaving. I was at the top of the stairs."

She shook her head. "You shouldn't spy on people."

He ignored this. "You do love him a little, don't you?"

"I'm . . . fond of him." Was she really having this conversation with her nine-year-old? "And you're right. Sometimes when you care about someone and that person gets upset, you get upset, too."

They were climbing Lilac Way. Jane turned into their driveway. As she pulled up to the garage she noticed that the front yard was thick with maple leaves of crimson and gold.

"Hey, let's do some raking!" she said.

"Raking!" He looked at her as if she were crazy. "That's boring."

"Nonsense. It's great exercise, and it needs to be done. *Jonny Quest* can wait."

"Mom," he said with forced patience, "*Jonny Quest* isn't on till five-thirty. *Rugrats* is on now."

"Well, the Rugrats can wait. We'll bring in our stuff and change into work clothes."

Despite a lot of whining, Jane got herself and Nick changed and back outside, where they got rakes from the garage and began dragging the leaves into two large piles, one on each side of the front walk. Nick had insisted that they leave the front door open so that Winky could watch them through the window of the storm door. She stood with her front paws up against the glass, opening her mouth wide in silent meows.

"Watch this, Wink!" Nick cried, and hurled himself into one of the leaf piles. He nearly vanished beneath the crunchy blanket of color, only his shiny brown hair showing.

"Hey, that was fun!" he said, standing and brushing off his jacket. "You do it, Mom."

"What! Are you crazy? And look at the mess you've made of our pile."

"Aw, Mom, loosen up. This is supposed to be fun."

She felt as if she were the child and he the parent. He was right. That was why she'd suggested raking in the first place—so they could have some fun, and she could get her mind off Roger and Marlene.

"Oh, what the heck," she said, threw down her rake, and fell into the pile of leaves. It felt wonderful, and she laughed as she couldn't remember laughing in ages.

"My, my, aren't you two having fun."

Jane poked her head up through the leaves. Audrey Fairchild from across the street stood on the walk between the holly hedges, smiling as if at two mischievous children. She wore a belted mauve sweater over a cream turtleneck and tan wool slacks. Her honey blond hair was pulled back in a ponytail, and her face was fully made-up, from her berry lips to her ashy eyelids.

Nick, as if sensing that the fun was over, the mood

spoiled, slouched into the house. Looking after him, Jane got up and brushed herself off.

"I feel so foolish," she said to Audrey.

"Foolish! Don't be silly. I think it's marvelous. I came outside to get the mail and heard you two." Audrey frowned in puzzlement. "I thought you had a lawn service."

"Yeah—us!" Jane said with a laugh. "Can't afford that quite yet, Audrey."

"Ah," Audrey said, but the expression in her blue-green eyes made it clear that the idea of being unable to afford something was completely foreign to her.

Jane, uncomfortable, added, "Not till I get that big best-seller."

"Mm," Audrey said. "By the way, I heard Marlene left."

"How did you hear that?" Jane asked.

"Roger told Elliott at their club."

Jane nodded.

"Any idea why she left?" Audrey asked.

"Apparently she'd just broken up with her boy-friend—"

"Boyfriend!" Audrey, to Jane's bewilderment, looked astonished. "Marlene had a *boyfriend?*"

"Yes, Audrey," Jane said, frowning. "Why do you find that surprising? She is quite a beautiful girl. . . ."

"Oh, I agree, I agree," Audrey blustered. "It's just that—well, did you *know* about that? You certainly never mentioned it."

"No, I didn't know about it, but it's true nevertheless. Anyway, she broke up with this young man. And she didn't like working for me, so"—Jane shrugged—"why stick around?"

"Why indeed . . ." Audrey said thoughtfully, eyes unfocused. For a long moment she stared down at the ground, crunching a leaf with the toe of her shoe. Then she looked up brightly. "So—have you hired someone new?"

"Yes, a lovely young woman named Florence Price. She's arriving tomorrow."

"Good," Audrey said, apparently no longer interested in this subject, because she was now studying the front of Jane's house, no doubt noticing that it needed a fresh coat of paint. She turned back to Jane. "Well!" she said briskly. "Don't forget my party Saturday night."

Audrey's husband Elliott was a cardiovascular surgeon, considered one of the best in his field. For that reason he was under serious consideration for the medical directorship of the New Jersey Rehabilitation Institute, one of the country's leading facilities. Which was why, as Audrey had explained to Jane, she was giving this cocktail party—to ingratiate herself and Elliott with the members of NJRI's board of trustees, who would ultimately appoint the medical director.

"Six-thirty," Audrey said. "Don't forget."

"I won't," Jane assured her.

At that moment a voice from across the street called, "Mother! I'm waiting!"

Jane glanced over at Audrey's house. Audrey's daughter Cara stood near the three-car garage, her hands on her hips.

Audrey laughed and rolled her eyes. "I promised to

take her to the Short Hills Mall. It's her favorite." Backing toward the road, she put out a cautionary finger. "Now don't forget—Saturday, six-thirty."

"Got it!" Jane said brightly.

"Bye, doll!" Audrey said, turned, and hurried toward her house, calling, "Coming, darling, coming."

Jane sighed and surveyed the masses of leaves. They didn't look like much fun anymore. She returned the rakes to the garage and entered the house through the kitchen. She peeked into the family room. Nick sat cross-legged on the sofa, engrossed in a cartoon. Winky lay asleep in his lap, a tight tortoise furball.

Jane poured herself a glass of Diet Coke and sat down at the kitchen table. She was glad Nick had Winky. Kenneth had given the kitten to Nick only a month before he died.

She remembered Nick's questions about Roger in the car. Did Nick think Roger would be his next daddy? Jane considered this extraordinary notion. Did she think so? Perhaps. It was possible. Though she and Roger had only made love that one time, they were becoming more and more intimate these days, and Jane felt ready now to take the relationship to the next level. She sensed that Roger felt the same way.

She roused herself from her reverie and got up to start fixing dinner.

"Mom?" Nick looked up from his spaghetti and meatballs, red sauce thick on his upper lip. It was two hours later. "Does Florence wear makeup?"

"I don't know, sweetie. You'll find out when she gets

here tomorrow. I don't think she was wearing any when I met her. Why?"

"Marlene wore a *lot* of makeup."

"Yes, that's true. She did."

"Marlene was mean."

"Was she?"

He nodded quickly.

"In what way?" Jane asked.

"She would never play with me. She was always watching TV or going to her room or talking on the phone."

"She talked on the phone a lot?"

"Not a lot, but sometimes."

"Any idea who she was talking to?"

"No."

"What she was talking about?"

He shrugged. "Sometimes she told people to stop bothering her."

"Really? Who was she saying that to?"

"Mo-o-o-om, I just told you, I don't *know*." He speared a meatball, looked up. "Mom, are ugly people nicer than beautiful people?"

She laughed. "What a question! No, what you look like has nothing to do with how nice you are."

He took a bite of the meatball and chewed it thoughtfully while patting Winky, who sat on the chair beside him, softly purring. He turned to her. "You're nice, and you don't wear any makeup, do you, Wink?" he crooned.

Jane smiled and shook her head.

The phone rang. Jane got up and answered it.

"Is Marlene there?" It was a woman's voice, whispery and unfamiliar.

Jane tightened her grip on the receiver. "Is this . . . Zena?"

The woman hung up.

Absently Jane returned to the table.

"Who was that?" Nick asked.

"Someone calling for Marlene."

"Who?"

"I don't know."

She picked up her fork, then had an idea and put the fork down. She jumped up, hurried to the phone, and dialed *69—Return Call. There was a pause; then a computerized voice told her the number of her last incoming call. It had a 212 area code. New York City. The telephone number itself Jane didn't recognize. She jotted it down on the pad of paper beside the phone. Then she dialed the number.

After two rings a woman answered. Jane could tell it was the same woman who had just called.

Jane said, "Is this Zena Harmon?"

There was a brief silence. Then, "There's no one here by that name," the woman said, and hung up.

Jane didn't try the number again immediately. She gave it about an hour, during which time she cleared the dishes, loaded the dishwasher, made Nick's lunch for school tomorrow, and watered her plants.

This time when she dialed the number an answering machine picked up. The message was in a man's voice, deep and booming.

"If you and I could just stay on this car," the voice said, "riding around and around like this forever, never coming up for air, I would die a happy man!"

Jane looked at the phone. "What on earth—?"

The man's voice continued, "Please don't miss the show—we need all the help we can get. Edith Mantell Theater, St. Marks. Oh, yeah, and if you want to leave a message, wait for the beep. Bye!"

Jane replaced the receiver while scribbling on the pad. She grabbed her briefcase from the floor beside the counter, opened it, and took out today's *New York Times*. Finding the theater listings, she took the paper to the counter and sat studying them.

When she had almost given up, she found what she was looking for in the Off-Broadway listings. Edith Mantell Theater. *Subways*, the play was called. "A true New York love story," a critic had said, "painfully real."

Jane tore out the listing and stuffed it into her briefcase.

The woman who had just called—Jane was sure she was Zena—was somehow connected to this man on the answering machine . . . who was appearing in *Subways*. Perhaps he could lead Jane to the elusive Zena, who in turn could lead Jane to Marlene.

It was a long shot, but worth pursuing.

She picked up the phone again and checked her watch. Six-thirty. Chances were good Daniel was still at the office. She punched out the number.

"Jane Stuart Agency," he answered in his soft smooth tones.

"Daniel," she said, "how'd you like to go to the theater tomorrow night?"

Nine

The next morning Jane sat in the car at the edge of the commuters' parking lot at the intersection of Route 46 and Beverwyck Road in Parsippany. She faced the highway, at whose edge stood a New Jersey Transit bus shelter. Florence was due to arrive at 10:38 on the bus from Randolph. Jane glanced at the dashboard clock: 10:34.

Last night Nick had pleaded with Jane to let him skip school today, or at least to let him take the morning off, so that he could come with Jane to meet Florence's bus. He'd pointed out that although Jane had met his new nanny, *he* hadn't, and wasn't it more important for *him* to meet her, since he was the one she'd be taking care of? Jane had laughed and called him a lawyer and told him he'd meet her soon enough. Besides, Jane felt strongly that school should not be missed except in the case of real illness.

At 10:48 she spotted the blue-and-red-striped bus in

the distance. She got out of the car and crossed the narrow strip of grass to the bus shelter.

Florence was the only passenger who got off. She saw Jane immediately and smiled a beautiful white smile as the bus's brakes let out a sigh and it pulled away.

"Hello, missus!" she greeted Jane cheerfully. She carried two large, tightly stuffed nylon duffel bags. Her coat, the same one she'd worn to her interview with Jane, was of navy blue wool with immense round buttons of light wood. Studying Florence more carefully now than she had during their interview, Jane realized that she was quite lovely, her dark complexion flawless, her black eyes large and slightly tilted, her hair cropped close to her small, well-shaped head. And all, Jane observed, without a touch of makeup. Nick would like that.

"Hello, Florence," Jane said, approaching her, and to Jane's delight Florence dropped her bags and gave Jane a hug.

"Welcome," Jane said. "It's good to see you." She led the way to the car, and they put Florence's bags in the trunk.

"So tell me a little about yourself, Florence," Jane said amiably as they headed north on Beverwyck.

"Well," Florence replied in her lilting tones, "you know that I have been working for the family in Randolph. The mister, he has been transferred to Chicago." Her face grew sad and she gazed out the window. "I will miss little Kerry."

"And before that?" Jane asked.

"I was in Trinidad," Florence said, cheerful again. "My family lives in a village just outside Port-of-Spain. My mother is there, and my brother. My father, he died many years ago when I was a baby. Also nearby are many aunts and uncles and cousins." She turned to Jane. "And you, missus? There is a mister?"

"No," Jane said, and Florence shook her head in sympathy. "He died two years ago. It's just Nick and me—and our cat, Winky."

"Ah, Winky!" Florence cried gleefully. "We will be in for some good times. Animals and me—we are very good together."

Jane smiled. She turned onto Cranmore Avenue, which would take them into Shady Hills. "Florence," she said, "I feel you should know that we had some trouble with the nanny we had before you."

"Trouble? Did she leave, or did you fire her?"

"She left. Without a word to me or anyone else, in fact."

"Whoo, just to disappear," Florence said, shaking her head.

"But that wasn't the only problem," Jane went on. "Even while she was with us she lived a rather—well, a rather wild life. She got involved with some people she shouldn't have gotten involved with. I blame myself partly for not keeping closer tabs on her, but . . . well . . ."

"You want me to behave myself?" Florence asked, her face all innocence.

Jane felt herself blush. "I'm sure you will, Florence. Please, I don't mean to offend you."

"Not at all, not at all," Florence said, making Jane feel more at ease. "I understand what you are saying and am happy to tell you that you have nothing to worry about with me. I am a good girl. I hope to make friends in your town, but I will make only good friends. If I go out, it will be on the weekends, when I am off." She looked at Jane, her face suddenly uncertain. "Sometimes during the week I like to go to Mass, but I would only do so if it was a good time for you. That would be okay?"

"Of course, Florence," Jane said, and gave the young woman a warm smile. They were passing over the one-lane bridge that crossed the Morris River. "Here we are in Shady Hills now. It really is a lovely place. I'll show you some of the sights."

And she began by pointing out Hadley Pond to the wide-eyed Florence, who Jane strongly suspected was a treasure.

That evening, in the darkened Edith Mantell Theater, Daniel's handsome profile turned toward Jane. He looked as if he were in excruciating pain.

"Was this absolutely necessary?" he whispered.

She gave him a warning look. The play *was* awful—three stories with no apparent connection to one another except that they all took place in the New York City subway system.

The sides of the scruffy little theater had been covered with Sheetrock that had in turn been covered with the most obscene graffiti Jane had ever seen—great sweeping rainbow scrawls of filth.

But she and Daniel weren't here for the play, she reminded herself. She scanned the audience. The theater was nearly full, mostly of people around Daniel's age, and they all sat in rapt attention as the play's lead, a mildly demented character named Sancho, whose dream was to charge at a subway car and win (whatever that meant), explained to a police officer what the subway system had always meant to him.

Jane, too, watched Sancho carefully, but not because she cared what the subway system had always meant to him. Ten minutes earlier, in conversation with an actress playing a ticket seller with whom he had fallen in love, he had said, "If you and I could just stay on this car, riding around and around like this forever, never coming up for air, I would die a happy man!"

The actor looked about forty. He was tall, well over six feet, and ascetically thin, with refined, aquiline features and graying blond hair that grew shaggy over his ears. Jane glanced down at her playbill. His name, it said, was Trevor Ames. She tapped the name with her finger and realized Daniel was watching her.

"What is it?" he asked.

"That's *him*," she whispered.

"Who?"

"The man on Zena's phone machine."

"*If* that was Zena."

A young man sitting behind Jane shushed them loudly. They returned their attention to the play, which appeared to be grinding toward the end of the second and last act.

A seeming eternity later the curtain fell, the cast took their final bows, and the lights came up.

"Now what?" Daniel said, putting on his coat.

"Now we go talk to him."

"Who?"

"Trevor Ames. That's why we're here, remember?"

"Well, I know we weren't here to see that play. Phew!"

"Come on, hurry up," she said, "before he leaves."

She led the way down the aisle, against traffic, and through a door to the left of the stage. The backstage area was a dank, old-smelling place that Jane thought bore more resemblance to the subway system than the graffiti-covered Sheetrock did. Actors hurried about in various stages of undress, but Jane didn't see Trevor Ames.

She squeezed her way through the crowd and into a narrow corridor with several doors on the left. On the second of these doors was a crudely lettered sign: TREVOR AMES. Jane raised her hand to knock, but at that moment the door opened and there he stood, tall and imposing in a billowing ankle-length gray-wool coat.

"Mr. Ames—" Jane began.

"Yes?" He smiled pleasantly, obviously mistaking her for a fan.

"Mr. Ames, I wonder if you could help me."

His smile was replaced by a look of confusion. His gaze darted to Daniel, who stood silently behind Jane.

"I'm looking for my son's nanny, Marlene Benson. She left without saying where she was going. Her mother and I are worried about her and are trying to find a friend of hers, Zena Harmon, whom I believe you know."

His eyes bulged from under bushy brows. "I—" he stammered, and shook his head.

"Trev!" a woman's voice called from behind Jane.

She turned. A young woman stood in the middle of the space they had just passed through, waving to Ames. She was petite, blond, and rather plain. Jane recognized her as the ticket seller to whom Ames had poured out his heart.

"Trev, honey," she said, "you'd better hurry or we'll be late for Gordon's party."

Jane turned back to Ames. He exhaled gratefully. "I'm sorry. I have to run." He moved Jane gently to one side and hurried off with the young woman.

"Come on," Jane said to Daniel, and she followed them. The stage door was just closing behind them. Jane pushed it open, Daniel behind her, and they emerged into the alley beside the theater. Glancing to her left, Jane saw the tail of Ames's coat vanish around the front corner of the building.

She ran after him. As she emerged onto St. Marks Place she saw him and the young woman getting into a taxi.

"Zena!" Jane cried.

The cab slid away from the curb.

"Zena!" she called again.

But the taxi picked up speed and pulled into traffic. As Jane watched, the young woman turned and shot Jane a hunted look through the cab's back window.

"I know that was Zena," Jane told Daniel, who had just caught up with her.

"*How* do you know that was Zena?"

"Because she was with Ames. She called him 'Trev, honey.' "

Daniel rolled his eyes in exasperation. "All you know is that you've found the man whose voice was on the answering machine—"

"—at the telephone number of the woman who called me yesterday."

"Who may or may not be Zena."

"Of course she is."

"How do you know?"

"Who else would she be?"

Jane stood on the sidewalk, uncertain what to do next, watching people pour out of the theater.

She took the playbill from her coat pocket, flipped through it, and found the biography of the young woman who had played the ticket seller. "Dorothy Peyton," she read.

"See!" Daniel said.

"Means nothing. It's Zena. Why do you think she won't tell her parents her phone number or her real address? Because she's living with a man twice her age! *Trevor Ames.*"

Daniel just shook his head.

Then Jane had an idea. Even selfish Marlene, if she knew how worried her mother and Jane were, would get in touch with one of them and let them know she was all right.

"We're going back in," Jane said.

"Back in? Why?"

"We'd better hurry before they lock up." She ran back down the alley, Daniel following, and they reentered through the stage door. The backstage area was quiet now, but all the lights were still on.

"Wait here," Jane told Daniel. "If anyone comes, start coughing."

He looked askance. "Coughing? Where are you going?"

She had already started down the narrow corridor where Ames had appeared. She went beyond his door to the next one, which was unmarked, and opened it. It was dark inside, and she found a switch and flipped it, illuminating two bare bulbs in the ceiling.

It was a storage room. Against the right wall stood a stack of immense, crudely painted panels. Jane surmised that the graffiti-covered Sheetrock would end up here at the end of the play's run, which she imagined would be soon.

Apparently the room also served as a dressing room. Along the left wall stood a long aluminum conference table. Three gray metal folding chairs sat before it, and on the table in front of each chair was a standing mirror and a discrete jumble of makeup, brushes, combs, pens, and candy.

Feeling like Goldilocks, Jane examined the first pile of clutter. Finding no clue as to its owner, she moved to the middle of the table. Beside the mirror sat a small stuffed panda, smiling mildly. Under it lay a slip of notepaper with words scrawled on it in ballpoint. Jane removed the paper and read:

Dorothy—Don't forget the party—7:00 tonight at Gordon's!

Bingo. Jane wished the note said where the party was. Then she could have followed "Dorothy" and Trevor. At least she'd found "Dorothy's" "dressing room." She took paper and pen from her purse and wrote:

Dear Zena,
   Marlene's mother and I are terribly worried about her and would like simply to know that she is all right. Please have her call her mother or me immediately. Thank you.
                                                    Jane Stuart

She added her home and office telephone numbers. She slipped the note underneath the panda, on top of the other note, then thought better of it and placed her note in the center of the makeup jumble, anchoring it with a lipstick.

At that moment, outside the room, Daniel began to cough loudly, a veritable attack.

Jane scurried to the door. As she reached for the knob, someone on the other side pushed it open, nearly smacking her in the face—Daniel, she assumed, come to warn her.

She found herself face-to-face with a bald young man with a trim reddish beard. Her heart began to pound.

The man's gaze bored into hers. "Who are you?"

"Jane Stuart," she said.

He glanced around the room suspiciously. "What are you doing in here?"

"I left my bag on the table."

"Why? Who *are* you?"

"I just told you—Jane Stuart."

He waited, blocking the doorway.

Daniel appeared behind him. "Jane, we'd better hurry or we'll miss the party."

Still the man waited.

"I," she said, haughty now, "am a literary agent." She opened her purse and made considerable business of removing one of her cards, which she handed to him. "Actually, I've been looking for the man who wrote this extraordinary play. I want him to think about writing a novel."

The man's face softened. "I-I wrote the play."

"Oh, dear." She looked him up and down, snatched back the card from between his fingers, and pushed her way past him. She took Daniel's arm and walked with him toward the exit.

"And what," she called back, "were *you* doing in there?"

Ten

It was nearly midnight when Jane walked in her front door. The house was quiet, Nick long asleep, Florence apparently having gone to bed, too.

In her study off the living room, Jane sat at her desk and phoned Ivy, who never went to bed before one.

"I think I found Zena," Jane said. "Petite blonde?"

"Yes, Zena's petite and blond. You don't *know* if it was Zena?"

"Well, no. She ran off before I could speak to her."

"Jane, what on earth are you talking about?"

Jane told her about the mysterious call, about dialing *69 and finally getting an answering machine with a message mentioning a play, and about going to see the play and trying unsuccessfully to speak to Trevor Ames and Dorothy Peyton.

"It's all clear now," Jane said. "I mean, why Zena wouldn't give her parents her phone number or address. It's because she's living with this older man, she's acting in this awful play instead of studying fashion design, and she doesn't want her parents to know."

"Well, I did speak to her parents today," Ivy said thoughtfully, "and they said they called FIT. Zena's never been there. She was registered but has never appeared. Bob and Jill are frantic. They've called the New York police."

"You see!" Jane said. "Zena never registered because she's acting in *Subways*."

"Why did she run away from you?"

"She wasn't really running away from me. I think she and Ames thought I was just a nutty fan. They were rushing to a party."

"Can't you reach Zena through the theater?"

"I left a note in her dressing room, telling her we're worried about Marlene and asking Zena to have Marlene call either of us to let us know she's all right."

"*If* this Doris Peyton is Zena."

"Dorothy."

"Whatever. It just doesn't make sense. . . . As far as I know, *Zena* had no interest in acting. And if, as you say, she knows where Marlene is, why did she call looking for her?"

"That occurred to me, too. I don't think Zena knew where Marlene was when she called, but I think she does now. Anyway, even if this woman isn't Zena—which I doubt—she still knows Marlene, and undoubtedly knows where she is."

"Jane, I want you to go to the police."

"The *police*?"

"Yes, that's who you talk to when someone's missing."

"Ivy, she's not missing; we just don't know where she is yet."

There was silence on the line.

"Give Zena a chance to read the note," Jane urged. "We'll hear from Marlene."

"I want you to go to the police," Ivy repeated. "If you don't, I will. I appreciate what you're trying to do, Jane, but it's time to stop fooling around."

"Fooling around!" Jane held her tongue. She sighed. "All right. I'll speak to the police in the morning. I'll let you know what happens." Better that Jane should go to the police than that Ivy should call them from Detroit in hysterics.

That night, Jane dreamed of graffiti come to life, malevolent rainbow-colored snakes that chased her up and down the twisting wooded roads of Shady Hills. She half woke with a start, reached out for Kenneth, but felt only the cold empty pillow.

Eleven

The next morning, Saturday, Jane drove to the Shady Hills Police Station, a one-story glass-and-brick building about a mile from the village center.

She explained to the officer at the front desk that she wanted to report her son's nanny missing and was shown into the office of a Detective Stanley Greenberg.

He rose from behind his desk, smiling politely but eyeing her in a strangely curious way. He was of average height and wore a tan tweed sport jacket that hung loosely from his broad shoulders. He had dark brown eyes and straight sandy hair that was combed neatly across his forehead.

He shook Jane's hand and motioned for her to sit in the chair facing his desk.

"What can we do for you?" he asked, sitting.

"It's my son's nanny. She's run off."

He opened a notebook on his desk and grabbed a pen. "Her name?"

"Marlene Benson."

"And I take it she lives with you?"

"Yes, for the past two months."

"I see," he said, writing. Even from where she sat Jane could see that his writing was small and precise, a schoolboy's cursive. He looked up. "And she came from—?"

"Detroit."

"Her age?" he asked.

"Nineteen."

"And when did you discover she was gone?"

"Monday."

"No word to anyone? A note?"

She shook her head. "Just took all her things and left."

He nodded. "How did she leave? Does she have a car?"

"No, she used my car. And it was in the driveway."

"So maybe someone gave her a ride. Any idea who that might have been?"

Jane shook her head.

"Do you know any of her friends?" he asked.

"I spoke with one of her friends, but the last time she saw Marlene was the day before she left."

"Did Marlene have a boyfriend?"

"Well, she had been seeing someone. A young man named Gil Dapero."

Greenberg's gaze snapped to her, his brows lifting. "She's involved with *him*?"

"Was involved. They broke up. I've spoken with him."

"How long was Marlene seeing Gil?" Greenberg asked.

"Since she got here—about two months."

He tapped his pen on his notebook. "I'd better get the basics. Your address?"

"Nine Lilac Way."

"You're Jane Stuart, you said. You're that . . . literary agent?"

"That's right. How did you know?"

Suddenly blood rushed to his face, an honest-to-goodness blush. Jane waited, smiling curiously.

"I was going to get in touch with you—someday, I mean."

"Oh . . . ?"

He nodded, his eyes lowered. "My sister went to a talk you gave about writing to her book group about a year ago. She really liked you, and, well . . . I've been working on this novel for a few years now. Kind of a police-thriller thing. 'Course it's not done yet. I haven't figured out the ending, and even when I do, the whole thing's gonna need a total rewrite. But when it *is* done . . ." He lifted his gaze eagerly to meet hers, his brown eyes bright. "Do you think you would—I could—"

"Of course," she said graciously, now understanding his strange stare when she'd come in. He really was very charming in a childlike way. "It would be my pleasure."

"Well, hey!" he exclaimed, tapping his pencil hard and fast now. "That's really nice of you. Thanks."

She nodded. Then all at once he seemed to remember why she was here. "I'd better get your phone number."

She gave him her home and office numbers.

He rose, all business now. "All right, Mrs. Stuart. Keep in mind that your nanny is a legal adult and has a right to go where she chooses. But we'll look into it, ask a few questions."

"Of Gil Dapero, you mean?"

He made no response.

"She spent a lot of time at the Roadside Tavern," she said. "You know the place?"

"Oh yes, that's where they all hang out. Peter Mann owns it."

She nodded. "That's where I met Marlene's friend, a girl named Helen. She works in the convenience store on the green. She said Marlene told her she was leaving because she'd broken up with Gil."

He chewed the inside of his lip as if considering his next words. "I'll be honest with you, Mrs. Stuart," he said at last. "Gil Dapero is the worst person she could have been involved with. I only hope for her sake that their relationship is really over. We'll see what we can find out." He rose. He seemed to be considering something; then he looked at her, and said, "Let me walk you to your car."

Emerging from the station, Jane noticed that a sharp wind had come up and that it had started to rain. Scattered droplets darkened the surface of the parking lot.

Greenberg walked with Jane to her car. She sensed that he wanted to say something to her. When she put her hand on the door handle, he finally spoke.

"Your nanny, Marlene . . . Did she get along with Gil?"

She frowned slightly. "Until they broke up, you mean. I really don't know. Why do you ask?"

"What I meant about Gil being the worst person she

could have gotten involved with is that— I shouldn't be telling you this."

She waited, watching him cast his gaze about.

"He's a violent man," Greenberg finally said. "A violent man with a wild, wicked temper. We had some trouble with him not too long ago. At the Roadside Tavern, in fact. Dapero beat a guy up real bad, but we couldn't pin anything on him."

"Why not?" Jane asked.

"Because everyone's afraid to tell us what happened, ed, especially the young man who got beaten up. Everyone in that crowd knows Dapero's reputation. They know—"

"That he once killed someone in Newark?" Jane said in a low monotone.

He glared at her. "How'd you hear that?"

"From Helen, Marlene's friend. Is it true?"

He shrugged, leveled his gaze at her. "Probably. We'll never know for sure. The guy we think he killed disappeared. But Dapero was the last person seen with him, and the motive was strong. Dapero owed the guy a lot of money."

"But surely those two things—the man disappearing and Gil owing him money—aren't enough to think Gil killed him."

"No," Greenberg agreed. "There's also the fact that Dapero has bragged about killing the guy."

"To whom?" Jane asked, alarmed.

"People . . . who talk to the police." Greenberg was clearly growing uncomfortable. "Listen," he said, lowering his voice, "I shouldn't have told you any of this, but I wanted you to know exactly what kind of character we're dealing with here."

"You mean . . . Oh my God. . . ." Jane's jaw dropped, and a violent shiver shook her. "You don't mean he might have—*killed* Marlene!"

For a terrifying moment he just looked at her, rain falling on his face. "I didn't say that. But we owe it to the girl to track her down as quickly as possible. You should follow every lead you've got. Keep us posted on anything that might help us. And as I said, we'll ask some questions, see what we can find out."

Jane was lost in a terrible mist of fear, as if reality had just been pulled out from under her. In a dream state she heard herself thank Detective Greenberg. She got into her car, started it, and waved to him as she glided out of the station parking lot, now uniformly dark with rain.

Marlene and Gil had quarreled violently, according to Helen. Whose idea had it been to break up, Marlene's or Gil's? If it had been Marlene's idea, could it have been because she'd been seeing another man? That would have maddened the hot-tempered Gil. Had his fury built until he was driven to punish her for abandoning him? Had it been *he* who came for Marlene on Monday?

The branches of the trees looming over Packer Road whipped and swayed in the rising wind, as if trying to convey a terrible message to Jane.

Twelve

At six-thirty that evening Jane stopped just inside her holly hedge, raked her fingers back through her hair, and gave her head a shake. Then she crossed the road to the Fairchilds' house. She'd been at the office since her meeting with Detective Greenberg—not the first time she'd worked on a Saturday—and it wasn't until she had arrived home and seen the cars lining the road that she had remembered Audrey and Elliott's cocktail party.

Jane was exhausted after a particularly trying day. Long ago she had made the mistake of mentioning to one or two of her clients that she sometimes came into the office on Saturdays. Now it seemed every writer she represented knew—they all talked to one another—she was sure of it—and the phone rang as often as on a weekday. Daniel, bless him, had started coming in on Saturdays, too.

Jane had decided this six-day workweek would have to stop. She needed to spend more time with Nick, and weekends were the only time that was possible. Though she tried to arrange play dates for Nick on Saturdays when she was working, she knew she herself should be with him. She wanted to take him places—the movies, museums, the park, and the town pool in the summer.

After all, Jane was all Nick had. Though he only occasionally asked questions about Kenneth, and showed no signs of trauma at having lost his father, Jane often worried that she alone was not enough. A boy needed a father. And if there was no father, he needed as much of his mother as possible. Yes, these working Saturdays would have to stop.

Today had been especially trying. Rosemary Davis had finally called to say she would not remove the dog from her mystery because, deal or no deal, doing so would spoil the integrity of the book.

Bertha Stumpf's friend Elaine Lawler, a writer whom Jane also represented, called complaining that her publisher never gave *her* fabulous covers like the one Bertha got for *Sunset Splendor*. When Jane reminded Elaine that covers like that would hardly be appropriate for her Regency romances, Elaine had said that was the trouble with publishing today—there were no freethinkers.

The last thing Jane felt like doing was mingling, but she'd promised Audrey. And Audrey and Elliott had come to Jane's party for Roger.

Audrey and Elliott lived in the biggest house on Lilac Way, a fifteen-room Tudor on a majestically landscaped lot. Jane climbed the wide brick front steps and rang the bell. The door swung open and there was Audrey, tall and busty in a snug lavender dress of some satiny material and matching high heels. She smiled a huge lavender smile and held out her arms to welcome Jane.

"Well, hi, doll! Come in, come in!" She grabbed Jane's coat and handed it to a maid, murmuring, "Guest room." To Jane she said, "I was beginning to think you weren't coming."

"No, no, wouldn't miss it," Jane said, grabbing a flute of champagne from a passing tray and taking a long gulp.

"Now," Audrey whispered conspiratorially, her sleek honey blond head close to Jane's, "let me point out the luminaries. Over there—the man with the little mustache—that's Allen Brown, who's on the NJRI board. You *must* talk with him a lot because he *loves* books. In fact I think he's even *written* one, and I told him our famous literary agent would be here...."

Audrey's voice drifted away as Jane, hypnotized by the sparkle of one of Audrey's swinging diamond drop earrings, was overcome by a wave of fatigue. She couldn't have avoided the party, but she didn't have to stay long. She really was too tired, and besides, she felt guilty leaving Nick alone with Florence so late again, especially so soon after Florence had started.

"... Okay?" Audrey finished.

"Okay."

"Have fun, doll," Audrey said, and hurried off to greet another guest.

" 'Evening, beautiful," came Elliott's baritone behind Jane.

She turned.

Elliott was one of the handsomest men Jane had ever known, perhaps even handsomer than Kenneth had been.

Elliott, who had once trained in javelin for the Olympics, was tall and matinee idol handsome, complete with crisp blue-black hair, dreamy amber eyes, and a wondrously deep cleft in his jutting chin.

He kissed her cheek. He smelled faintly of expensive citrus cologne. "Lots of people want to meet you tonight."

She smiled.

"You all right?" he asked. "You look tired."

That meant she looked terrible. She grinned and forced her eyes open wide, like Jacqueline Onassis. One thing about doctors, they could always see right through you. "No, I'm fine, El. Long day, that's all." She gestured toward the teeming living room. "Some do."

He shrugged, looking a little embarrassed. "You know Audrey."

A waitress appeared with a tray. "Cheese puff?"

"No, thank you," Jane said, and turned back to Elliott. "Now where is that little man with the mustache I'm supposed to meet?"

"Oh, you mean Allen. Yeah, he's been asking for you since he got here. He's got a novel he's working on, a serial-killer thriller set in a rehab clinic. He wants you to have a look."

"Mmm, does he now?" She pursed her lips politely. "There he is—by the piano."

Jane tossed her head and growled, "Let me at him."

"Thanks," Elliott said, winking. "You're a real sport. See you in a bit."

Jane headed for Allen Brown, the balding little man with the Chaplin mustache who was leaning drunkenly on Audrey's beautiful baby grand. Some champagne sloshed from his glass onto the instrument's mirrorlike black surface. Jane hated his novel already. She'd get this over with, plead a headache, and leave.

Passing the archway that led from the living room into the dining room, she caught a glimpse of the balcony that ran the length of the back of the house. Abruptly she stopped and looked again.

There was Roger. On the balcony, drink in hand, chatting and laughing with a willowy redhead in an emerald velvet cocktail dress. What was he doing here? Damn, and she looked like hell.

She straightened her shoulders, put on a bright smile, and made her way through the dining room. As she approached the balcony, Roger saw her and did his own double take. His smile vanished. He raised his free hand in feeble greeting, then returned his attention to the redhead, whose face Jane could now see. She looked unutterably bored, nodding every so often and stealing glances into the dining room.

Jane stepped through the French doors onto the balcony. Roger and the redhead were the only ones here.

"Hello, Jane," Roger said. Clearly uncomfortable to see her after his second walkout, he turned back to the redhead, not introducing Jane, who just stood there, unsure what to do.

Roger, apparently, had decided to proceed as if she weren't there. "So anyway," he said to his companion, "here's this hideous armchair, abandoned by the previous tenants, filling half my study—and I can't get rid of it! Soon it becomes an obsession—I simply have to get rid of that chair at all costs!"

He was talking rapidly, the way he did when he was nervous.

"Well," he went on, "one day at my health club I mention my little problem to Elliott, and he tells me about a cliff very near here, where for years people have thrown away their . . . unthrowables! Even local builders dump all their scraps there by cover of night!

"Well, you can imagine my joy. Somehow I get the monstrous thing into the trunk of my car, rope it down, and drive it over to this cliff. I untie the chair and am about to heave it over, when out of the blue appears this fierce troll of a man who tells me I can't! It seems he's bought this land to build houses—'luxury homes,' he calls them—and how dare I 'defile' his property by dumping my garbage on it? I point out that people have been doing so for years, but he says it doesn't matter, they have to stop—"

"Will you please excuse me?" the redhead broke in, clearly unable to bear more. "I see someone I know." She made a fast escape, shooting Jane a beleaguered look as she passed into the dining room.

Still Jane stood, saying nothing.

"How are you?" Roger asked stiffly.

"Fine, Roger, and you?"

"Just fine, thank you. I wasn't aware you knew Elliott and Audrey."

"I live across the street, Roger, remember? They were at the party I threw for you."

"Ah, yes, that's right. Well, I didn't know them then. I only just met Elliott at my health club."

"So I heard. Roger, what's wrong? Why are you acting so strange?"

His gaze darted about, as if he were seeking an escape route. But she kept her eyes trained on him, holding him there.

At last he said, "I gather you haven't received my letter."

"Letter? What letter?"

"I sent you a letter. I'm ... dismissing you."

A violent chill passed through her. "You're what?"

He brought himself up, swallowed. "Your services are no longer required."

Her heart began to thud. She breathed out through her nostrils. "And may I ask why?" she asked, equally formal.

"I'll be giving my new book—without revisions—to an agent who believes in it."

"I see. And have you found this agent yet?"

"Yes, as a matter of fact I have."

"Roger," she said, the stiffness falling away, "*why*? Why are you doing this?"

"Because you failed with Millennium. You know that. What did you expect me to do? When I needed you most, you caved in."

For a moment she simply stared at him. She could tell he was trying hard to look unruffled, but his voice had held a whiny tone, and there was a look of hurt and shame in his eyes.

"What about ... us?" she asked.

He looked down.

"I see," she said, fighting to maintain her dignity.

"Roger, you know I wish you only the best, in your career"—her voice broke—"and your life."

His gaze remained downcast.

She turned and walked off the balcony. She hurried upstairs, found her coat on a rack in the guest room, and left the party without speaking to anyone.

Thirteen

Daniel stared harder at the contract, but the words refused to unblur. It didn't matter; he no longer comprehended their meaning. And this was no way to read a contract, especially for the first book he'd ever sold.

He rubbed his eyes and put the contract, along with his three pages of notes, in his top drawer to finish on Monday. He would ask Jane to go over the contract for him, of course, but he wanted to do as careful a job as he could. Tanya Selman, the author of *Sea Glass*, the quiet literary novel Daniel had sold to a small publisher called Oasis Press, was especially naive about publishing, and that made Daniel want to do an especially thorough job.

He got up and stretched, arching his sore shoulder muscles, then slipped on his blazer and got his coat from the closet.

He went to the window that looked out on the green. It had grown dark hours ago, but in the glow of the gas lampposts that studded the perimeter of the green he could make out the lone figure of a woman walking crisply along Center Street toward him. He realized it was Jane's friend Ginny Williams, who worked at Whipped Cream. He liked her; she was an honest, straightforward person. As if sensing his thoughts, she looked up and saw him in the window. Her face broke into a sweet smile, and she waved, then marched determinedly on, her hands shoved deep into the pockets of her windbreaker.

Daniel pulled down the blind. Then he went into Jane's office as he always did last thing before leaving for the day. She was so absentminded that she almost always left something important behind—a manuscript, a contract, some important phone number—which Daniel would drop off at her house on his way home. Other times she left things at home. Like when she'd left Roger's awful manuscript at home on Monday, and Daniel had driven over to Jane's house to get it.

He didn't want to think about that.

Jane's desk looked as if someone had stood over it and dumped out a barrel of papers, pens, napkins, and notes. When Daniel, fresh out of Yale, had started to work for Jane and Kenneth, he had tried to make some sense of Jane's desk each night, sorting the mess into stacks: contracts, manuscripts, negotiation notes, correspondence, and so forth. Jane hadn't even noticed. Falling into her chair the next morning, she would run her splayed hands over his perfect stacks, like a blind person seeking an object by feel, until she'd found what she was looking for, and very soon the stacks were one great heap again. Daniel had realized that Jane liked her heap, and he had never touched it again.

Standing at the desk, he reran the day's important events in his mind, trying to think of anything Jane might need tonight. That fool Rosemary Davis had told Jane to turn down the offer on her mystery because Rosemary had decided not to take out the dog. So Jane wouldn't need her negotiation notes on that deal. Which was a pity. Jane, in her shaky financial situation, could have used the commission.

Daniel had asked Jane to read the manuscript of a novel he wanted to represent. He could see a corner of the manuscript peeking out from under last Thursday's *USA Today*. He wished Jane had taken it home with her, but he wouldn't press her.

In the center of the heap, right on top, was a yellow legal pad on which Jane had written the heading *Roger Haines*. Under that she had written *In the Name of the Mother*, the title of Roger's new manuscript. Then there were comments, many of which Daniel had contributed, pages and pages of them. And none of those comments could ever save that pile of paper Roger called a novel. Not that Roger would ever consider them anyway.

Daniel realized that Roger hadn't called today. That was decidedly odd, considering the mess he and Jane were in with Arliss. Oh well, Roger was one more aggravation Jane hadn't needed today—though Daniel was aware that Jane saw Roger as anything but an aggravation. Poor Jane had romantic designs on Roger. If she could only see him for all he was. . . . But Daniel had already decided he wasn't going to think about that.

Daniel left Jane's office, grabbed his briefcase on his way past his desk, and went out the front door and locked it. Then he started for his car, parked not far away in the municipal lot.

All the lights were on upstairs when Daniel pulled into the driveway. He hoped Laura wouldn't be annoyed that he'd stayed at work so late. She'd said she was going to do some errands and just relax today. Climbing the stairs to their apartment on the top floor of the two-family house, he checked his watch. It was nearly eight.

She opened the door just as he reached it. She was in jeans and a baggy pale blue T-shirt and had tied back her light brown hair.

He wrapped his arm around her tiny waist, pulled her to him, and kissed her.

"Mmm, nice." She took his briefcase from him and led the way into the kitchen. "I picked us up some lasagna from Giorgio's on the way home from the mall. It's in the oven."

"You were right near my office. Why didn't you come in?"

"I didn't want to bother you," she said dutifully.

She plunked down at the table and beamed at him as if she knew a secret, her gray eyes huge in her pale heart-shaped face.

"All right," he said, "what's going on?"

"Sit down."

His heart leaped. Please, don't let her be pregnant. They'd agreed they couldn't possibly afford a baby. "What is it?"

"Don't look so terrified! It's something good."

He waited.

"Now, Daniel, you have to promise to be open-minded."

He laughed. "I'm marrying a white woman, aren't I? Wouldn't you say that makes me open-minded?"

"No, Daniel," she said seriously, "in most ways you're not. Now, you know we've been worried about money. You know we love Jane and everything. But, Daniel, you don't make much money at your job, and—"

"Just say it!"

"All right." From the pocket of her jeans she took a slip of paper and handed it to him. On it she had written *Beryl Patrice*, and under it *Silver and Payne*. There was a New York City phone number.

He frowned down at the note. "Silver and Payne? That's where Jane and Kenneth used to work. Beryl Patrice—"

"Runs the agency."

"So?"

She looked as if she would burst. "So she called you!"

"Called me? Why?"

"Now, Daniel, you're not looking open-minded. Just listen to me. She was very nice. She said she would like to talk to you about—now don't say anything—about the possibility of your coming to work there."

"Work there! At Silver and Payne? *Me?* Why?"

"As an agent, idiot. Isn't that what you are?"

"No, not really. I have three clients. I've sold one book. Laura, what is this all about?"

"That's all she said. Well, actually she said she'd heard wonderful things about you and was eager to meet you."

"Heard wonderful things from whom?"

"I asked her that. She didn't say."

He was still glowering at the note.

"Just say you'll call her back."

"Oh, I'll call her back. I return phone calls. But I'm sure you've got it wrong. They probably need an assistant and somehow got hold of my name. But I'm already an assistant. And more important than that, I'm happy working with Jane."

"Working *for* Jane."

"No, *with* Jane. Laura, what's gotten into you? You know how I feel about her. She's like family to me."

"Family wants what's best for family."

He got up and opened the oven door. The lasagna bubbled invitingly. "I'm starving. Let's eat."

"Subject changer."

He spun around and tickled her ribs through her over-size T-shirt.

She squealed. "Stop. She said she'd heard you were brilliant."

"Brilliant! Oh, Laura, please." *Who* could have given her his name? "Is that all she said?"

"Mm-hmm. I'm sure she'll have more to say when you call her. Which will be when?"

"Monday—when else?"

She looked disappointed. "Not tonight?"

"Of course not tonight. It's after eight."

"But that's her *home* number. She wants to talk to you as soon as possible."

That stopped him short. Now he really was curious. "All right, after dinner."

"Good," she said, clearly restraining herself.

He served them lasagna while she put ice in glasses and poured iced tea.

"How was your day?" he asked when they were both seated.

"Okay. I bought some jeans and a sweater at the Gap. Yours?"

"Tiring. Aggravating." He told her about Rosemary Davis.

"What about Roger? Wasn't he aggravating today?"

"Actually, no. He didn't call."

"Any word from Marlene?"

Laura had met Marlene only once, at Jane's party for Roger, but that one meeting had been enough for Laura to dislike Marlene intensely. A manipulative bitch, Laura had called her. Daniel didn't disagree, but also wondered if Laura, though herself lovely, wasn't envious of Marlene's incredible looks.

"No word," he answered. "Jane went to the police this morning."

"The police! To report her missing?"

He nodded, chewing. "I actually thought Marlene might call today, after Jane left that note for Zena at the theater." He'd told her all about last night's escapade.

"Well, what did the police say?"

"That they'd ask some questions. They didn't like hearing she'd been involved with that Gil guy."

Laura sipped her iced tea and rolled her eyes. "The girl is trash. Why can't we all just forget about her and get on with it?"

"Because that 'trash' is the daughter of Jane's oldest friend."

"You certainly seemed interested in her at Jane's party."

He stared at her in amazement. "I *chatted* with her."

"About what?" she asked innocently.

He shrugged, shook his head. "I don't know, nothing really. She asked me if I was married—"

"Aha!" she cried.

"Aha what?"

"She was interested in you. Were you interested in her?"

"Laura, of course not," he said impatiently. "I told her you were my fiancée. I pointed you out to her. Then I brought her over to meet you. You remember."

"Mm-hmm. What did she say when you pointed me out?"

"She said you were pretty."

Laura raised one eyebrow. "Did she now? She's pretty, too. Beautiful, I'd say. Prettier than me."

"Laura! What's gotten into you?"

"Nothing," she pouted, twirling her fork in her lasagna. "I just don't like beautiful women sizing you up, that's all."

"Sizing me up!"

"Yes," she insisted, leaning forward in her chair. "You happen to be a very handsome man. And from my brief meeting with Marlene, I'd say she considers *all* men who appeal to her fair game."

How right you are, Daniel thought.

"That may be," he said quietly, meeting her gaze, "but the only woman *I'm* interested in is you."

She allowed a tiny smile, tilted her chin as she pondered. "You know, if you made more money, we could maybe get married sooner. . . ."

"Subject changer!" he said with a laugh. He wiped his mouth with his napkin and picked up the note from the table. "I'll make you a deal. You clean up, I'll call Beryl."

"Deal!" She jumped up and started clearing the table.

"But no listening in!" he warned her.

"Damn," she said, stacking plates in the sink. Then her face grew serious, and she gave him an imploring look. "Daniel, really, honey—open-minded, okay?"

He was already heading for the bedroom. "Okay, okay."

"I mean you have to at least *see* her. You can't just say you're happy where you are and that there's no point."

"Fine," he said, though not liking that, and closed the door.

From what Jane had told Daniel about Beryl Patrice, he disliked her already. According to Jane, Beryl had been a secretary at a major women's magazine in the sixties when Henry Silver was selling serializations of his best-sellers to Beryl's boss. Beryl, an ambitious beauty, had targeted Henry and taken full advantage of his business relationship with her magazine to work her way into his affections and his bed. They had embarked on a torrid affair, though Beryl and Silver were both married— Beryl to an advertising executive, Silver to the Broadway actress Dinah Calhoun.

Eventually Beryl left her magazine and went to work

for Henry as his assistant. She rose quickly to become a
successful and respected literary agent in her own right,
as well as director of the agency. Silver, now in his eight-
ies, was long divorced from Calhoun and his two subse-
quent wives. Beryl, according to Jane, was still married
to her advertising executive. As for Silver and Beryl's
relationship, it had apparently evolved into an intimate
friendship.

Kenneth, though always discreet, had clearly disliked
Beryl. As Jane told it, Beryl had made a pass or two at
the handsome Kenneth, who'd had no easy time rebuffing
her without jeopardizing his status at the agency. It
wasn't surprising that Jane disliked Beryl as well, calling
her "a woman of monstrous appetites."

A great intro, Daniel thought as he dialed the number
on Laura's note.

"Ah, Mr. Willoughby!" Beryl Patrice's voice was mel-
low and smooth, at once grand and girlish. "I'm so glad
you called."

"My fiancée said you were looking for someone for
your agency . . . ?"

"Indeed we are, indeed we are. Tell me, Mr. Willoughby," she said, all business now, "can you come in
and see me? The sooner the better."

Open-minded. Open-minded. "Uh, yes, that's possible,
Ms. Patrice, but can you tell me—what position, exactly,
are you looking to fill?"

"Why, we need an agent, of course. One of our people
has left, and we have a spot to fill. So can you come in?"

Feeling like a complete traitor, he made an appointment

for the following Tuesday morning. He'd have to make up some story to tell Jane.

"Very good, then, Mr. Willoughby. I look forward to meeting you. I've heard such wonderful things."

He was about to ask from whom, but she had already hung up.

Fourteen

Jane took the nine-hundred-page manuscript of *In the Name of the Mother* in both hands and held it high above her head. "CONTEMPTIBLE PIECE OF GARBAGE!" she shrieked, and hurled it across her office. In midair the rubber band snapped and it was as if the manuscript exploded, pages flying everywhere like a paper blizzard.

That felt great. She cast about for more and on the credenza behind her desk found the copy of *A Better Place* that Roger had inscribed to her. She opened the book, savagely tore out the autographed page, and threw the book across the room with all her might just as the door opened and Daniel poked his head in. He ducked, the book missing him by a fraction of an inch.

He surveyed the office floor, a sea of paper. "Jane! What are you doing?"

For a moment she just stood there, staring at him belligerently. Then her shoulders slumped, and she dropped into her chair, thoroughly defeated.

"He's gone."

Daniel came into the room. He was carrying the mail. He bent down to examine the carpet of manuscript pages and held one up. "Roger?"

She nodded.

"Just a minute." He went out to the reception room; through the open door she could see him switching on the answering machine. Then he came back in, closed the door, and sat down in her visitor's chair. "What happened?"

Slowly, calmly, trying not to cry, she told him everything that had happened Saturday night at Audrey's party.

" 'I'll be giving my new book to an agent who believes in it,' " she finished, mimicking Roger in a pompous tone. "The coward. And to do it in a *letter*."

Daniel looked down at the stack of letters in his hands and began leafing through them. He pulled one out and offered it to her.

"Read it to me," she said.

With a sickened expression he opened the envelope, unfolded the sheet of Roger's heavy cream-colored stationery, and read:

Dear Jane,

This is a very difficult letter for me to write, but write it I must. I'm sure you know I've been unhappy with the way things have been going with A Better Place. *I won't embarrass you by dredging up details. Millennium broke all of its promises to me, and you as my agent failed to correct the situation. Equally troubling has been your response to my new manuscript,* In the Name of the Mother, *which as you know means a great deal to me, more than any other novel I have written. Perhaps because of Millennium's recent loss of faith in me, you have lost your own faith in my talent and my vision. The last person in whom I will tolerate a lack of faith is my agent.*

I thank you for all you have tried to do for me, and of course wish you well.

Very truly yours,
Roger Haines

Jane shook her head. "An ego run amok. Completely out of control."

"As always."

She looked at Daniel searchingly. "He always was an egomaniacal asshole, wasn't he?"

"Yes."

"And I didn't see it."

"No."

"I was fond of him. I really was. I thought our relationship was actually going somewhere. How could I have been such a fool?"

He smiled sadly. "You're lonely, Jane."

She looked down at her desk for a moment, then heaved a great sigh. "A terrible fool."

"Jane," he said gently.

She looked up.

"There's something I think I should tell you now. Something I . . . something I just couldn't tell you before. I didn't want to hurt you."

She shrugged, gave him a dopey smile. "Hurt me, what the hell."

"I don't think it matters now, as far as Roger goes, but it's also about Marlene."

"Marlene? What has she got to do with this?"

"Monday, when I went to your house to get Roger's manuscript . . ."

Jane was sitting up now, frowning in bewilderment. "Yeah?"

"Well, I got out of my car and walked up the driveway, but as I was about to go into the house I heard voices. One was a woman's—I recognized it right away as Marlene's. The other was a man's voice. It was familiar, but I couldn't place it."

"Where were these voices coming from?"

"From behind the house. I'm not sure why, but I crept around the side of the house and peeked through the bushes to the back to see if I could see them. I did. Marlene was with Roger."

"Roger! What was *he* doing there?"

"They were arguing. Roger had his arms around Marlene. He was trying to pull her toward him and kiss her, but she pulled away. He said, 'Come on, you little bitch, you owe me,' and yanked her toward him again, but she broke free and slapped his face. Hard. She was crying. There was hair in front of her face and her eye makeup was all smudged. She screamed at him, told him if he didn't leave her alone, she'd tell you everything."

"Tell me everything? What's everything?"

Daniel shook his head. "I have no idea."

For a moment Jane just stared, at a loss for words.

Roger, who had made love to her so tenderly that day in his apartment ... who had kissed and touched her countless times since ... How could he have betrayed her like this, led her on all this time? Her eyes filled with tears. "What did Roger do then?" she managed to ask.

"For a minute he just stood there. I've never seen him look so angry. His face was dark red, almost purple. He muttered something I couldn't quite make out, something like, 'You're going to pay for this.' Then he turned and stormed off. I pulled back into the bushes. He walked right past me."

"Where was he going? Was his car there?"

"That's what I was wondering. Because when I arrived at your house, there was no car. But when he got to the street he walked up the hill, and a moment later he drove past, going down the hill really fast. So he must have parked up the road."

Jane seethed, her eyes slits. "That bastard! Hitting on my nanny! What did she do?"

"She must have gone into the house by the back door. I still had to get Roger's manuscript. I decided that if I ran into her in the house, I would pretend I hadn't seen anything. But when I went inside, she wasn't around. I figured she'd gone upstairs to her room. So I went into your office, grabbed the manuscript, and left."

Jane nodded thoughtfully. "No wonder he'd been drinking when he got here. He always has a few drinks when he's upset. To think he had the nerve to come here and see me after trying to put the moves on Marlene."

Daniel held up Roger's letter. "Does anything he does surprise you now?"

"No, and that's what worries me." She got up and grabbed her bag.

"Where are you going?"

"To talk to Roger."

"Why?"

"Believe me, it's not that I want to see him again. But Marlene's gone, and Roger knows something." Raising her chin determinedly, she tossed her bag over her shoulder and headed for the door. "I owe it to Marlene and Ivy to find out what it is."

Fifteen

Roger's bungalow was in the hills, not two minutes from Jane's house. She'd wanted him close, idiot that she was.

She parked at the gate, walked up the path to the vine-covered cottage, and rang the bell. She waited for several moments and was about to knock hard when she heard the bolt turn and the door opened. Roger looked shocked and unhappy to see her.

"Jane. Hello."

"I want to talk to you," she said coldly.

"I'm writing now. This really isn't a good time. Is it some—old business?"

"You bet your ass it is." She pushed past him into the dark living room and sat in one of the overstuffed armchairs. "Sit down."

Eyes wide, he obediently complied, choosing the chair farthest from Jane's, directly opposite her. Then he seemed to make a decision to take charge, made his face angry. "Jane, what is it that couldn't be dealt with on the phone?"

"A lot." She looked him up and down, full of loathing. "You really are the lowest life-form."

"Jane! How dare you come into my home and—"

"How dare *you* lead me on, make me think there's something between us, *manipulate* me—for your career! Is that what life is to you, one big manipulation? Say something, damn it! Deny it."

He sat very quietly, gave her a level gaze. "I don't deny it, Jane. I'm sorry I hurt you—I truly am. But you have to understand something. My career . . . I'm in trouble, Jane. My publisher doesn't want me anymore; my new book stinks . . . I was desperate."

"And you had so little faith in my abilities as an agent that you felt the only way you could get me to work effectively for you was to romance me?"

He looked down. "I never had any doubts about your abilities, Jane. You are a good agent. I mean that. It's just that I needed to be your top priority. I couldn't take any chances. And I did feel for you—"

"Stuff that shit. If you have such faith in my abilities, why didn't you take my advice and rewrite your manuscript?"

He threw out his hands. "It would have done no good. Jane, you don't understand. I've lost it. The young genius your Kenneth discovered all those years ago is an old has-been. It's gone. I'm yesterday's news. Publishing has changed, and I'm no longer the fashion. And this is no recent development. When I came to you after Kenneth died and you'd taken over the agency, and I told you I'd left my previous agent—that was a lie. *She* dropped *me*. She said my work had lost its magic—I'll never forget those words. That's when I started to panic. I knew you were hungry. I believed your aggressiveness would make up for the weaknesses in my work."

She shook her head. "No agent can sell bad work. And I don't buy that nonsense about your talent. It's still in there somewhere. But when it's not drowning in Bloody Marys, it's trying to get past what a shit you are."

"I'm not a shit, Jane. I did what I did out of desperation."

"No. Sorry. None of that 'desperation drove me to it.' You're a shit. It's as simple as that."

"If you've come here to insult me—well, you've done it, and you can go now."

"No, I can't, because that's not even the real reason I'm here—though I have enjoyed insulting you. I'm here about Marlene."

He swallowed. "Marlene? You mean that girl—your baby-sitter?"

"Oh, come on, Roger! Don't even try it. I mean that 'girl' you were putting the moves on."

"What?" He sat up, outraged. "I did nothing of the kind. Did she say—?"

"Daniel saw you."

"How? When?"

She repeated what Daniel had told her.

"Oh," he said, defeated again.

"How *could* you, Roger? My son's nanny! A girl young enough to be your daughter. Your granddaughter."

He winced. "She's no girl. She's one-hundred-percent woman, believe me.

"I met her at the party you gave for me. I thought she was the most exquisitely beautiful creature I'd ever seen. That face, that body . . ."

"Spare me the inventory."

"She looked like a living angel." He laughed at the irony of that. "I couldn't help myself. I made a pass at her. And to my complete amazement, she took me up on it. She was interested. I couldn't believe my good fortune. We went into your pantry and—and we kissed, touched each other. She was as hot for me as I was for her. It was a miracle.

"The day after the party I called her at your house and invited her here. She came right over. We—we made love all afternoon. I tell you"—he shook his head in wonder—"it was like a dream."

"All right!" Jane interrupted, her face growing hot. "I got that part."

Roger's expression grew dark. "But I soon found out it wasn't me she was interested in. She was interested in my money. Or in the money she thought I had." He laughed. "She said a big best-selling writer like me must be rich. I didn't correct her."

"What did she want money for?" To get as far from Shady Hills as she could?

"I asked her that. She wouldn't say. She just said it was very important and couldn't I just help her out."

"How much did she want?"

"Five thousand dollars."

"Five thousand dollars!"

He nodded.

"And you gave it to her?"

"Yes," he said, his eyes pleading with her to understand. "I couldn't lose her."

"You *had* five thousand dollars?"

"Just barely. She said it was just a loan; she would pay it back within a few weeks. She was *extremely* grateful."

Jane looked down, embarrassed.

Roger went on. "But the next day when I called her, she was like a different person. She was so cold. She sounded annoyed, as if I was *bothering* her. She said we couldn't get together. I thought she meant that day and asked her when I could see her again. She said she didn't know. She made some excuse, said she had cleaning to do, and hung up. I called her back and she said maybe we could meet the following week. I called her the next day, and she got mad and said I was hounding her and that she would call me when she was ready."

He took a deep breath and blew it out. "Three days passed and I never heard from her, so I called her again. This time she screamed at me to stop bothering her. Well, I'd already figured out what had happened, though I didn't want to believe it. I called her a conniving bitch and said I wanted my money back. She said not to worry, that she'd pay it back, that she'd call me when she had it."

He laughed ruefully. "Well, I don't have to tell you, Jane, that to me—these days—five thousand dollars is a lot of money. I didn't even have the next month's rent on this place! I knew if I called her again, she would just scream at me and hang up, so I drove over to your house."

"That was this past Monday?" Jane asked.

"Yes. I parked up the hill. I didn't want anyone to know I was there. And also in case you came home," he admitted sheepishly. "I rang the bell, but there was no answer. So I just stood there on your front steps like a complete idiot for what must have been fifteen minutes, hoping she'd appear. I was that furious."

He shook his head. "Finally I gave up and started to leave, but as I started down the path, I saw her come out of the Fairchilds' house across the street. That in itself surprised me—I couldn't imagine what she'd be doing visiting Audrey or Elliott. Then it occurred to me that maybe she had something going with Elliott, too. She was clearly upset. She was crying, and one side of her face was bright red.

"When she came through the space in the hedge I stepped out and surprised her. I started hollering at her, and she looked terrified that we'd be heard or seen and pulled me around to the back of the house. I told her I knew she'd used me and that I wanted my money back right then. She refused, said she didn't have it. I asked her when she would have it, and she just shook her head and said she didn't know. Then she said, 'So you'd better leave, old man.' "

His face grew furious as he relived the moment. "That really made my blood boil. I grabbed her, and said I'd be happy to take it out in trade. Not that I was attracted to her anymore. I just wanted to hurt the little whore, show her I knew I'd paid dearly for her favors. I told her she owed me. We struggled. I tried to kiss her. She hit me, hard. She said she would tell you everything if I didn't leave her alone."

He threw out his hands in defeat. "That's when I gave up. I knew it was over, I'd been a complete fool, used. I was never going to see that money again. And there was no one I could go to. I'd done it to myself."

"Yes," Jane said quietly, "you had." And to us. . . .

"I was more agitated than I can ever remember being," he said. "I needed a drink, badly. I needed several drinks. I drove over here, fortified myself, pulled myself together as best I could, and drove down to the village for my meeting with you. Daniel gave me a strange look when I came in. Now I know why."

Jane nodded. "On Wednesday, at Whipped Cream, when I told you Marlene had left, what did you think? Where did you think she'd gone?"

"I didn't know what to think! Of course I was glad she wouldn't be around anymore, that there would be no danger of her talking about us. Later I thought her leaving must have had something to do with whatever she'd needed the money for. We still don't know why she wanted it, what she did with it."

"No," Jane said with a sigh, "we don't." She rose to leave.

"What do you think?" he asked.

"What do I think?" She shook her head sadly, looking at Roger and seeing him as she had never seen him before—as a pathetic middle-aged man terrified to face what he really was.

"I think," she said at last, "that we've both been terrible fools."

Sixteen

"Well, hi, doll! Isn't this an unexpected surprise."
Audrey's pale blond hair was in a ponytail. Over her
black slacks and fruit-print rayon top she wore an indigo
apron with not a speck on it. In her ears were large
diamond studs. Audrey's working clothes.

"I hope this isn't a bad time," Jane said.

"No, of course not. It's great to see you. Come in, come
in." Audrey urged Jane in and shut the door behind her.
"Let me take your coat. You'll have some coffee?"

"Sure, that would be great, thanks."

Audrey hung Jane's coat in the foyer closet and led
the way through the dining room into the vast white
Smallbone kitchen. "How come you're not at the office
at this time of day?" she asked, measuring coffee.

Jane sat down at the kitchen table. "I wanted to talk
to you about something."

Audrey turned to her and smiled a big red closemouthed smile, eyebrows raised. "Oh?"

"It's about Marlene."

Audrey shook her head thoughtfully. "I still can't believe she'd just leave like that, boyfriend or no boyfriend. You know, Jane," she went on, sliding into a chair facing Jane, "I hope you'll forgive my saying this, but as a nanny, Marlene was just *awful!* How in heaven's name you ever chose her is beyond me." Quickly she added, "I mean, I'm sure that if she hadn't left, you'd have fired her."

"Actually, I *was* planning to. I wanted to give her a decent trial period. She is my best friend's daughter."

"Oh, right, I forgot that. Well, water under the bridge, as they say. Moot point. And I understand you've already hired a new person. Florence, is it?"

"Yes. How did you know *that?*"

"My Cara saw her with Nick the other day after school. Cara says she's marvelous—though she didn't use that word, of course." Audrey laughed, eyes to the ceiling.

"I'm very pleased with her," Jane said.

There was a brief awkward silence, during which Audrey waited, her smile frozen.

"Audrey," Jane said, "last Monday, the day Marlene left, Roger saw her come out of your house."

Audrey blinked. *"Roger* saw her?"

"Mm, he was at my front door, looking for me, and happened to see Marlene leave here. What was she doing here?"

"Oh, that's easy. I had asked her to do me a favor. Elliott was expecting a very important package of materials from NJRI—you know, the institute he's up for—"

"Yes, I know."

"Well, the package had to be signed for, but *I* had an appointment down in the village for my nails. So I asked Marlene if she would mind waiting for the package while I was out. I mean, I knew she couldn't screw *that* up." Suddenly Audrey looked concerned. "Oh—I hope you don't mind that I asked her. And that I didn't tell you. It really was no big deal."

"No, that's okay. And did the package come while she was here?"

Audrey seemed surprised by the question. "Yes, as a matter of fact it did. When I got back from my nails, I thanked Marlene—gave her a twenty, actually—and she left."

"Roger said she was upset. She was crying, and her face was red."

"Oh. That. Well. I suppose I may have overreacted, but really, the girl is too much."

"What did she do?"

"Well, as I was seeing her out, I happened to glance over at my Lladro collection on the mantel in the living room, and I noticed something funny about one of my pieces. I went over to it and saw that the figure's arm was missing—broken off! I asked Marlene if she knew anything about it. At first she said no, that my cleaning lady must have done it and why was I blaming her. But Rosa would never be so clumsy, and the figure had been fine that morning."

"You *check* them?"

"Well . . . yes," Audrey said defensively. "They're worth a lot, Jane." Her tone implied that Jane wouldn't know about such things. "Anyway, I could tell from Marlene's face that she was lying, and I told her so. She finally admitted she'd picked up the figure and accidentally broken off the arm."

"I'll be happy to pay you for it," Jane said.

"That's very sweet of you, Jane, but I wouldn't dream of letting you do that. *You* didn't do it—she did. And she had the arm in her pocket, the little sneak. Well, I just lost it. I screamed at her that she had no right to touch my things and that to try to cover it up made it twice as bad. Elliott's parents gave us that piece for our tenth anniversary."

"Which piece was it exactly?"

"The shepherd girl. It was a large piece, worth a lot."

"What did you do with it?"

"Threw it away, of course. If it's not perfect, I don't want it."

How fortunate to be able to live life that way, Jane thought. "Roger said one side of Marlene's face was red. Did you . . ."

"Slap her? Yes, Jane, I'm afraid I did. She called me something quite horrible and I couldn't help myself. . . . I wasn't going to tell you about any of this."

"Where was Elliott at this time?" Jane asked.

Audrey looked puzzled. "He was at his office, or at the hospital—I don't know, what does that matter?"

"He wouldn't have had any reason to stop here while you were out?"

"No, Jane," Audrey said coolly, understanding now, "he wouldn't. Jane, I don't think I like the way this conversation is going. If you resent my having asked Marlene to do me that little favor, why not just say so instead of making insinuations about Elliott?"

"I'm not making insinuations about Elliott. It's Marlene's character that's in question. I've learned that she was rather . . . loose. If she made a pass at Elliott, and he of course would have rebuffed her, she might have become upset."

"She was upset about the Lladro and my slapping her. And as I just told you, Elliott wasn't here. That's why I asked Marlene to wait here in the first place. I would have asked Rosa, but Monday's not her day."

"When is her day?"

"Thursday," Audrey said icily, and turned toward the counter. "Coffee's ready. You'll have?"

"No, thanks, Audrey. I'm afraid I can't after all. I'd better get back to the office."

That seemed just fine with Audrey. She followed Jane out to the foyer.

"Audrey," Jane said, shrugging into her coat, "Marlene didn't happen to say anything to you that might have suggested where she was going, did she?"

"No, nothing. Do you really care? I mean, good riddance, right? Gorgeous girl, but terrible nanny. Sometimes I'd see her with Nick, and she looked as if she didn't even know he was there."

Jane felt another sharp pang of guilt. She loved Nick so much she couldn't express it, yet she had been too preoccupied—with her work, with her relationship with Roger—to see that she had entrusted her son to a woman who cared nothing about him. And Nick, even sensing that himself, had simply borne it, saying nothing. How could she have been so selfish, so unfeeling? She had betrayed not only Nick but also the memory of poor Kenneth. Would she ever have behaved this way if Kenneth were still alive? No, decidedly not. But if Kenneth were still alive, everything would be different. . . .

Audrey was still talking. "Just let her go!" she said.

Jane took a tissue from her bag and wiped the tears from her eyes. Audrey seemed to take no notice.

"It's not that I want Marlene back," Jane said. "Her mother and I are worried about her. She was seeing a dangerous young man. We want to make sure she's okay. She had a right to leave. We just need to know where she went."

"Mm. Speaking of running off, doll, what happened to you Saturday night? You couldn't get out of here fast enough. Headache?"

"Yes, that was it," Jane said, buttoning her coat. "A real killer."

Audrey laughed airily. "I thought maybe our friends had bored you."

Jane looked scandalized at the thought. "Your friends? Not possible." She went out the door and down the steps. "Bye, doll!"

"Mm," came Audrey's thoughtful murmur behind her.

Seventeen

Jane crossed the road and walked up the path to her house. It was a little after two. Florence would be picking up Nick from school at 2:40. Jane decided not to go back to the office. She was tired, and besides, she had plenty of work she could do at home. Daniel had asked her to read a manuscript by a writer he wanted to represent, and Jane felt she should get to it quickly. She wanted to encourage Daniel to take on his own clients, just as Kenneth had encouraged her so many years ago.

She made herself some coffee and settled in her study off the living room, pulling the manuscript out of her briefcase and dropping it on her desk.

Winky padded silently into the room and leaped into Jane's lap. Purring loudly, practically rumbling, she rubbed her head against Jane's blouse.

"I know, Winky, I know," Jane said. "You've been kind of neglected lately with all of our running around looking for Marlene." She took a sip of coffee. Winky rubbed harder. "I'll bet even when Marlene was here you didn't get much attention from her, did you, baby? Bet she hated cats." *If only Winky could speak,* Jane thought. What had the cat seen and heard that might tell them where Marlene had gone? "Bet you didn't like that bad old Marlene one teensy-weensy little bit, did you?"

"Mom, who are you talking to?"

She turned in her chair. Nick stood in the doorway, looking amused.

Jane laughed. "To Winky, who else? I didn't hear you come in. How was your day?"

He shrugged. Florence appeared behind him. Her dark brown face beamed; her pretty dark eyes were cheerfully bright. She wore a navy nylon running suit that looked good on her slim frame.

"Afternoon, missus! We didn't expect you home now."

"I know. Last-minute decision. Just make believe I'm not here."

"Will do," Florence said, putting her hands on Nick's shoulders. He smiled and spun around, clearly quite willing to remain under Florence's supervision despite Jane's presence in the house. He liked Florence—that was plain. Jane, too, liked her more and more.

"First we will have a nice little snack," Florence said in her faintly singsong Caribbean tones. "Then we will do homework."

"Are you doing it, too?" Nick asked.

"Funny, funny little wiseguy. No, I will be making something supernice for dinner. My special meat and rice. That okay, missus?"

"Perfect," Jane said.

They trotted off, and Jane started Daniel's manuscript. Even from the first few pages she could tell it was quiet, rather literary. Maybe a hard sell. Needed the perfect editor. She would keep reading so she could give Daniel her opinion in the morning.

Then she remembered she hadn't told him she wasn't coming back today. She dialed the office. He answered on the first ring.

"No problem," he said. "It's been kind of quiet. Oh—some good news. Barbara called from Silhouette to make an offer on Pam Gainor. Wants to do a three-book contract. I told her you'd call her back."

"Great. Anything else? Mail?"

"Some rejects."

"Nope—don't wanna hear about those. I've been rejected enough today."

"Gotcha. Well, enjoy the rest of the day. Call if you need me. See you tomorrow.

"Oh, Jane—" he said before she could hang up. "I forgot to tell you I have a dentist appointment tomorrow morning. I won't be in till around noon. I hope that's not a problem." He sounded oddly apologetic.

"Hey, don't worry about it," she said. "I'll see you and that gorgeous white smile whenever you get there."

"Thanks," he murmured, and hung up.

Jane hung up smiling. Thank heaven for Daniel, a marvelous assistant and a dear friend. She needed all the dear friends she could find right now. She honestly didn't know what she would do without him.

"Excuse me, missus."

Florence stood in the doorway.

"Sorry to disturb, but I have a question. When I make my special meat with rice, do you like spicy, not so spicy, what? My boyfriend, he always liked *super*spicy, but American people, they say they like spicy but they usually don't really. My family in Randolph didn't like spicy one bit at all. So I wonder about you and the little one."

"It's thoughtful of you to ask, Florence. I think just regular spicy. You have a boyfriend?" she ventured.

"When I was in Randolph, yes, but we broke up about six months ago. It was very ugly, and I was embarrassed." She looked truly upset at the memory of whatever had happened.

"Really? Embarrassed in front of whom?"

"In front of my Randolph family. I didn't know the missus was home, and my boyfriend and I, we had a big fight with screaming. The missus, she heard the whole thing. I told her I was very sorry for the unprofessional behavior."

"Oh, well," Jane said sympathetically, "these things happen and aren't necessarily our fault. I wouldn't give it another thought."

Florence nodded happily. "You are very kind, missus. I am going to like it here. Regular spicy."

"Florence!" Nick called from the kitchen. "It's boiling!"

"I'm coming just now!" Florence called back brightly, and jogged back to the kitchen. Winky, perhaps interpreting Florence's haste as a sign of food, jumped from Jane's lap and followed.

Jane returned her attention to the manuscript but couldn't concentrate. Words blurred, replaced by images of Roger fondling Marlene in the pantry, of Marlene slapping Roger, of Roger sitting forlornly in the big shabby chair in his bungalow's dark living room.

Had that really been the last Roger saw of Marlene? Had his fury at being rejected and humiliated escalated to the point that he had gone back to see her? He could have gone to Jane's house right after his meeting with her. Perhaps he had confronted Marlene again, this time inside the house. He might have hit her . . . might have *killed* her?

No, that didn't make sense. First of all, Roger, for all his faults, was no killer. Second, Marlene had left on her own, packing up all her belongings. . . .

Jane shook herself, forcing the images away. But then a new one came, of Marlene emerging from Audrey's house, crying, her face red. . . .

The phone rang.

"Jane, it's Ivy." Her voice was like ice, dark with reprimand. "What happened with the police? You never called me. Did you go?"

Damn. Jane had completely forgotten. "Yes, Saturday morning," she said meekly.

"And you didn't call me?" Ivy's voice rose in anger. "Really, Jane, that was unbelievably thoughtless. Here I've been thinking that for some reason you hadn't gone yet—though I couldn't imagine why not—and that you'd call me the minute you spoke to them."

"I'm sorry, Ivy. I really am. But I did go, the morning after we spoke."

"And?" Ivy demanded. "What did they say?"

"They took down the important information and said

they would ask some questions and let me know what they found out."

"Ask some questions? Of whom?"

Jane drew a shaky breath. She twisted the phone cord tightly around her index finger. "Ivy, I didn't tell you this before, but—"

"Tell me what?" Ivy shouted.

"I didn't tell you Marlene had a boyfriend while she was here. I went to see him. A young man named Gil Dapero."

"And what did he say? Does he know where she is?"

"No. In fact, they broke up a couple of days before Marlene left. He says he has no idea where she is."

"No idea at all? She never said anything to him about where she was going? Nothing?"

"No, nothing. At least that's what he said." Then a thought occurred to Jane: Why was she protecting Ivy? "Ivy, this boyfriend—he's . . . tough. Not a good choice of boyfriend, according to the police."

There was a long silence on the line.

"What are you saying, Jane?" Ivy growled. "That the police think this boy is lying? That he does know where Marlene is? What?"

"I don't know, Ivy. The police don't know either. They're going to ask him some questions."

"If this thug did anything to my Marlene . . ." Tears came into Ivy's voice. "I can't believe this," she sniffed. "What were you doing while this affair was going on?"

"Sleeping."

"Are you being funny?" Ivy snapped.

"No! Marlene went out at night and stayed out late.

This is what she was doing. Seems she had quite a wild secret life."

"Marlene is not a wild girl, Jane. Can you blame her for wanting to have some fun? Cooped up with you and Nick all day—what kind of life is that?"

"A hellish one, I'm sure," Jane said sarcastically, "and I don't begrudge her her nightlife. I'm just saying she's a big girl, and I let her have her privacy on her own time."

"I'm coming out there," Ivy said suddenly.

"Ivy, there's no point. I'm sure Marlene will call one of us. Just give her some time."

"I want to talk to the police there myself. What's the name of the person you spoke to?"

Jane supposed she couldn't stop Ivy from doing that. In fact, it might be a good idea to let Ivy hear all this for herself. "Detective Greenberg." She opened the phone book and read Ivy the number for the Shady Hills Police Department.

Ivy read the number back to her. "Jane, if you find out anything, I expect you to call me immediately."

"I will. Ivy. I promise. Did the New York police find out anything about Zena?"

"No, nothing yet," Ivy said, and hung up.

The clock on Jane's desk read 4:30. She'd gotten virtually nothing done. A delicious aroma of meat and spices wafted in from the kitchen, and Jane realized she was hungry and looked forward to Florence's dinner.

She hoped Florence didn't find a new boyfriend here in Shady Hills. That was selfish, Jane knew, but her experience with Marlene had shown her that a nanny with too wild a nightlife had little energy left for nannying.

It was unfair, perhaps, to apply that to Florence, who was far more mature than Marlene. Florence had clearly been mortified at having her violent breakup overheard by her employer.

Marlene's friend Helen said Marlene and Gil had had a violent breakup, too. Screaming at each other in the Roadside Tavern's parking lot.

What had they fought about? Gil had been unwilling to say. Had Marlene left because of her breakup with Gil? Or was it the other way around? Had Marlene decided to leave, thus causing the breakup? Perhaps something had been said in their argument, something that pointed to where Marlene had gone. Something someone might have overheard.

It was worth looking into.

"Ready!" Nick called from behind the closed door to his bedroom.

"Twelve!" Jane cried out, smiling, enjoying their nightly ritual. Nick, wrapped in a towel, would run from the bathroom while Jane counted, Nick's goal being to get into his pajamas before she reached twenty. "A new record," she said, entering the room. Nick sat on the bed, his arms wrapped around his knees, his face red and clean and alight with a huge smile. He wore his white pajamas with baseballs and bats all over them.

"Did you brush?" she asked him.

"Yup. Smell my breath." He rose up and exhaled the scent of peppermint into her face.

"Kissing sweet!" she exclaimed, as always, and grabbed him and showered his head and neck with kisses. He giggled uncontrollably, breaking free to burrow under his green flannel comforter.

"Hey, Mom," he said, "look," and whipped back the covers. "Surprise!"

Winky lay sound asleep in the bed, her head on Nick's pillow, her legs limp before her.

Jane laughed. "How will you be able to sleep?"

"Easy," he said, and carefully cuddled up next to her. Jane reached for his lamp.

"Hey, wait a minute!" he said indignantly. "I'm not ready yet. First"—he leaned over to the framed picture of Kenneth he kept on his night table—"say good night to Daddy."

No matter how many times they performed this ritual—and they'd been doing so for as long as Jane could remember—it invariably brought tears to her eyes. Perhaps one day it wouldn't; but then, how long would Nick keep this up? Maybe forever. She hoped so. And she promised herself, not for the first time, to find more ways to help Nick remember his father.

Nick had gently taken the photo from the night table and was holding it in the air in front of him. "Good night, Daddy. I love you." He kissed the glass and handed the picture to Jane.

"Good night," she said softly, looking hard into Kenneth's handsome smiling face. "I love you."

"And second . . ." Nick said, reaching under his bed and brandishing a small hardcover book, "is *Clue of the Screeching Owl!*" He gave Jane a serious look. "You know,

Mom, you should represent an author like Franklin W. Dixon."

"Yes, darling, I know," she said, and added cheerfully, "I'm always on the lookout!"

He sank down into the pillow and opened the book to the page he had marked with a Magic card. At that moment Winky awoke, sat up, and mewed softly. "Oh, Wink!" he greeted her. "You're just in time for the Hardy Boys." He held the book a little to the side so that Winky could see, too.

Jane bent and kissed Nick's forehead. "Good night," she said softly. "I love you." And because she knew he would remind her if she didn't, she added, "Good night, Wink."

Quietly she stepped from the room, taking one last look at Nick and Winky staring up at the book in the lamp's glow.

Eighteen

When Jane left the house ten minutes later it was bitter cold, that kind of perfectly still cold that penetrates deeply. She turned the car heater up all the way and drove with her gloves on.

The Roadside Tavern was just as busy as it had been on her first visit, but this time the music was at a bearable level. In the bar, the slight blond bartender leaned against the counter, chatting with two bearded young men in red-and-black-plaid lumber jackets. Intending to ask him where she could find Peter Mann, Jane stepped into the bar. The bartender glanced up and, to Jane's surprise, came out from behind the bar and walked over to her.

"Heard you're lookin' for Marlene."

"That's right. Do you know her?"

He laughed as if she were crazy. "Everybody knows Marlene. Didja find her?"

"No. Any idea where she might have gone?"

He shook his head, his brow wrinkled in thought. "I was kinda surprised she left."

"Why is that?"

"She always seemed to be having such a good time. I thought she liked this town. She go back home, d'you think? Where was it she's from—Chicago?"

"Detroit. No, she didn't go home. Tell me, uh . . ."

"Steve."

"Steve. Do you think her breakup with Gil had anything to do with her leaving?"

He looked down at the bar, licked his lips nervously. "Wouldn't know about that."

"Apparently she wasn't having such a good time after they broke up."

"Mmm, really wouldn't know."

"Yo!" a man at the far end of the bar called to him.

"Sorry, better help this guy. Listen, when you find Marlene, tell her we really miss her. Tell her to come back and see her friends."

"Will do," Jane said. "Is Mr. Mann here tonight?"

"Peter? Yeah, he was in the dining room. Hey, Vicki!"

Jane turned and saw the waitress she'd spoken to on her first visit look up from a table she was waiting on at the front of the bar.

"Go get Peter," Steve told her.

She gave him a resentful look but crossed the entryway to the dining room. A moment later she returned with Mann not far behind. Tonight he wore enormous baggy jeans and a white sweatshirt. When he saw Jane, his eyes grew wide in inquiry.

"You find Marlene?"

Jane shook her head. "May I speak to you?"

"Shoot."

"Somewhere more private?"

"My office." He led the way across the bar and through a door at the back into a tiny room paneled in knotty pine, furnished with only a desk and two battered metal chairs. "Make yourself at home."

"Thank you."

"Now, you wanted to ask me somethin'?"

"Yes. When I was here last week, Marlene's friend Helen said Marlene and her boyfriend Gil broke up in your parking lot. That was only two days before Marlene left. I'm wondering if their breakup had anything to do with her leaving. Did you happen to hear them arguing?"

"Hell, yeah. He was makin' so much noise I ran out to see what was goin' on. Gil was screamin' in Marlene's face, and she was cryin', beggin' him for somethin'. But he wouldn't have none of it. He just kept screamin' at her."

"What was he saying?"

Mann shook his head, laughed a little. "It's gonna sound really weird, but the only two words I heard were 'porn star.' "

"Porn star?"

He nodded. "Beats me what that meant. I think I don't wanna know! Your Marlene, she is one unbelievably hot young thing. I wouldn't put it past her . . ." He trailed off. "Anyway, right when I was comin' out, Gil turned and walked away from Marlene. She kept cryin' and beggin' him, callin' after him, but he got into his car and drove away. She just wandered off cryin'. It was pathetic. I went back inside."

"Do you think anyone else might know what they were arguing about?"

"Don't think so. There was no one else out there. I asked Helen, and she had no idea. I asked a few other people, but nobody knew."

He leaned over to the door and pushed it shut. "Listen," he said, his voice low. "I'm gonna tell you about some trouble I had with Gil and the police because I want you to know what the guy's capable of. So you'll look into possibilities, if you know what I mean."

Jane nodded, waiting.

"About two weeks before this argument we're talkin' about, this guy named Vernon who comes here a lot must have come on to Marlene out in the parking lot. Marlene screamed, and Gil ran out to see what was goin' on. He beat the livin' shit out of Vernon, hurt him so bad Vernon ended up at St. Clare's over in Denville. Didn't come out for a while. You understand what I'm sayin'?"

This must be the incident Detective Greenberg had been referring to. "Yes, I understand," Jane replied. "I'd like to speak to this Vernon. Any idea where I can find him?"

"Oh, he won't know where Marlene went. She didn't want nothin' to do with him—gorgeous girl like her, nerdy guy like him."

"Still, I'd like to talk to him."

Mann shrugged. "Suit yourself. He works at Harmon's—you know the building-supply store over in Boonton?"

"No, but I'll find it." Jane rose. They walked together through the bar to the entryway.

"I appreciate your help," Jane said.

"Hey, no problem. I just hope you find Marlene. We miss her here."

"Tell me," Jane said. "Do you like Marlene?"

He looked at her and frowned, as if that was a strange question. " 'Course I like her. Everybody likes Marlene."

"Why?"

"She's a real party girl. And she's a knockout! What's not to like?"

Jane just shook her head and shrugged.

Sitting in the car in her coat and gloves, waiting for the air blasting from the vent to heat up, Jane regarded the entrance to the Roadside Tavern. A black pickup truck with a deep diamond-shaped dent in its side rumbled into the parking lot and a couple got out, a young man with a crew cut who wore only jeans and a black T-shirt, and a girl—she couldn't have been more than seventeen—with a mop of black hair who wore a black micro-miniskirt and a purple halter top. From the look of them, it might have been July rather than the middle of October. They walked into the Tavern, the man far ahead of the girl, as if they were strangers.

Jane shivered, suddenly feeling old at thirty-eight. The car was just beginning to warm up. She put it in gear and drove out of the lot onto Highland.

Peter Mann's perplexed voice seemed to echo in the dark car. *It's gonna sound really weird, but the only two words I heard were 'porn star.'*

What on earth had Gil been talking about? Assuming, of course, that Mann had heard him correctly. If only Jane could just ask Gil—but she daren't go near him again.

The most natural conclusion was that Marlene had been carrying on with Vernon, the man who had "come on" to Marlene and whom Gil had beaten up. But why would learning of Marlene's affair with another man cause Gil to use the words *porn star?*

Jane chewed her lower lip, pondering as she followed Highland Road's frequent twists. What could Marlene have done that would have caused Gil to use those words? What did porn stars do? *Well,* Jane thought, *they have sex. Lots of it. Often with a variety of partners.*

Like Roger, and Vernon, and Gil himself, and . . . ?

It was all too much to think about. Jane felt a dizzy headache coming on fast. She switched on her high beams and leaned forward in her seat, forcing herself to concentrate on the road ahead.

Nineteen

The next morning, Florence waved cheerily from the front steps as Jane backed out of the garage. Jane and Nick waved back.

Jane pulled onto Lilac Way and headed up the hill. "You've got your dollar for the fifth-grade bake sale?" she asked Nick.

"Yup, in my backpack. Why couldn't you give me five dollars?"

"Too much sugar."

"Florence said she's going to bake an American apple pie."

"How nice. You're lucky to have Florence."

"Yeah, *she* doesn't care how much sugar I have."

She'd have to have a word with Florence about that.

"Mom, drive faster. I'm going to be late." Nick was leaning over the seat, staring at the clock in the dashboard, which read 8:12. School started at 8:15.

"Buckle up and stop worrying," she said. "You've never been late yet."

She turned onto Magnolia Lane, Roger's street. As they passed the bungalow, she looked away. She continued along the winding road and came to Hawthorne Place, a short road leading off Magnolia that ended in a cul-de-sac at the edge of a cliff.

Suddenly Jane realized this must be the cliff Roger had been going on about at Audrey's party. Parked at the cliff's edge was a dump truck loaded high with building debris—a mountain of wood, plaster, and rock. A short bearded man stood beside the truck, gesticulating wildly as he spoke to the truck's driver.

"Mom," Nick whined, "why are you slowing down? Come *on*."

She hadn't realized she had slowed the car. At that moment the little man turned and saw Jane. To her dismay, he stomped over.

"Mom, what does he want?"

"I don't know, darling. Hello," Jane greeted the man. Up close he looked like a troll out of a fairy tale, with a red bulbous nose and a bushy gray beard that came halfway down his chest.

"If *you're* thinking about dumping something here, you can forget it," he said angrily.

Jane shook her head quickly in denial.

"I own this land. Don O'Rourke, O'Rourke Development. You people can find someplace else to get rid of your shit."

Nick giggled in the backseat.

"I have no intention of dumping anything here," Jane said.

"Then why'd you stop?" Before she could reply, he rushed on. "I'm clearing this land, from the top here all the way down to the bottom of the cliff. Building luxury homes. I've got enough crap to get rid of down there without you people adding more, so you can just shove off."

Furious, Jane opened her mouth to defend herself, then decided it wasn't worth it. "Oh, for Pete's sake!" she blurted out, and drove away, leaving him standing there. In the rearview mirror she saw Mr. O'Rourke watch her briefly, then stomp back to the dump truck.

"What an impossible man," Jane fumed.

"He said 'shit' and 'crap.' "

"I know it, darling. A very rude person."

She drove quickly the rest of the way to school, but it was 8:17 when they arrived. Jane went in with Nick and explained to Mrs. Glenn that it was entirely Jane's fault, that something had come up on the way. When Jane was finished explaining, Mrs. Glenn handed Nick a late pass. "Fill this out and give it to your teacher," she said in her dead monotone.

Jane's mouth fell open. "But I just told you it's my fault."

"Late is late," Mrs. Glenn said, and returned to her desk.

"Thanks a lot, Mom." Nick led the way out to the lobby. "My first tardy."

"I'm so sorry, darling." She kissed his head and

watched him trudge down the corridor toward his classroom.

From Nick's school Jane drove directly to Harmon's Building Supply in Boonton, the town bordering the northwest end of Shady Hills. As she pulled into the parking lot, she realized she hadn't told Daniel she'd be in late. Then she remembered he'd said he had a dentist appointment and wouldn't be in till noon.

Harmon's was a vast hardware warehouse that smelled of paint and fresh-cut lumber. Jane went directly to the customer-service desk.

"I'm looking for Vernon List."

The woman at the counter referred to a chart on the wall. "Fasteners, aisle six."

Jane thanked her and found aisle six. Halfway down, an elderly couple stood talking to a young man in a bright yellow Harmon's apron. Jane went close enough to read his name tag: Vernon.

He was of medium height and average build. What first drew your attention was his hair, the wiry kind that's impossible to do anything with. It stuck out from his head in strange brown lumps. His eyes were small and brown, his features unremarkable. He was neither handsome nor ugly, just an average young man one would have been unlikely to take much notice of if not for the raw-looking red scar running from his left temple to his jaw.

He finished with the couple, who bustled off with a handful of screws, and turned to Jane. "Need help?" He spoke in a dull monotone, totally lacking in effect, as if he were in a trance.

Jane found it difficult to imagine that Marlene would have been interested in this young man, bland of personality and appearance—certainly no comparison to the dangerous and handsome Gil Dapero.

"Yes. Mr. List, I—"

"How'd you know my last name?"

"I wonder if I could talk to you for a minute."

He frowned. "About what?"

"Marlene Benson."

He flinched, his mouth dropping slightly. "Marlene?"

"Yes. My name is Jane Stuart. Marlene took care of my little boy."

"Yeah?"

"You probably know she's gone away."

He nodded. "So?"

"So I'm looking for her. Her mother and I are concerned. Do you have any idea where she might have gone?"

"Why would I?"

"I understand you were . . . interested in her. I heard about what happened with Gil Dapero."

For the first time he showed some feeling, tilting his head and directly meeting her gaze as if willing her to believe what he was about to say. "Gil thought I was interested in her, but I wasn't. I was just talking to her. Then he came out and went crazy."

"What made him come out?"

He glared at her resentfully. "How the hell should I know? He came out. He thought I was comin' on to her or something and"—he gently touched the scar on his face—"beat the shit out of me."

"And that's all that happened?" Jane asked.

"Yeah, that's all." His expression suggested that it was all as puzzling to him as it was to her.

"So you're saying you have no idea where Marlene might have gone? You haven't heard anything, maybe at the Tavern?"

"No, I haven't heard anything. And I don't go there anymore."

"And the last time you saw her was when?"

"That night," he whined. "When this happened." He touched his cheek again. Then he frowned as a thought occurred to him. "How'd you know I work here?"

"Peter Mann told me."

He nodded, shrugged.

Jane fished a business card out of her bag and handed it to him. "If you think of anything that might help us find her, will you please give me a call?"

"Yeah, sure," he said, but from his belligerent expression she could tell he thought taking the card was pointless.

Twenty

As Daniel sat in the reception area of Silver and Payne, it occurred to him that he had never seen any literary agencies other than Kenneth and Jane's. He'd had no reason to until now. Posh was the only word to describe these offices, and he wondered if other large old agencies looked the same.

Silver and Payne's reception area was larger than Jane's entire office suite. At the back of the room stood a massive curved desk in blond wood, behind which sat a polished young dark-haired woman with a British accent who had invited him to make himself comfortable while she let Beryl know he had arrived. In the wall behind the receptionist, recessed glass shelves displayed the agency's latest releases, four of them current *New York Times* bestsellers. A similar display in the wall opposite the cream leather sofa on which Daniel sat offered a selection of books for children and young adults. The walls were covered in cream grass cloth. On the polished pale wooden floor lay two enormous Oriental carpets in shades of cream, lichen, and gray.

The door to the elevator area flew open and a skinny young man in baggy jeans and a knitted cap sauntered in. "Pickup for Random," he said. Wordlessly, without looking at him, the receptionist produced a large padded envelope from her desk and handed it to him.

"Many thanks, my pretty," the messenger said jauntily. He waited for a response but, getting none, gave an exaggerated shrug and sauntered out with the parcel under his arm.

"Mr. Willoughby."

Daniel turned toward the double doors in the far right wall of the reception area. Beryl Patrice was easily sixty, but Daniel could tell she'd been a beauty. Still a handsome woman, she was tall and slim and wore a gray wool suit. Her salt-and-pepper hair was pulled back tightly into a bun. Most striking about her were her eyes, a bright cornflower blue, which radiated acute intelligence.

Daniel rose and shook her hand. "It's a pleasure to meet you, Ms. Patrice."

"Oh, please, call me Beryl," she said, leading the way into the office. "May I call you Daniel?"

"Yes, of course."

He followed her down a corridor between cubicles at which young men and women sat talking on telephones, clacking away at computer keyboards, or poring over manuscripts. There was an air of busyness, of deals—and money—being made.

"Here we are." Beryl opened a door at the end of the corridor and she showed Daniel into a spacious corner office with views of Fifth Avenue to the south and west. She indicated a cluster of chairs around a marble coffee table, and they both sat.

"Now." She crossed surprisingly shapely legs. "Thank you so much for coming in. Would you care for some coffee?"

"No, thank you."

She became all business. "As I told you, we recently lost one of our agents. Dana Ashton has gone to the Morris office." She waved dismissively, as if to say, "Gone and forgotten."

"So we need someone new. I've heard such impressive things about you. How would you like to come and work here?"

"Well, I— May I ask how you heard about me?"

"Ah," she said, her eyes twinkling, "that's our little secret. But you should know that you are very highly regarded."

By whom, he couldn't imagine, since most people knew him only as the voice of Jane's assistant. "That's very kind."

She just smiled. "How do you like working with Jane Stuart?" she asked, her tone casual.

"I'm quite happy there."

"Mm. You know, she used to work here."

"Yes, I know."

"So did her late husband, Kenneth. So sad."

He nodded.

"Do you feel that Jane is ..." She searched for the words. "Do you feel she's allowing you to grow, to handle the projects you'd like to?"

"My first responsibility is as her assistant," he said dutifully. "She encourages me to take on clients if I have the time. But I only have a few." Laura would have killed him for being so honest.

"What sort of projects are you taking on?"

"Novels. Mostly literary. That's what I like best."

"And do you feel that Jane is a good teacher, that you're learning the right kinds of things from her?"

Beryl hated Jane—that was clear. Daniel fought to control himself. "She's the best teacher I could have. She's also my friend."

Beryl's brows rose ever so slightly. Only her mouth smiled. "I see. Well. At any rate, you would no doubt like to get more into the mainstream of things. If you're interested in working here, Henry and I would love to have you."

"That's extremely flattering, but I—"

"We pay a draw against commission. Our attorney produces a document, of course, but the main points are that we're offering you a draw of sixty thousand dollars a year. When your draw is earned back, we will split any remaining money with you fifty-fifty."

A chill began in Daniel's shoulders and traveled down his chest into his legs. Sixty thousand dollars. Nearly three times what Jane paid him. Laura would faint dead away.

"You will have complete freedom with respect to the writers you take on. I assume you're interested in African-American writers, being African-American yourself."

"I'm interested in any writer with talent."

"Good answer," she said, like a teacher to a student. "It's just that it *is* the hot new area in publishing."

He said nothing.

"You would have complete access to Henry and me for advice. And I'm sure any of our other eight agents will be more than happy to help you. Silver and Payne is, of course, one of the most prestigious and successful literary agencies in the world," she said proudly. "Henry founded the firm in 1947, after the war. We handle more best-selling authors than I can name, and of course a tremendous number of authors' estates. You would have access to all of our contract files to guide you. I daresay Jane's files are lacking in that respect."

"She's done her share of big deals," he said, trying not to sound defensive, "and Ken did, too. Jane has some pretty big names."

"Oh," she said politely. "Like who?"

He felt his face grow hot. What was he going to say— Bertha Stumpf? Pam Gainor?

"She's just lost one of her biggest," Beryl went on before he could speak. "If not *the* biggest."

"Oh?"

"Roger Haines, of course—but I'm sure you know that. He's come to us. Forgive me when I say he was not well served by Jane. I was horrified at the things Roger told me."

Daniel stared at her in surprise. "Like what?"

"Oh, I'd really rather not say. . . ."

"Please."

"Well," she said quickly, obviously quite happy to say,

"in order to get Roger to sign with her, she . . . slept with him."

"What!"

She nodded simply.

"That is absolutely untrue," he said, seething with fury at Roger, the worst kind of cad. "Jane would never do something like that."

"It is difficult to learn unpleasant things about a friend."

"Friend or not, Jane would never do that. Is that how Roger says he selects his agents?" He leveled a meaningful glance at her.

Her jaw muscles tensed, but she pretended not to understand. "Of course, that wasn't why he ultimately signed with her. He actually thought she could do him some good, thought she was an effective agent." She threw her hands out. "We have big plans for Roger, but it won't be easy to repair the damage that has been done to his career."

Daniel felt his face grow hot. Fighting to remain calm, he sat up, dropping his hands on his knees in a gesture that indicated he was ready to leave. "I do appreciate your time, Ms. Patrice."

"On the contrary," she said, rising, "I'm grateful you'll consider us. Perhaps you could give me your answer in a week?"

Her smile as she turned to lead the way out was smugly assured, as if the week was merely a quaint formality.

Twenty-one

Jane found Daniel at his desk, quietly reading, when she arrived at the office. The room was chilly, and he wore his jacket, a charcoal gray one she couldn't remember seeing before.

"Don't we look spiffy today," she said, hanging up her coat. "I finished the manuscript you gave me." She pulled it from her briefcase and handed it to him. When he stood to take it from her, she noticed that his trousers matched his jacket.

"A suit! My, my. You sure do it up for the dentist."

He gave her a wan smile. "Laura and I are going to dinner after work."

She sat down in his visitor's chair. "Special occasion?"

"No. Just for fun."

"Good. I like that. Now, about that manuscript. In my opinion, it's a no-go."

"Really?" His eyes showed his deep disappointment. "You didn't like it?"

"She shows promise, but she doesn't pull it off. The whole bit about the daughter's suicide doesn't ring true, and that's the basis of the whole story. Plus the book is quiet to begin with—already a difficult sell."

He looked down at the stack of paper, then back at her. "It's literary. Not everything we sell has to be *Sunset Splendor*."

She stared at him, shocked. "I'm aware of that. I think I know the difference between a historical romance and a literary novel. I also think I know what criteria to apply to each."

"I'm sorry," he said, looking down again.

"Is something wrong? You're not yourself today. Did the dentist hurt you?"

"No. I'm just a little down today."

"Let me take you to lunch. I had planned to invite Roger—today's his birthday—but obviously that's off. You're more fun than Roger anyway."

"Thanks, Jane, but I'm not in the mood. Another day, maybe?"

"Sure, sure. Say when. And listen, about that book. You do what you think is right. My opinion is just my opinion. But if you take her on, you should have her do some revisions. I'll give you my notes."

"Thanks," he said, and smiled. "Any word from Marlene?"

"No. And Ivy's frantic."

She brought him up to date, ending with her visit to Vernon List, who was reportedly hot for Marlene but denied any interest in her.

"I feel I've hit a dead end."

"Then let it go. Why keep looking?"

"I owe it to Ivy. And to Marlene herself. I feel very guilty about her. I disliked her so much it never occurred to me that she was my responsibility—not just while she was taking care of Nick, but all the time. And I let her down. I should have watched her more closely, imposed some discipline. Set a curfew."

"She *is* nineteen."

"A child. Forgive me—I know you're not many years past that. I have no trouble caring about you because you're like family to me. It's when you don't like someone that you have to make a special effort and force yourself to care."

She rose, shaking her head. "I owe the girl an apology."

She opened the door to her office and stopped. "Something's different."

"I picked up the papers."

She gave him an affectionate smile. "You didn't have to do that."

"I know."

"Thank you."

He nodded. She went into her office, leaving the door open. Sitting down at her desk, she picked up a thick stack of pink message slips and riffled through them. She still hadn't called back Barbara at Silhouette about Pam Gainor. She'd do that now. She could certainly use the commission on that signing payment, the sooner the better. She was grateful for deals like this—steady, reliable sources of income. Without Roger, now even her top authors were B-level at best.

She realized she hadn't told Daniel about her visit with

Roger yesterday, and Daniel hadn't asked. That was just like him.

Jane also realized now that in her fury about Roger and Marlene, she'd forgotten to ask Roger who his new agent was. Not that he would necessarily have told her.

"Daniel," she called.

"Yes?" came his voice through the intercom.

"Do me a favor. If you hear through the grapevine what agency Roger's gone to, will you let me know?"

There was a strangely long silence. Then, "Yes."

"Thanks."

With a deep sigh, Jane picked up the phone to make the Pam Gainor deal.

Twenty-two

By lunchtime she actually felt cheerful—something she wouldn't have thought possible in light of the last few days' events.

She'd gotten Pam Gainor a four-book deal at Silhouette, with a decent increase in her advances from her last contract.

Gary Kostikian at St. Martin's had called to start negotiations on a new contract for Bill Haddad, a thriller writer they published in hardcover and paperback.

And, most important of all, Jane already felt herself getting over the whole Roger situation.

She decided to take herself to lunch.

"Sure you won't come?" she asked Daniel on her way out.

"No. Thanks again." He gave her a decidedly forced smile.

Something was definitely bothering him. She hoped things were okay between him and Laura. Jane liked

Laura, but the girl was intense. It amazed Jane that Laura hadn't strong-armed Daniel into setting a wedding date yet. Could they be breaking up? Jane fervently hoped not. Daniel loved Laura deeply. That would destroy him.

She'd give him his space. He knew he could always confide in her if he wanted to.

It was raining lightly when she left the office. She had decided to eat at Whipped Cream, which had recently begun serving sandwiches and salads to the lunch crowd. If Daniel had come along, she would have taken him to Eleanor's, but Whipped Cream would do for her just fine. She hoped her table would be free.

Popping open her umbrella, she set off across Center Street and down one of the brick paths that cut across the green. She was alone except for a young woman in a hooded raincoat pushing a baby carriage covered with clear plastic against the rain. The woman could have been the baby's mother or nanny.

Had Marlene ever taken Nick for a walk after school? What exactly *had* Marlene done with Nick after school? Probably nothing. Probably left him to watch TV, something Nick would never have complained about. Jane wanted him to spend more time with other children, to play outside, to read.

More guilt. She had to stop this. You live and you make mistakes and you learn—and you don't make the same mistakes again. They had Florence now, an entirely suitable choice. A find, a treasure.

Nearing the bandstand, Jane passed the woman with the carriage and smiled at her. The woman smiled back and nodded demurely.

Jane reached the other end of the green, crossed the street, and started along the line of shops toward Whipped Cream. She came to the Village Shop and stopped. Marlene's friend Helen worked there. Jane peered through the window and saw the stocky dark-haired girl behind the counter, ringing up a sale, her face expressionless.

It occurred to Jane that Helen must know Vernon, if they all hung out together at the Roadside Tavern. Maybe Helen could tell Jane more about him. It was a long shot, but Jane had nothing to lose.

The man Helen had been serving was on his way out as Jane entered the cluttered little convenience store. Helen had sat down on a stool behind the counter and was reading the *National Enquirer*. She didn't look up.

Jane approached the counter. "Hello."

Helen looked up blankly, clearly not recognizing Jane.

"We met at the Roadside Tavern last week," Jane said. "I spoke to you about Marlene . . . ?"

"Oh, yeah, right." Helen's expression barely changed. "What do you need?"

"Nothing—nothing to buy, that is. I'd like to talk to you."

Helen waited, staring blankly.

"I spoke with Peter Mann, who told me about Gil beating up Vernon List because Gil thought Vernon was interested in Marlene. I went to see Vernon, hoping he might know where Marlene went, but he said he had no idea. He also said he'd never been interested in her."

Helen let out a derisive chuckle. "What do you expect Vernon to say after Gil almost killed him? Vernon *was* interested in Marlene. Did Marlene ever tell you about her birthday party?"

Jane shook her head.

"Vernon was always bothering Marlene, trying to talk to her, but he was the worst at this party I threw for her at the Tavern in September."

Jane had forgotten Marlene's birthday. Marlene would never have volunteered it. Another wave of guilt swept through Jane.

"I did it up real nice," Helen said. "Balloons, streamers—I even got a cake. We were all having a great time when Vernon walked in with one of those camcorder things. He started taping the party, which kind of freaked us out, but nobody said anything. Then he started aiming the camera at Marlene and not taking it off her. Marlene told him to knock it off, but he wouldn't. Then Peter saw what he was doing and yelled at him to cut it out or leave. Finally Vernon stopped, the nerd. He took a piece of cake, stuffed it into his mouth, and walked out. It's a good thing Gil wasn't there."

"Gil wasn't there?" Jane asked. "At Marlene's birthday party?"

"No, they weren't going out yet," Helen explained. "Gil's not there every night anyway, not like the rest of us."

"You told me Marlene was interested in Gil pretty early on. *She* would have wanted Gil at her party, wouldn't she?"

Helen gave a little shrug. "I guess so, but she didn't know about it ahead of time. It was a surprise." She chuckled again. "So when Vernon says he wasn't interested in Marlene, he's full of it. And he's also lying when he says he didn't come on to her, because he did, and I saw the whole thing."

"What whole thing?" Jane asked, frowning in puzzlement.

"Gil beating Vernon up."

"You were *there*?" Jane faltered. "Why didn't you tell me that before?"

"Why would I?" Helen's voice rose defensively. "What did it have to do with Marlene leaving?"

Jane nodded concedingly. "All right. Can you tell me now what happened?"

"Sure. It was late, and Marlene and I were leaving. She was going to give me a ride home. As we were getting into the car, Vernon drove into the parking lot and jumped out of his car. He ran up to Marlene. They went off to the side for a minute. I figured she was telling him to bug off. He took something out of his jacket."

"Something?"

"A smallish package—I couldn't see it so good. It must have been a present. Marlene grabbed it like she didn't want anybody to see it and stuffed it into her bag. She looked really embarrassed. Then she walked back to the car."

"Did Vernon go into the Tavern?"

"No," Helen replied, her eyes growing wide. "He *chased Marlene.* He said, 'Marlene, wait—I want to talk to you,' but she just ignored him." She shook her head. "Marlene could do that real good."

Yes, Jane thought, recalling the times she had addressed Marlene and received no response.

Helen went on, "She told me to get in, which I did, and she got in, and Vernon started banging on her window. She looked totally aggravated and rolled down the window and said, 'I told you to leave me alone.' Then she rolled the window back up.

Helen held out clawed hands. "That made Vernon nuts! All of a sudden he yanked open her door and grabbed her arm. I don't think he meant to hurt her, but he pulled her too hard, and she fell right out of the car onto the ground. She screamed—really loud."

"That's when Gil came out?" Jane asked.

Helen nodded. "And Mann, and whoever else was inside. Gil was holding a beer bottle. He ran up to Marlene, saw her on the ground, took one look at Vernon, and hit him right in the face with the bottle." She might have been describing an everyday encounter in the supermarket.

Jane screwed up her face in horror. "How awful!"

Helen gave a nonchalant shrug. "Yeah, lots of blood. Vernon was on the ground, moaning, and Gil picked him up under his arms and dragged him around behind the building. That's where he finished the job. Beat Vernon up really bad."

"How do you know if you didn't see it?" Jane asked.

"Because about five minutes later Gil came back around to the parking lot—"

"You were still there?" Jane cried.

"Yeah, Marlene wanted to see what happened. Gil told us to get the hell out of there, which we did. The next day we heard that Mann called the ambulance and you know the rest. Vernon was in St. Clare's about a week and a half."

"What was it Vernon gave Marlene?" Jane asked.

Helen shook her head. "No idea. She never showed me, and I never asked."

"Why not?"

"Why didn't I ask?" Helen glared at her defensively. "Because it wasn't any of my business."

"I thought you were friends," Jane said, dryly sarcastic.

"We are, but I could tell she was embarrassed, and I didn't want to make it worse. Did she tell *you?*" Helen demanded, leaning forward slightly. "She worked for *you*, lived with *you*."

"No, of course she didn't tell me," Jane admitted.

Helen smiled triumphantly.

The door opened, and a woman entered and headed for the milk section of the refrigerator.

"I better get back to work," Helen said, turning toward the woman, who was approaching the counter with a gallon of milk.

Reluctantly Jane drew her gaze from Helen and left the shop.

Twenty-three

Now the rain was a torrent that beat down on the sidewalk and splashed cold against Jane's legs. Beneath her now barely adequate umbrella she scurried to a few shops farther along and pushed her way into Whipped Cream. The small café was full almost to capacity, with only a few tables free.

"Hi, Jane!" Ginny called from behind the counter.

Jane waved, struggling out of her raincoat and hanging it on a hook near the door. She propped her umbrella against the wall underneath. Two young women Jane recognized as Nell and Ann, the owners of the gift shop next to Jane's office, sat at Jane's usual table. She took a free one near the register, where Ginny was handing a young man his change. Then she came over to Jane.

"What's wrong?"

Jane blinked. "Who said anything was wrong?"

"Your face." Ginny glanced behind the counter to make

sure Charlie wasn't looking, then sat down at Jane's table. "Come on . . . Is it Roger?"

Jane nodded. "Over."

Ginny gave Jane a pained smile and patted her arm. "I'm sorry, hon. I know how much he meant to you. Jeez, you and he were here less than a week ago— though that didn't seem to end too well. . . . Why'd you two end it?"

"Let's just say his attentions were not sincere."

Ginny frowned. "Wha—? Very literary. Now what does it mean?"

"It means," Jane said, lowering her voice, "that he was leading me on so I'd work harder for him."

Ginny looked horrified. "I never liked the guy, but that's the lowest."

Jane nodded.

"You need a good lunch." Ginny rose and took her order pad from her pocket. "We've got great soups today. How about chicken soup with matzo balls?"

"Mm, love it." Jane smiled gratefully. "Thanks, Ginny."

"You got it, babe. You coming tonight?"

"Tonight?" Then she remembered that this was Tuesday and that their knitting club met tonight. "I forgot all about it. I don't know. I'm not sure I'm in the mood."

"Oh, come on, Jane. It's exactly what you need. Besides, I need your help with my sweater. It's a mess."

"Okay," Jane gave in. "I guess I can ask Florence to watch Nick. But, Ginny, do me a favor and don't mention Roger at the meeting."

"I promise," Ginny said, patting Jane's shoulder. "We'll have fun. We always do. I'll get your soup." She hurried off to the kitchen.

Jane folded her arms against a slight chill in the air. She wished her table near the fire were free. If Nell and Ann finished soon, she'd move. Behind them the flames roared and crackled invitingly.

She let her gaze travel around the room. Someone had taped a flyer to the front of the counter below the cash register. It was for the Halloween party Shady Hills sponsored every year at the high-school gymnasium, an event at which children could have safe fun instead of risking being the victims of pranks—or, especially in the case of the older kids, perpetrating them. Jane and Kenneth had always taken Nick to this party, having fun dressing him up as a daisy or a dragon or a frog.

Jane couldn't believe Halloween was so soon, only two weeks away. It had crept up on Jane, the season rushing by. Nick had said nothing about a costume this year. She would ask him tonight what he wanted to be and whether he might like to go trick-or-treating this year instead of going to the town party.

She let her gaze continue to wander. Two tables away from Jane sat a man and a woman. The man was a handsome fiftysomething, old enough to be the father of the woman, a stunning redhead who couldn't have been more than twenty-five. Jane was reminded of the redhead on Audrey's terrace—and quickly put the image out of her mind. Jane wondered how she herself would look with hair that red, instead of the auburn she had lately begun to assist chemically against an alarming number of gray hairs. No, a red like that would be too harsh for her; she'd look like Woody Woodpecker. She'd leave well enough alone.

The man, definitely not the young woman's father, had his arm on the back of her chair and occasionally stroked her cashmere shoulder. The woman turned away from him for a moment, looking for something in her purse. As she did, the man reached into his pocket, withdrew a small square box wrapped in shiny red paper, and quickly placed it in front of her. When she turned back and saw the box she squealed in surprise. The man, all smiles, watched her unwrap the gift. It was a black velvet ring box. She opened it and squealed again, then threw her arms around the man's neck and kissed him hard on the mouth. Definitely not her father.

"Some nice fresh rolls," Ginny said, arriving with a tray. "And your matzo-ball soup, super yummy with carrots and chicken in it, just the way we like it."

"You sound like my mother. She used to talk about food that way."

Ginny chuckled. "Guess I'm a natural for mother-hood." She looked a little sad. She had been seeing Rob for six years, with no engagement in sight. Yet Ginny loved him dearly, and he her. From things Ginny had said, the reluctance was on Rob's side.

"Did you get a load of what's going on over there?" Ginny asked softly.

"A special occasion?" Jane said.

"You might say that." Ginny gave the man a look of pure loathing. "That's David Kagan."

"*Rhoda's husband?*" Rhoda Kagan was a member of

their knitting club, a lovely woman who had been trying valiantly to save her ailing marriage. Obviously she had failed.

"Rhoda called me last night," Ginny said. "He asked her for a divorce. He's marrying Bimbo. She's his hygienist. Lola," she said, dwelling on the *l*'s. *"Whatever Lola wants . . . Lola gets. . . ."* she sang softly.

They both looked over with distaste.

"He sure picked a romantic place to pop the question," Ginny said. "Cheap son of a bitch. He coulda sprung for Giorgio's."

Jane burst out laughing. Bimbo was slipping the ring onto her finger. The diamond was immense; Jane could see that even from here. She snarled.

"Rhoda will appreciate your loyalty," Ginny said. "She's taking it well, but these things are always hard."

"There's one person who won't be at the club tonight."

"Oh yes, she will. I made her promise. Told her it's the best therapy she could get. Same goes for you."

"True, true," Jane said, and tasted a spoonful of her soup. The broth was rich and piping hot, perfect for this grim gray day.

"I better get back to work," Ginny said, "before David whips out the Frederick's of Hollywood. I don't think I could survive that."

She went behind the counter to help the customers lined up at the register waiting to pay. Jane sipped her soup and laughed to herself. If Kenneth had asked her to marry him in a storefront coffee shop, she would have refused him. No, she corrected herself, she wouldn't have done that; but then, Kenneth wouldn't done *that*, either.

Looking at David Kagan, who was rising to help Bimbo with her coat, Jane now understood perfectly everything Rhoda had told the club. To give a woman a ring at Whipped Cream! How embarrassing. Not that Bimbo had looked embarrassed.

Marlene, according to Helen, had been embarrassed by Vernon's gift. What could he have given Marlene in his pathetic attempt to make her like him? Embarrassment was not a feeling Jane would have thought Marlene capable of. The gift must have been something especially embarrassing—so much so that Marlene hadn't wanted anyone to see it or know what it was. Not even Helen, her close friend.

Would Marlene have thrown it away? Maybe—if it had been worthless. But what if it had had some value? What if it had been, say, a piece of jewelry? Did young men give young women jewelry anymore? Even though Marlene had disliked Vernon, she would have kept the gift if it had been worth something. But she still wouldn't have wanted anyone to see it. What would she have done with it? Where would she have put it? In her room, of course. But not in plain sight. . . .

She would have hidden it. Would it still be there? No. Unless . . .

Jane quickly finished her soup. She left the rolls and didn't ask for coffee. She left a nice tip for Ginny and took her check to the register.

"What'd you do, inhale it?" Ginny said, taking Jane's check and twenty-dollar bill.

"It was as good as you said," Jane said cheerfully.

Ginny gave her a funny look as she handed Jane her change. "See you tonight."

"Right," Jane said, hurrying toward her coat and umbrella.

Twenty-four

It was one-thirty when Jane entered the house, Winky
instantly mewing at her feet. Florence was out, as Jane
had known she would be. They had agreed that Tuesday
would be Florence's grocery-shopping day, and that Florence would go to the supermarket between lunch and
picking up Nick at school.

Without stopping to take off her raincoat, Jane went
directly upstairs, Winky close behind, and down the hall
to Florence's room. She pushed open the door and
stepped inside.

Jane realized she hadn't been in this room since Florence had arrived. Florence was as tidy as Marlene had
been sloppy. On the dresser near the door, in front of the
Hümmel figurines, stood three framed photographs. The
beaming man and woman sitting arm in arm on a sofa
must be Florence's parents. The sweet little boy in a Yan-
kees cap must be the nephew she had mentioned, Rodney.
In between was another little boy who Jane guessed was

Kerry, whom Florence had taken care of in Randolph. Near the photos sat a large seashell, tan mottled with brown, presumably a souvenir of Trinidad.

Carefully, feeling guilty, Jane opened the dresser drawers. Florence's clothes were neatly folded and stacked. *This is silly,* Jane told herself; *Marlene would never have hidden Vernon's gift here, and if she had, Florence would have found it.*

As she turned from the dresser, her gaze lighted on the closet. A long shot, but still a possibility. She crossed to it and opened the door. Winky ran inside and began pacing between the walls of the small space. The closet wasn't nearly as full as it had been when Marlene had lived here. Just a few cotton-print dresses and blouses. Jane pushed the hangers to each side, revealing only the white wall behind them. Then she searched the floor of the closet, finding it bare except for two pairs of shoes and a pair of worn slippers. She looked up. Above the rod was a deep shelf. Jane ran her hand over it but found only a thin layer of dust. The shelf was too deep for Jane to see all the way back, so she stood on her tiptoes but still found nothing.

She closed the closet door, thoughtfully chewing the inside of her lip.

"What do you think, Wink?"

"Mew," Winky replied.

Jane went to the night table, on whose surface sat a reading lamp and a Bible. The table contained two drawers. Jane opened the top one and found writing paper, an assortment of pens and pencils, and a roll of postage stamps. The bottom drawer was empty.

Jane sat on the bed and tried to put herself in Marlene's place. If she were living in someone else's house, in a room anyone might enter at any time, where would she hide something she wanted no one to see? The dresser, the closet, the night table—these were the only possibilities, for otherwise the bedroom was bare, a simple square space with one window and nothing on the walls. The only other object in the room was the bed.

The bed. Jane got up and considered the bed, which Florence had meticulously made, the rose-covered bedspread tucked neatly around the pillow. When Jane was twelve, her friend Gretchen had lent her a copy of *The Pirate* by Harold Robbins. At night, when her parents thought she was asleep, Jane had read it under her covers by flashlight. At all other times she had hidden it between her mattress and box spring.

She eyed the mattress. A silly idea . . . Feeling foolish, she knelt and inserted her hand up under the bedspread and between the mattress and box spring, past her elbow. She felt around. Nothing. She got up and tried the other side of the bed, sweeping her arm as deeply as she could.

Her wrist hit something. She touched it with her hand. It felt like hard plastic. She grasped it and drew it out.

It was a black videocassette, unlabeled.

Quickly Jane neatened Florence's bed and hurried downstairs with the tape, Winky in close pursuit. She practically ran to the family room, closing the double doors in case Florence came home unexpectedly. She turned on the TV, then the VCR, popped in the video, and pressed PLAY. What could it be? Had Vernon given

Marlene a tape of her own birthday party? Surely she would have just thrown it away.

Jane watched the TV screen. First there was sky blue, but only for a moment. Then there was soft rock music, and she was looking at something she couldn't identify. Flesh—close up. Moving, shifting. And there was sound. Moaning. A woman moaning.

Porno? Had Vernon given Marlene a *porn video?* Jane supposed she wouldn't be surprised.

Porn star . . .

"Winky—don't look at this," Jane murmured, but the cat practically had her nose on the screen.

The camera pulled back. Jane could tell what she was looking at now. There were two women, naked on a bed, making love. Jane watched, transfixed. Was this what Vernon had given Marlene—a lesbian porn video?

One of the women, who had a smoothly voluptuous yet athletic body and long silky blond hair, had her face between the legs of the other woman, obviously the moaner. The camera moved up the moaner's body—not a bad body, firm and smooth, but not as beautiful as the other woman's. Jane guessed this woman was older.

The camera reached her face.

Jane gasped. She reached for a chair, missed, and fell on the floor.

It was Audrey.

Twenty-five

On the screen, Audrey moaned and her eyes rolled back in her head. A thin film of sweat glistened on her forehead and upper lip.

How could this be—?

Who could—?

The camera moved back to the younger woman, who now rose up on her haunches and turned toward the camera with a triumphant smile.

It was Marlene.

She winked at the camera, tossed her hair the way she did, and returned her attention to Audrey, now running her hands slowly up Audrey's torso and caressing her breasts, taking one of Audrey's nipples in her mouth . . .

With a sudden movement Jane pushed the EJECT button on the VCR. Then she turned it off. The TV screen went sky blue. She turned it off too.

Her heart thudding, she sat on the carpet where she had fallen, staring into nothingness.

Audrey and Marlene—*lovers?*

Jane could see why Marlene wouldn't have wanted anyone to see this video. But who had made it? Vernon? Had Audrey known she was being taped? Clearly Marlene had known, as evidenced by her conspiratorial wink at the camera operator.

From the front of the house came the soft rumble of the Corolla. Jane looked at her watch: 2:30. Florence must have finished the grocery shopping early and come home to unload before picking up Nick.

Jane pulled herself together, or tried to. She got up from the floor, straightened her clothes, and shook back her hair. Florence wouldn't know she was in here, though she might notice the closed doors and wonder. Jane slipped the videocassette into her skirt pocket. She hurried to the kitchen, went to the back hall, and opened the door to the garage. Florence was leaning into the Corolla's trunk, reaching for a bag of groceries. When she straightened and saw Jane standing in the doorway she jumped.

"Oh, missus, you startled me!" Her face broke into its beautiful white grin. "Home so early? Just in time to help with these."

"Yes, of course." Jane took the bundle from Florence.

Florence was watching her. "What's wrong, missus?"

Jane looked at her sharply, forced a smile. "Wrong? Nothing. Why?"

"You're as white as flour."

"Am I? Oh, dear, I must need more makeup." Jane laughed. "Pasty old me."

Florence shrugged, clearly unconvinced but aware that

Jane had no intention of disclosing what was troubling her. "It's okay, missus. I'll do these. You can go do your manuscripts."

"Don't be silly." Jane carried the bag into the kitchen, deposited it on the counter, and moved around Florence to return to the garage for another bag. Within a few minutes all the bags stood lined up in a row.

"*Now* I'll go do my manuscripts," Jane said, "but at the office. I'll see you around five-thirty."

"Very good," Florence said, stacking cans in the cupboard. She looked over her shoulder at Jane, concern in her eyes. "You need anything, you be sure to come to Florence."

Jane smiled gratefully. "Thank you, Florence. I appreciate it—I really do." Perhaps one day their relationship would be such that Jane *could* confide in her—though she would never be able to confide in her about what she'd just found.

Jane went out through the garage but walked right past her car. She wouldn't go to the office just yet.

First she had to talk to Audrey, much as she dreaded it.

She crossed the street toward the majestic house that seemed to glare down on her in haughty defiance.

returned a moment later with Audrey in tow. She wore a little scowl of irritation that vanished when she saw Jane, a huge closemouthed smile taking its place.

"Janey, howdy there, doll! What brings you here today?"

"I wanted to chat with you about something," Jane said, wishing Elliott would leave already.

Audrey looked puzzled. "Chat?"

"Yes. Can we have some coffee?"

"Sure," Audrey said.

"I'm out of here." Elliott took his coat from the closet. "You two stay out of trouble, now, you hear?"

"Yes, darling," Audrey said, and kept her smile pasted on only until he was gone. "He took today off, as you can see."

Jane nodded. "Racquetball."

"Mm," Audrey said. "Let's go in the kitchen. I've got coffee just made."

In the kitchen they put everything on a tray, and Audrey carried it to the living room. She set down the tray on a cocktail table between two plump periwinkle sofas.

"So," Audrey said, pouring, "what did you want to chat about?" She handed Jane her cup. "Jane, you look positively terrified."

"Audrey, I . . . I found . . . I don't know how to say this . . ." Finally Jane gave up and reached into her skirt pocket for the videocassette.

Audrey, blond brows knitted, watched Jane in bafflement. Then, when the tape was completely visible, her face underwent a terrible change. Her brows relaxed and

Twenty-six

It was Elliott who opened the door. "Well, say, beautiful, looks like you're off today, too!"

Smiling and animated, he wore gray wool slacks and a red V-neck sweater over a crisp white shirt open at the collar. His hair was a mass of glossy black curls; clearly he'd just showered.

"Come in, come in. Business slow today?"

"Not really, no. I just wanted to talk to Audrey about something."

"Audrey's doing laundry, and I'm on my way to play some racquetball with our mutual friend Roger."

Then Roger had said nothing of recent events to Elliott. If Roger had, Elliott was one hell of an actor. But then, what reason would Elliott have to pretend he didn't know? Embarrassment? Maybe—men were like that.

"Aud!" he called. "Jane's here."

"What?" Audrey called from the back of the house.

Elliott rolled his eyes. "Excuse me." He jogged off and

her jaw dropped and her eyes widened and she drew in her breath as if she were looking at a hideous monster. "Is that . . ."

"Yes." Intently Jane studied her coffee, deeply embarrassed.

Audrey put her hands over her face. "I knew it. I knew it. She gave it to you, the conniving bitch."

"She didn't give it to me. I found it."

"You found it? Where?"

"Under the mattress in Marlene's room. Well, Florence's room now."

"Under the mattress? Why would she have put it there?"

"So no one would find it, obviously."

"Well, *obviously*, Jane. What I mean is, why did she leave it there?"

"Good question. Not one I have an answer to yet." Jane reached for her coffee, made a business of adding milk and sugar. "Do you have any answers for me, Audrey? Answers you didn't share with me before?"

Audrey let her shoulders slump, thoroughly defeated. "I'm ashamed, Jane. I'm really ashamed. I can't imagine what you'll think of me."

Jane said nothing, waited.

"All right," Audrey said bravely, "I will tell you. I might as well, right? I can't shock you any more than you have been."

She gazed down at the tray. "Not long after Marlene got to Shady Hills, she started to . . . flirt with me."

"*Flirt* with you?"

Audrey nodded quickly, her eyes beseeching Jane to

believe her. "There was no mistaking it. The first time was when you sent her over here with that money you owed Cara for baby-sitting. Remember?"

"Yes."

"We were right over there in the foyer. She held out the money, and as I took it, her hand stroked mine and she looked me straight in the eye and her eyebrows went up a little.

"I can tell you," Audrey said with a shocked laugh, "I was thrown for a loop. I—I didn't know what to make of it. I figured, well, that's what she is, and I left it at that. Highly inappropriate of her, but it won't happen again.

"But it did happen again. This time it was at the Labor Day picnic. Right there on the green! Remember, Marlene and I were both helping with the little kids' games. It was during the egg-and-spoon race. We were near the bandstand. Somebody's egg rolled underneath, and I knelt down to reach for it. Next thing I knew, Marlene was kneeling beside me, and she—she touched my breast. Then she gave me that look again.

"Jane, I'll be completely honest with you and say this time I wasn't horrified—I was interested." She looked straight at Jane, as if in defiance. "Think what you like, but I couldn't help it. Marlene is probably the most beautiful girl I've ever seen. I'd never had thoughts like that before, but now I did. Her wanting me was—*flattering*. It was just nice to be wanted."

Jane looked at Audrey in surprise.

"I know what you're thinking, Jane. She's got Elliott, the rich, handsome cardiovascular surgeon who'll probably be executive director of NJRI, who treats her like a queen. He treats me like a queen, all right—he never touches me!"

Here her voice broke and she started to cry. "We haven't had sex in over a year, Jane. He's screwing one of his nurses; I know it for sure. That's where he's going now—not to play racquetball with Roger. But Roger covers for Elliott. You know, male solidarity and all that bullshit.

"So I was flattered—and interested, damn it." She took a napkin from the tray and used it to dab at the corners of her eyes. "Think what you want—I don't care. I wanted to see what it was like. So the next time it happened— this time it was when she brought over a letter that had been delivered to your house by mistake—the next time she gave me that look, I smiled and gave her a look right back. She said I was beautiful and that she'd wanted to make love to me since she met me.

"We agreed to meet a week later at a motel—one of those dumpy by-the-hour places on Route Forty-six." She shook her head. "I've never been so scared as I was that week. But I met her. It was in the evening. I told Elliott and Cara I had a meeting about some school event I was helping with.

"When I got to the motel and Marlene and I went into that room, I thought my knees would give out under me. But we—we did make love, and, well"—she looked away—"you've seen the tape—you know I enjoyed it."

Audrey threw out her hands. "I thought that would be the end of it! We'd gotten it out of our systems. I told her it couldn't happen again. She said she was disappointed but understood." She laughed ruefully. "She'd had no intention of repeating it. You have in your hands the only reason she came on to me in the first place."

"But *why?*" Jane asked.

"Why do you think?" Audrey knocked twice on the side of her head. "M-O-N-E-Y. Blackmail. Two days later, she came over here with the tape and played it for me. I thought I would die. Truly. My heart was beating so fast I really thought I would have a heart attack."

"But who took the video?" Jane asked, baffled.

"I have no idea," Audrey said, and then her eyes narrowed as she said, "But I know *how* it was done. I remembered there'd been a big armchair right next to the bed. When I entered the room, Marlene had already taken the bedspread off the bed and folded it and draped it over the back of the chair. Someone was hiding under there with a video camera. They had to be. You saw how close up the tape was."

"Yes," Jane admitted.

"Your little nanny wanted money. A lot of it. And fast."

"How much?"

"Ten thousand dollars," Audrey said.

"Ten thousand dollars!" Jane cried.

Audrey nodded.

"And you gave it to her?" Jane faltered.

"What was I supposed to do? It was the only way she'd give me the tape. She said if I didn't give her the money, she would make the tape public, send it to the local news."

Audrey gave a bright artificial smile, eyebrows raised.

"Can't you just picture it? Wife of prominent surgeon stars in lesbian porn flick with neighboring nanny! I truly believe she would have done it." Her face darkened with hatred. "She was like that, Jane—spiteful. And if she had, it would have ruined everything; it would have destroyed my life. I would have lost Elliott, this house, Cara, everything." She nodded. "Oh, I know what you're thinking. Elliott's a jerk and he's not much interested in me anyway. But we're a good team. We've worked hard to get here. I wasn't going to let some cheap slut take it all away."

"But ten thousand dollars. . . ." Jane began.

Audrey shrugged. "That's not a lot for us, Jane. The hard part was getting it quickly, and in such a way that Elliott wouldn't find out."

"And did you do it?"

"Yes. I liquidated some of my own investments. I got the little bitch her money. I called her, and we agreed on a time when I would give it to her." She looked straight at Jane, her eyes bulging. "But when she got here, she didn't have the tape. When I asked her where it was, she said she'd decided she hadn't asked me for enough money, that for rich people like Elliott and me, ten thousand dollars was nothing. She wanted twenty thousand more."

"Good heavens!" Jane cried.

"I should have told her no. But I believed that would be the end of it. So I went back to the bank and got the money. I'd already made arrangements to liquidate more of my assets, and the people at the bank had it ready, though I can't imagine what they were thinking.

"When I got home, I called Marlene and told her to

come over with the tape. *That* was why she was here, Jane." She lowered her gaze. "I'm sorry I lied to you."

"So what happened?" Jane asked.

"Marlene came over, took the money, *and still refused to give me the tape!* She said she'd decided to extend her payment program for a while and would be back for more.

"Well, Jane, I saw red." Audrey was practically growling now, as if reliving those moments. "I grabbed her, called her horrible things. I told her I'd tell you everything she'd done, and she dared me to do it. I was so scared and frustrated. That's why I slapped her across her smug face, not because of any Lladro—another lie. She ran out of here in a fury, and on her way out she said she'd show the tape to Elliott and send it to the news."

Audrey shook her head and leaned forward now for some coffee. "I didn't know what to do," she said, tearing open two packets of Equal. "I paced and cried and paced. Then I realized there was only one thing I *could* do. I had to tell you everything. You were responsible for her. You needed to know what she'd been up to. I prayed you'd understand. If you thought badly of me, well, that would be my problem, but I was going to tell you—right in front of her, if need be."

She stirred her coffee, sat back with the cup. "I thought you were home, because when I'd come back from the bank, I'd seen Roger's Jaguar parked up the hill and I figured he was visiting you. Of course, if he'd still been there, I would have waited until he was gone before I told you."

Audrey sipped her coffee, then went on. "When I went

outside, I looked up the road and saw that Roger's car was gone. I was glad—that simplified matters. I started to cross the road, but as I did, a different car pulled up in front of your house. A grotty old gray sedan. I stepped behind a tree and watched. A big heavy girl with a dark braid got out of the car and went up the path to your front door. I could see her through the space in the hedge. She rang the bell. Marlene opened the door. I figured the girl was a friend of Marlene's.

"It was then I noticed that *your* car wasn't there, Jane. Not in the driveway or the garage. I assumed you'd left when Roger did. I was terribly disappointed. I'd worked up the courage to tell you everything, and you weren't home."

"You could have called me at the office," Jane said. "You could have come to see me there."

Audrey looked shocked at this suggestion. "No, it wasn't something to discuss downtown, Jane. I promised myself I would just tell you later, when you got home."

"But you didn't," Jane pointed out.

"No. I was going to the next day, but I lost my nerve and swore I'd do it the next day. Then I heard Marlene had left. That made sense. She knew I wouldn't give her any more money, so she got out while the getting was good. That made things easy for me." Her face grew worried. "Of course, there's no telling when she'll come back. . . ."

Jane shook her head, smiling sympathetically. "You don't have to worry anymore, Audrey. It's highly unlikely she'll come back." Jane got to her feet and laid the videocassette on the tray beside the coffeepot. Sadly, she gave Audrey's hand a reassuring pat. "Your secret is safe."

Jane took the long way back to the office, taking Lilac Way up the hill to Christopher Street, then following it to where it intersected with Packer Road. She needed quiet, away from the phone, to think about what Audrey had told her.

To a woman like Audrey, there was no darker secret than the one she had just been forced to reveal to Jane. According to Audrey's story, the last time she'd seen Marlene was when the girl stormed out of Audrey's house in a fury. Could Audrey be lying? Audrey herself had explained to Jane how much was at stake, how much Audrey stood to lose if Marlene didn't keep quiet.

And in the end, Audrey had refused to pay any further blackmail money to Marlene. Marlene had promised to go public with the tape. Audrey now claimed that she'd intended to put a stop to Marlene's game by confiding in Jane and enlisting her help. That was what Audrey said *now*, now that Jane had found the tape.

Had Audrey really intended to confide in Jane? Or had she found another way to end Marlene's game? How far would Audrey have gone to keep her shameful secret? As far as killing Marlene? Audrey could have walked right up to Jane's front door, confronted Marlene ... They could have struggled, perhaps one of them had screamed—in that quiet neighborhood, where most people were gone from early morning until dinnertime, probably no one would have heard it.

How could Audrey have done it? Stabbed her? With

a knife she brought over for the purpose? With one of Jane's knives? No, then Jane would surely have found blood. Unless Audrey had cleaned it up.

Strangled her? Yes, that would work. Audrey was a big, healthy woman. Strong. Easily a match for the petite Marlene. Audrey could have strangled her, then dragged her body out to the dense woods behind the house.

But then who had removed all of Marlene's belongings from her room? Audrey? Where would she have put them?

Jane turned the car onto Center Street and into the alley that led to the lot behind her building. She cut the engine and just sat for a moment, thinking.

It just didn't hold together.

Twenty-seven

When Jane entered the office, Daniel was on the phone, answering someone's questions and trying to remain calm.

"No, I'm afraid I don't know when she'll be back." He saw Jane and his eyes widened in appeal. "Yes, Rosemary, I do realize she's been out more than usual lately, but she's had some personal matters to attend to. If you'll just tell me what you're calling about, I'll be more than happy to—" He broke off and stared at the phone, then looked up at Jane. "She hung up on me!"

Jane's jaw dropped. "Why, that rude bitch." She stomped into her office, fell into her chair, and flipped open her address book to Rosemary's number. She punched it out, seething with anger.

Rosemary's voice when she answered was its usual meek whine, as if her conversation with Daniel had never taken place.

"How dare you hang up on Daniel!" Jane said.

"Oh, Jane, then you *are* there."

"Yes, Rosemary, I just walked in—in time to witness your rudeness."

"*My* rudeness! I've left four messages for you and have received no return call. You're supposed to be my agent. You're my only connection to the publishing world. . . ."

Jane drummed her fingers on the desk. How often had she heard this from her clients?

"You know how lonely and isolated it is for a writer." Tears came into Rosemary's voice. "I just don't know what to think anymore, Jane. Am I important to you anymore? Do you care about my career? Are you still there for me? Do you still want to represent me?"

"No, Rosemary, I don't."

"I beg your pardon?" The tears had disappeared.

"I don't want to be your agent anymore, Rosemary." Jane looked up and saw Daniel standing in the doorway, his mouth open in astonishment. "You're a whining, ego-maniacal passive-aggressive with only a fraction of the talent you think you have. Besides which, lately there's been nothing *to* represent for you, because you turn down deals—"

"Only the last deal."

"Because of a frigging dog!"

"That dog is important to me!"

"Good. Keep the mutt in. I'm out." Jane slammed down the phone.

She sat there, breathing hard. "What did I just do?"

"You fired Rosemary Davis," Daniel replied, smiling in wonder. "Brava, Jane!"

"Brava? I guess. Crazy, maybe, but it sure felt good.

Nah, not crazy. Something I should have done ages ago."
She laughed. "And to think I was just passing through
the office!"

"I'd hate to see what happens when you plan to stay."

"I have been out a lot lately, haven't I?"

"Yes," he answered shyly.

"I can't help it. I've got to find out what happened
to Marlene." She wouldn't tell Daniel about the video,
despite what its presence under Marlene's mattress signi-
fied. She couldn't ever tell him about that.

"Speaking of Marlene," he said, "Ivy called."

She sighed. "You might as well bring me all the message slips."

He disappeared and returned with a thick stack of pink
paper.

"Good heavens."

"It's not all bad," he said brightly. "Holly Griffin at
Corsair wants to buy Carol Freund's novel."

"You're kidding!" This was fabulous news. Carol
Freund had written a riveting literary thriller that Jane
had been trying to sell for nine months, collecting more
than a dozen rejections. Yet she'd believed in the book
and refused to give up. "Please call her back and tell her
I'm thrilled and will call her ASAP, but that I've got some
personal matters to attend to, as you so well put it."

"Will do. So . . . any progress on Marlene? Ivy was—
well, she was pretty upset. She said she'd talked to the
police—"

"Here in Shady Hills?"

"Yes."

"Great. It's my own fault. I should have called her before this. What did she say?"

"That they had nothing to report. She wants to talk to you right away. She's threatening to fly out here."

"All right. Put her message on the top." She took the slips from him and placed them in the center of the mess on her desk. "I will call her, but first I have to see someone." She got up and hurried out to the front office, stopping at Daniel's desk. "And if Rosemary calls back to whine an apology—which she will—tell her we'll be sending along an official letter of termination shortly."

"Gotcha. Will you be back today?" he called after her.

"Not sure. I'll call."

She left the office by the front door, crossed Center Street, and started across the green. She glanced at the Village Shop, and as she did its door opened and Helen emerged, a heavy dark-haired figure in a tight tan raincoat. She crossed the street and started down Jane's path. She walked with her head down and didn't notice Jane until they were less than ten feet apart. Even then Helen's face registered no emotion, nor did she even stop walking.

"Hello, Helen," Jane said. "I'd like to talk to you, please."

Now Helen stopped and drew in her breath in annoyance. "I've talked to you twice already. I told you I'd tell you if she called."

"Yes, you talked to me twice, but you didn't tell me everything. Please, it won't take long."

"Where?"

"How about over there?" Jane indicated the bandstand. Helen shrugged. "Fine."

Jane led the way to the ornate white structure, and they climbed its four steps. They sat on the bench that ran around the inside.

"I have to be home in ten minutes." Helen took a cigarette and a book of matches out of her bag and cupped her hand around the match to light the cigarette. "My mother needs me. She's got MS. She's in a wheelchair, can't leave the house."

Without preamble Jane said, "You lied to me when I asked you about Marlene."

Helen shot her an angry look. "What do you mean, I lied to you?"

"You never told me you went to see Marlene the day she left. Why not? Because you gave her a ride? Where did you take her?"

Helen fixed her gaze on a squirrel sitting on a branch of a lilac bush beside the bandstand. Finally, she blew out smoke and turned to Jane with an expression that surprised her—a look of disgusted defiance.

"What do you think, that you *own* Marlene? That because you paid her practically nothing to take care of your whining brat, you have a right to chase her around? Why don't you give it up, give the girl some space?"

Jane gritted her teeth. *This is a young woman*, she reminded herself, *barely more than a child. I must remain calm, mature.*

"No," she said evenly, actually smiling a little, "I don't think I own Marlene. But you have to understand, she's my responsibility. At least, she was my responsibility while she worked for me, lived with me. She left without telling me where she was going. I have no way of knowing that she's safe, or even where she is. I'm sure I told you her mother is a dear friend of mine, one of my oldest friends, from college. I owe it to her to find out where Marlene is and make sure she's all right."

Helen seemed to consider this. Then she shrugged indifferently. "All right, I did go to your house that day."

"Why?"

"To give Marlene a ride, like you said. And no," she said nastily, "I didn't tell you, because Marlene made me promise not to. Marlene, she's *my* dear friend—you can understand that, right? So I was protecting her."

"Protecting her?" Jane said, brows knitted. "From whom?"

"From *you*," Helen exclaimed. "She knew if she told you she was leaving, you would have tried to talk her out of it, made things hard for her. You would have called her mother. She didn't need that kind of trouble. So she just left."

"Where did you take her?" Jane asked.

"To the station. Her bags were ready, and we loaded my car and I took her downtown and saw her off."

"Where did she go?"

"To New York, to stay with Zena. That's the girl you asked me about at the Tavern, right? So you had it figured all along. Why didn't you just call her?"

"That's a long story," Jane answered. "Why hasn't Marlene called her mother? I can understand her not wanting to talk to me after leaving the way she did, but to not even call her mother—"

"Who would try to pressure her into coming back to *you*." Helen shook her head slowly. "She's not coming back to you, and she's not going back to Detroit. She's having too much fun in New York."

"Then you've heard from her?" Jane pounced.

"Yeah, sure." Helen's tone was casual.

"When?"

"A few days ago."

"What did you talk about?" Jane asked.

"None of your business."

Jane stared at her, waiting.

Finally Helen relented. "She wanted to know how Gil was. She's still stuck on him, still wants him. But that's over. I told her to get on with her life, find someone new. She started crying. She wanted to come back and see Gil, plead with him to take her back. I told her not to waste her time. It's not gonna happen."

"Did you ask Marlene to call me or her mother?"

"I told her you wanted her to."

"Did you get her address or phone number?"

"No."

Liar, Jane thought. She considered all Helen had said. "So Marlene is living with Zena, and doing what?"

"I don't know, partying, shopping—what difference does it make?"

"She'll have to earn money."

Helen smiled slyly. "Maybe she'll find somebody with money."

"Has she?" Jane asked.

"I said maybe she *will*." Helen met Jane's gaze. "Listen. Now that she's gone, I don't see much future in my relationship with her. I don't think she'll be keeping me up to date on her life in the Big Apple." Her voice dripped with sarcasm.

"Really?" Jane said, equally sarcastic. "A good friend like you?"

"You can stuff that." Savagely Helen ground out her cigarette on the white enameled surface of the bench.

Jane winced.

"I gotta go," Helen said flatly, and left the bandstand.

Jane watched the girl's back as she crossed the green, the too-tight raincoat pulling with each step, the fat brown braid swinging heavily from side to side.

Helen's admission explained a lot. Marlene had simply gone to New York to be with Zena. And, judging from Helen's supposed speculation, Marlene had probably found a man to live on, just as Zena had found Trevor Ames.

Her bags were ready, Helen had said. Marlene would have been in a rush to leave before she was caught. And in her haste she forgot the videotape she had hidden under her mattress. Most likely she had already realized she had no further use for it: Audrey had made it clear she would pay no more blackmail. And as for showing it to Elliott or sending it to the local news out of spite, Marlene must have seen there was no future in that. After all, she herself was the tape's other "star."

Porn star . . . Once again, the words Gil had purportedly spat at Marlene during their parking-lot breakup echoed in Jane's head. Had Gil *seen* the tape? Yes, Jane believed he had, and she had a pretty good idea how.

Mesmerized by this new train of thought, Jane left the

bandstand and started back along the path toward her office.

Sitting at her desk, Jane regarded with dread the steadily growing pile of letters, manuscripts, book contracts, advance reading copies, and message slips. She knew what she should do first: call Ivy. She dreaded that most of all. But, as Kenneth had always said, "Do the worst first," so she resolutely picked up the phone and dialed Ivy at work.

Ivy's tone was cold, her voice tight. "Your not calling me back tells me a lot, Jane. This is my *daughter* who's missing, and you put me off like one of your trashy writers."

Jane decided not to respond to that. "Ivy, I don't blame you for being angry. I apologize for not getting back to you before this. But looking for Marlene is what's kept me so busy."

"Oh, really? And have you made any progress?"

Jane couldn't possibly tell Ivy about the video. "Not much yet, I'm afraid. I'm still waiting to hear from the police, but I understand from Daniel that you called them."

"Yes, I did," Ivy said defiantly. "The reason you haven't heard from them is that they have nothing to tell you. They spoke to that Gil character, and he denies having anything to do with Marlene's leaving. Really, Jane, *I* shouldn't have to be telling *you* this."

Jane decided to hold out a crumb of hope to poor Ivy. "Actually, I have learned something encouraging. Marlene's friend Helen has admitted she gave Marlene a ride to the train and that Marlene was going to New York to stay with Zena."

"Well!" Ivy said. "Why didn't you tell me that in the first place? That means when we find Zena, we'll find Marlene."

"Have Zena's parents heard from her?"

"No."

"Have the New York police found out anything?"

"They spoke to the post office about Zena's post-office box. On her application, Zena put down a phony address. It turned out to be a Korean grocery store. The police went there. No one had ever heard of Zena. Now why would Zena do that?"

"Because she didn't want to put down the address of the place she's really living—Trevor Ames's apartment. Did you tell the Harmons about my going to the play? About Dorothy Peyton really being Zena and that she's living with that actor, Trevor Ames?"

"No, Jane, I didn't."

"Why on earth not? That's the trail the New York police should be following."

"Because that theory's flimsy at best."

"Flimsy! I told you, I got a call from this girl. She was looking for Marlene, and when I called her back, I got this Trevor Ames's answering machine."

"Yes, but there's one problem. You have no way of knowing that the girl who called was Zena."

Jane decided not to pursue this conversation, which she'd already had with Daniel in the middle of St. Marks Place. "Well," she said with a sigh, "let me know if the Harmons hear anything."

"I will, Jane, but I won't count on hearing from you."

"What is that supposed to mean?"

"You don't care about Marlene. You don't really care about me. Our friendship . . . well, I just don't know what our friendship has been about. If you—" But Ivy's voice broke, and Jane could hear her weeping. There was fumbling on the phone, then a loud sharp click.

Jane sat perfectly still, a coldness filling her. She saw now that their friendship all these years since college had been tenuous at best. It was not a friendship born of similar values and interests, or even of an abundance of mutual affection, but rather a friendship born of a shared experience. How often did one remain friends with someone for that reason alone?

Would Jane and Ivy have become friends if they were to meet today? Jane asked herself. No. Decidedly not. But weren't many friendships like Jane and Ivy's? Perhaps, but it seemed to Jane that for a friendship to continue to survive, there had to be more, an evolving of the friendship so that it was based on more.

Of one thing Jane was sure: When this mess was cleared up, when Marlene was found, Jane and Ivy's friendship, whatever it had been about, would end.

In the meantime, Jane would do all she could to locate the poor misguided girl who might well have paid the ultimate price for her beauty, lust, and greed.

Twenty-eight

Jane left the office early, despite the backlog of work. Most pressing was Holly Griffin's interest in Carol Freund's novel, but Jane was in no mood to negotiate. She made it a policy never to work on a deal when she was sick, tired, or depressed, and she definitely fit the last two categories.

She arrived home around three. Florence and Nick weren't home yet, but as she passed the living-room window she saw the Corolla pull into the driveway. Nick jumped out of the car, his green backpack still on, and ran up the path to the front door. Jane went to the foyer and opened it.

"Mom!" Nick cried in surprise.

She grabbed him and hugged him tight. To her delight, he returned the hug with equal enthusiasm.

"Have you forgiven me for making you late this morning?" she asked, letting him go.

"Yeah," he said nonchalantly. "It was kind of cool walking into the classroom like that."

"We still won't let it happen again," Jane said, remembering the horrid Mr. O'Rourke. "How was your day otherwise, darling?"

He shrugged. "Okay. Johnna Cartwright barfed in phys ed."

"Oh!" Jane said, unsure of the correct response to this. "Poor Johnna."

Winky had appeared in the foyer, and Nick had already picked her up and started for the dining room.

Florence, coming up the front path, smiled warmly. "Hello, missus. What are you doing home so early?"

"Oh, just catching up on some work here," Jane said vaguely.

"You're looking tired or something," Florence said, studying her closely. "Maybe a nice nap."

Jane managed a smile. "I'm fine. It's been a difficult day."

"Well, don't you worry about us. Nick has his homework to do, and I am going to wash curtains."

"Curtains?"

"Yes, in the kitchen. No offense, please, missus, but they are disgusting. The last girl, Marlene, she never cleaned them?"

Jane burst out laughing; it really was the funniest thing she'd heard in a long time. "Oh, Florence, if you'd only met her. The idea of Marlene washing curtains—well, it's just priceless."

She was still laughing as she took Nick's backpack from him and helped him get set up at the dining-room table, his favorite working spot. He gave her the day's notices and flyers. One was an appeal from the Home and School Association for volunteers for the school's annual Holiday Craft Fair, to be held in early December. Another was a reminder that the school's Halloween parade would take place on Halloween morning and that children were to come to school in costume.

"Hey," Jane said, mustering enthusiasm, "we've got to decide what you're going to be for Halloween! Any ideas?"

He was already at work on a math ditto, writing furiously, his face inches from the page, his tongue hanging out one side of his mouth. After a moment he looked up at her and frowned in thought. Before he could speak, Winky suddenly appeared as if from nowhere, jumping onto the table with a little rumbling sound of greeting. Nick started patting her hard and fast.

"Easy," Jane said, "and put down the pencil or you'll stab her."

He dropped the pencil and resumed patting. Then he took Winky's face between both his hands and squished it tightly so that her features were almost lost in folds of fur. "I wouldn't stab you, would I, Wink?" Terrified, she pulled herself from his grasp, scampered off the table, and dashed from the room.

"I think I want to be a mouse," Nick declared.

"Oh, we have enough of mice where I come from in Trinidad," Florence put in, passing through the dining room, her arms loaded with yellow-and-white-checked curtains that Jane could see were indeed filthy.

"A mouse is a great idea," Jane said, suddenly bursting

with enthusiasm. "We can make a really adorable costume. Now, let's see ... I'll buy some gray felt at the Fabric Barn for the ears, and we can make whiskers out of brush bristles ..."

"Mom, I don't want you to *make* me a costume. I want to *buy* one."

"Buy one?" she said, crestfallen. "But we've always made your costumes. Remember last year you were a sandwich, and we used foam rubber to make cheese and ham and lettuce?"

He shook his head firmly. "Kids my age don't make costumes. We have to go to that place in Boonton where they have the best costumes. It's called Master of Disguises."

Jane had heard of it. It was a serious costume shop where grown-ups rented Halloween and costume-party gear. "Well, I suppose we could look into renting something, if it's not too expensive."

"*Renting?*" He looked at her askance. "I'm not wearing some old costume somebody else wore."

"Listen, young man," she said, anger building, "I am not made of money. We will do what we can afford. We may *have* to make a costume, and if *that's* not good enough, you can go without one."

She waited for him to slam down his pencil and storm from the room, but he only set his mouth firmly, squinted, and returned his attention to his math, continuing to work as though she weren't there.

Fine, she thought, and went to see Florence in the laundry room.

"Florence, I'll be out for the rest of the afternoon and

then I have my knitting-club meeting. Would you mind baby-sitting Nick?"

"Not at all," Florence said, measuring detergent. "I will give you the coconut bread I made this afternoon to take to your meeting."

Jane realized that it was her turn to bring something. She would have stopped at the bakery, but this was much nicer.

"That will be lovely," Jane said. "Thank you, Florence. Very thoughtful."

Florence gave her a huge smile. "You are very good to me. I appreciate that. Things like this are my way of saying thank you."

How very sweet, Jane thought as she walked away. Had she been especially good to Florence? She hadn't noticed.

She should have made an *effort* to be good to Florence. From now on, Jane vowed, she would. No more ignoring of the nanny, the way she had ignored Marlene.

How selfish she had been, not even trying to see Marlene as a person, to take an interest in what she was doing, in her life in Shady Hills. If Jane had shown this interest, would things have turned out differently? Would Marlene not have felt a need to seek companionship at the Roadside Tavern, not met Gil Dapero, not entangled herself in sordid intrigues with Roger and Audrey?

Jane would never know.

She felt quite ashamed.

Twenty-nine

This time Jane found Vernon in Paint. At the end of the aisle stood a counter, behind which he concentrated on mixing a custom color for a young woman with a toddler in hand.

Jane stood off to one side, waiting for him to finish. When he had put the paint can into the mixing machine, he glanced up, noticed her, and did a double take. Then he seemed to make an effort to ignore her, puttering behind the counter, straightening color cards, handing the woman a few mixing sticks, and asking her how she was fixed for brushes.

Eventually, however, he was finished, and as the woman placed the paint can in her shopping cart and wandered away, Jane approached the counter. Reluctantly, he met her gaze.

"We need to talk," she said softly.

"About what?" he asked, his gaze darting about.

"I don't think this is the best place for our conversation. Will you be finished soon? Can you take a break?"

He looked around furtively. "I can take a few minutes. Follow me."

He came out from behind the counter and led her all the way to the back of the store, through a set of swinging doors into a vast concrete-floored storage area. He walked to an empty corner and turned to face her, waiting.

Jane put her hands on her hips. "I know all about it," she said flatly.

"About what?" He gave her a blank look.

"About the videotape. How you hid under the bedspread in the motel room and taped Marlene with—that woman. How you gave the tape to Marlene outside the Roadside Tavern."

His face had gone deathly white. He drew a ragged breath. "If you know, then why do we need to talk?"

She poked her index finger in his face. "I want you to tell me exactly what happened, and I want you to tell me the truth. If you don't, I'll tell the police the exact extent of your interest in Marlene. I'm sure they'll have a lot of questions to ask you."

"Okay, okay," he said, putting up his hands. "So I liked her. I thought she was really hot—the hottest girl I ever saw." He hesitated, then continued. "Helen gave a party for Marlene's birthday. I thought that would be a good excuse to take some video of her. So I took my camcorder to the party and started taping her, but she got all upset. So I stopped."

He gave Jane an imploring look. "You gotta understand something. To Marlene, I was invisible. Dirt. Nothing.

She made that real clear. I could understand that, beautiful chick like her, but I could still look, right? I didn't mean no harm."

He grew animated. "But then, a few weeks after the party, she started noticing me. She talked to me—and she *never* talked to me before. I thought I must be dreamin', but she actually started, like, comin' on to me. I couldn't *believe* it. She said I was a nice guy, and she was sorry she didn't see that before. Then she asked me to do something for her. We went out to her car and sat there, and she told me what she wanted."

"What was it?" Jane asked, though she already knew.

"She told me she was gettin' it on with another chick. She said she swung both ways, and that she was interested in me, too."

"What about Gil?" Jane asked.

"That's what *I* wanted to know! She said she was sick of him bossing her around. She said he was boring. She wanted me. She said she'd spend more time with me, go out with me, you know, if I'd do this certain kinky thing for her."

"Kinky thing?" Jane repeated.

He nodded. "She wanted me to tape her makin' it with her friend. She said it had to be done secretly so she could surprise her friend with the tape as a special present. I asked her how the hell I could tape them without the other chick knowin' about it. Marlene said she had it all figured out. She told me to meet her on a certain night at the Sunrise Motel on Route Forty-six."

"And you did," Jane said.

"Yeah." He laughed ruefully. "She had it figured out

all right. In the motel room there was this big chair, and
Marlene pushed it right up next to the bed. Then she
took the bedspread off the bed and folded it and draped
it over the back of the chair so it hung down to the floor.
She told me to hide under there and just stick the camera
lens out when it was time to tape. I asked her what if
her friend noticed it, and she laughed and said not to
worry—her friend would have her mind on other things.
Then I asked her what if I made a noise or something,
and she said don't worry about it and turned on the radio
next to the bed."

He exhaled sharply, remembering. "So I hid under
there, feeling like an idiot, and Marlene left the room.
About ten minutes later she came in with her friend, this
older chick. And they took off their clothes and started
gettin' it on right there on the bed, about a foot from
where I was hidin'. It was *hot* under there, and I was
getting pretty hot myself, these two chicks naked, Marlene going—"

Jane put up her hand to signify that she got the idea.

"Anyway," he went on, "finally they finished, got
dressed, and left the room. I waited about ten minutes;
then I went home."

He couldn't suppress a smile. "The tape was unbeliev-
able. I knew Marlene would love it and so would her
friend. Marlene was like a real actress. She even winked
at the camera, like it was our special secret. . . ." His eyes
unfocused as he remembered.

"What did you do with the tape?" Jane asked.

"Two nights later I took it to the Tavern to give it to
Marlene. When I got there, Marlene and Helen were in

the parking lot, about to leave. I said I needed to talk to Marlene, and when I had her alone I gave her the tape."

His face darkened. "She was like a different person. She grabbed the tape and stuffed it into her bag. She got furious at me and said I was an idiot to give it to her there, right out in the open like that. I asked her when we could go out, like she said, and she *just walked away*. She just turned and walked away without saying anything.

"I followed her," he went on, his eyes blazing with anger. "I reminded her about what she said about us going out if I did this special thing for her. But she still ignored me. She and Helen got in the car. I went up to Marlene's window and told her she was a user, and she'd better at least talk to me or she'd be sorry. She rolled down her window and told me to leave her alone. Then she rolled it back up and just stared straight ahead, like I was air."

He paused, clearly trying to collect himself. "I lost it. Before she could start the car, I pulled at the door handle. I didn't expect it to be open—I figured she'd locked it— but it opened. She was scared—she looked at me with her eyes huge. She screamed at me to get away from her. She said she would never be interested in somebody like me. I grabbed her arm. I didn't mean to pull her out of the car, but she fell out onto the ground. Then she started screaming.

"People came runnin' out of the Tavern." His hand went to the scar on his face. "Gil hit me with a beer bottle. Then he dragged me behind the building. . . ." He shut his eyes as if feeling the pain all over again.

"An ambulance came and took me to the hospital. I was there for twelve days. I needed a lot of stitches from the broken glass, and my jaw was dislocated. I still can't open my mouth all the way." He carefully lowered his jaw to demonstrate.

"Did you press charges against Gil?" Jane asked.

He looked at her as if she were crazy. "No, no way. You do something like that to Gil, and you're history. Everybody knows Gil offed some guy in Newark about some money Gil owed the guy. I was already half-dead; I didn't need the other half. The cops tried to get me to tell them what happened, but I said it was an accident. They didn't believe me, but they couldn't get me to say anything."

"What about all the people at the bar who saw what happened? You wouldn't have had to press charges for Gil to be charged."

Vernon shrugged. "Nobody else wants to make Gil mad either. And I guess the cops knew they had no way to prove Gil did it."

"But you got back at Gil in your own way, didn't you, Vernon?"

A sly smile curved his lips. "Sure did. I'd made myself a copy of that tape—you know, for my own personal use. Soon as I got out of St. Clare's, I wrapped that sucker up and mailed it to Gil. I thought, 'Let's see how interested he is in Marlene when he finds out she's doing chicks.'"

"And you were right. He didn't like it, did he?"

"Nope, not one bit," Vernon said triumphantly. "Somebody at the Tavern told me he screamed at her right out there in the parking lot, called her a whore and a porn star." He giggled. "He was right—she coulda been!"

"So that fixed Marlene, too, didn't it?"

"Sure did. She screws with me, uses me like some—cameraman—that's what she gets. She begged Gil to take her back, but I knew he never would. Gil's never gone for that kind of stuff."

"How do you know?"

"I've known Gil since the second grade. We all grew up together in Shady Hills. Gil, Helen, Steve—he's the bartender at the Tavern. Peter Mann is older, but he grew up there, too. We're a tight crowd."

"Yet you let Marlene in."

He looked at her thoughtfully, paused a moment before speaking. "You know, she never really fit in. She and Helen got to be friends, but Marlene was still an outsider. Gil was hot for her, but I never really thought they'd stay together. She was different, not like us."

"Different how?"

"Well, being so great-looking, for one thing. Always dressed up and . . ."—he searched for the word—". . . glamorous, like some kind of actress. We're not like that. And she acted different. Like she always had a secret. You never knew what she was really thinking; she always seemed to be after something she wouldn't tell you about. I guess she got it."

"What do you mean?"

"I heard through the grapevine she's in New York, living it up."

"What do you mean by 'the grapevine'?" Jane asked.

He shrugged. "Somebody I know who still hangs out

at the Tavern told me. But it's no secret. She's with some old friend of hers from wherever she used to live— Denver?"

"Detroit."

"Right, Detroit. Some old friend. Zara, Zelda . . ."

"Zena."

"Yeah, that's it, Zena. She and Marlene are shopping and partying and having a great time."

"It's certainly a good story," Jane said.

He frowned, puzzled. "What? You don't believe me?"

"Oh, I believe *you*. It's the New York jet-set stuff I'm not sure about."

"Does it matter?"

"Yes, Vernon, it does," she said, her tone ominous. She stepped closer to him, her face only inches from his. "Where Marlene is now matters a lot. And if there's anything you haven't told me, if you have harmed Marlene in any way, you're going to be one very sorry young man."

He licked his lips nervously and swallowed, his gaze fixed on her face.

Jane regarded him a moment longer, then turned and found her way out.

Thirty

When Daniel arrived at Eleanor's that evening, Laura was already seated at a table in the restaurant's small back room that overlooked the mill wheel and millpond. By now it was completely dark outside, and the immense picture window loomed like a smoky mirror.

Laura had obviously stopped at home after work to change for dinner. She wore a cowled wool dress the same pale gray of her eyes. Her fair hair fell loose about her shoulders. She looked very beautiful.

She rose and kissed him as he reached the table.

"Why so glum?" she asked. "We're supposed to be celebrating."

"Celebrating what?" he said, sitting.

"Your exciting new opportunity. *Well?* How did it go?"

He shrugged, fiddling with his silverware.

She frowned. "What's the matter with you? You seem depressed."

He looked her in the eyes. "I am. I don't like lying,

especially to Jane. We've always had an open, honest relationship."

She rolled her eyes in exasperation. "What do you want to do? Tell her you're going after a new job?"

"I'm not 'going after a new job,' and if I were—yes, I would tell her. I *should* have told her I was going to see Beryl."

"Ooh, so it's 'Beryl,' is it? What's she like?"

"I hated her. She's a cold, manipulative monster. She said some awful things about Jane, things that aren't true."

"Really? Like what?"

"It doesn't matter what. It's all lies anyway."

"Where did she get these lies?"

"Roger."

"Roger?" She looked baffled. "Roger Haines?"

He nodded.

"How does she know him?"

"He's signed with her."

"Beryl Patrice took *Roger?*"

"Yes, and believed everything the lizard told her to place all the blame for his dying career on Jane."

"That's terrible! How could he do such a thing?"

"Easy. He's Roger."

Laura pondered this for a moment. "What does Beryl look like?"

"What a strange question. What does it matter?"

"I'm curious, that's all."

"An attractive older woman, well groomed, beautiful once."

"And . . ." Laura prompted. "Did she offer you a job?"

He nodded reluctantly.

She squealed and reached across the table to squeeze his hands. "What? What? Tell me, tell me."

"I don't want it, Laura. It's not me. She's got some notion I'll be the African-American agent. African-American is very hot right now, you know," he informed her with a wry smile.

"You've always been pretty hot," she said, and when he didn't smile she grew serious. "So? What's wrong with that? I'm sure you'll be free to handle other books, too."

"Laura, I'm not ready to just sit myself down and be an agent yet. I've only sold *one book*. I have more to learn. I don't think I would like it there, anyway."

"How can you possibly know that? Did you meet anyone else? Henry Silver?"

"No."

"Then you can't possibly know if you'd like it there!"

"Meeting Beryl was enough. She's a barracuda."

Laura's face was sullen as she sipped her water. A waiter appeared, and she ordered a glass of white wine. Daniel asked for Perrier.

"It's natural to be afraid of change," Laura said, choosing her words carefully. "But you can't let your affection for Jane stop you from taking risks, from rising in your career. I'm doing okay at Unimed, but at the rate we're going we'll never have enough money for a down payment on a house."

"I can rise in my career with Jane, the same way Jane rose in her career with Kenneth."

"That was different," Laura said. "Jane built up her

clientele while she was still with Silver and Payne. She had the agency name as a draw. What do you have?"

"Jane's agency is highly respected," he said defensively. "All kinds of writers approach us. We just have to be more aggressive. Jane's thinking of going to some writers' conferences to get her name out there."

"All that takes so much time. And who knows if it will even work?" Her shoulders slumped.

"And if it doesn't work? What have we lost?"

"I've told you—time and money."

"What about happiness? What about fulfillment?" He shook his head. "I got bad vibrations from that place."

"What kind of vibrations did you get about money?"

He looked at her frankly. "The money would be very good." He sounded almost sorry.

"How good?" Laura asked, and sipped her water.

"A draw of sixty thousand against commissions."

She nearly choked, and carefully set down her glass. "Dollars?" she asked in a high, thin voice.

"No, yen. Of course dollars."

"Oh my . . . Daniel, honey," she said, her face becoming solemn, "I want you to be happy and fulfilled, but we can't turn down sixty thousand dollars. It's three times what you're making. How can you even *consider* turning it down? If you'd told me that in the first place . . ."

"Nothing else would have mattered?" he asked sardonically. He shook his head. "That's not true, Laura. At least not for me. If it's true for you, and I don't take this job, and that comes between us . . . well, I think we have a serious problem."

"What are you saying?"

The waiter brought their drinks. Daniel kept his gaze lowered to his plate, concentrating on its border of tiny pink roses.

"Would you care to order?" the waiter asked.

"Not yet," Laura told him, and he went away. "No," she said to Daniel, "we wouldn't have a problem. I'm not like that, and you know it. I would never expect you to take a job you hated. I love you. I want you to be happy. But I also know you very well, Daniel. You're not good with change. It scares you. And your friendship with Jane doesn't make it any easier.

"I'm not saying you should take a job you'll hate, just for the money. I'm saying you shouldn't be so positive you'll hate it. Give it a chance. Think about it. You only saw her this morning."

"All right," he said, looking up with a wan smile. "I'll think about it."

"Good." She opened her menu, started to read, then put it down. "By the way, did you find out how she knew about you?"

"She wouldn't say, but I'm pretty sure it was Roger."

"Why would he do that?"

"To get me away from Jane—an extra twist of the knife. And Beryl would take pleasure in it, too. She clearly dislikes Jane. After all, Jane got Kenneth, and Beryl wanted him."

"From what you've told me, it sounds like Beryl wants everybody."

"Including me."

Her gaze snapped to him. "Daniel, do you think—?"

He threw back his head and laughed. "She's in her sixties!"

"So what? You think women shut down at sixty? Think again."

"Hmmm," he said, opening his menu. "Maybe you don't want me to consider this job after all. . . ."

Laura, engrossed in the menu, didn't respond.

Thirty-one

Jane drove carefully down Plunkett Lane, a narrow dirt track that snaked through the thick woods at the south end of town. The car's headlights pierced the darkness, throwing bare branches into stark relief. A light wind tossed dead leaves against the windshield. The clock in the dashboard said it was ten minutes to seven. Jane would make the meeting, which always began at seven, in plenty of time.

Jane had been a member of the Defarge Club for nine years, since she and Kenneth had moved to Shady Hills. In all that time, the only change in the club's membership had been due to the death of poor Karen Richardson of breast cancer during Jane's first year in the club. The club's meeting time and venue had not changed at all: seven o'clock every other Tuesday night at Hydrangea House, the only inn in Shady Hills.

Plunkett Lane wound deep into these woods, more than two miles, and ended at Hadley Pond. The pond was fed by the Morris River, which had once driven Hadley's gristmill, now Eleanor's.

Hydrangea House had once been the home of William Hadley, the mill's owner. For the past twelve years Louise and Ernie Zabriskie had owned the sprawling Victorian (it was they who had given it its name) and run it as an inn and a setting for weddings, company parties, and the like.

Jane stopped at the white wooden posts that flanked the inn's driveway, also just a dirt track, and turned in between them. She drove up the long, sloping lawn and parked just to the left of the inn's wide white wooden steps.

Grabbing her carpetbag from the passenger seat, she got out and took from the trunk the foil-wrapped plate containing Florence's coconut bread. She gazed up at the inn. Warm golden light glowed at several of the upstairs windows: Louise and Ernie were never without a few guests—people in the area on business, or sightseeing bed-and-breakfast types.

Jane climbed the stairs and crossed the wide porch, full of white wicker chairs and love seats and sofas piled with plump floral-chintz cushions. In the spring and summer, Louise added hanging baskets of flowers overflowing with vivid color, and often the club met on the porch, as lovely and peaceful an experience as Jane had ever had.

Before Jane reached the front door, Louise opened it, smiling in her brisk way. Jane was exceptionally fond of Louise, though this had not always been the case. Louise, the only daughter of an alcoholic mother whom Louise had cared for until her mother died of cancer, had built a wall around herself, a wall meant to keep people from seeing her pain at never having been loved by her parents. As a result she could be brisk and cold and sometimes rude, but one had only to spend some time with Louise to realize that this was not the true woman. In actuality, Louise was a caring, deeply empathetic person, the first to offer help, comfort, or sympathy to a friend in trouble.

She was a tiny woman, no more than five feet, and invariably wore tidy blouses and skirts and, on cold nights such as this, crisp cardigans. She had brown hair that she kept cropped close to her head because she couldn't be bothered, and fine, birdlike features—a tight little mouth, a sharp nose, and small brown eyes.

"Come in, come in," she said, graciously accepting Jane's kiss on the cheek. She took Jane's coat and hung it in the closet. "How are you, dear?"

"Exhausted." Jane followed Louise across the foyer and into the living room on the right. A fire roared in the hearth at the back of the room, at the center of which two fat sofas upholstered in a green-and-gold tapestry print faced each other across a large coffee table. Completing the square were two chairs in solid hunter green, one with its back to the fireplace, the other facing it.

"Is something the matter?" Louise asked.

Jane waved in a dismissive gesture. "Same old trouble. Trying to find out what happened to my nanny."

"Oh yes, I heard. Left, I understand."

Jane set down the coconut bread on the coffee table, plunked her carpetbag on the sofa on the right, and sat down beside it. "How'd you hear?"

Louise frowned in thought. "I think Ginny told me. But you've found a wonderful new woman, she said."

"Yes, Florence. A treasure. She made that." Jane indicated the plate.

"Mmm, can't wait to try it."

Ernie appeared in the doorway—dear plump Ernie in his snug fisherman's knit and heavy black-framed glasses. " 'Evening, Jane."

"How's it going, Ernie?"

"Not bad, not bad. Can't stop to talk, though. Gotta get that coffee made, or I'm in trouble." He winked.

"Oh, please," Louise scoffed. "The poor overworked slave." She sat down in the chair that faced the fireplace. "Penny can't come tonight. Alan's got the flu and can't watch the baby."

"Poor Alan. Everyone else coming?" Jane asked.

Louise nodded, eyes wide. "Even Rhoda. I guess you know."

"About David. Yes. In fact I saw him in Whipped Cream with *her* today. Gave her a ring, right there in the coffee shop. Made Ginny and me sick."

"He's a pig," Louise said, as if stating an absolute fact. "I warned Rhoda trouble was coming. I must say she's taking it well. She says she's not going to be one of those pathetic abandoned middle-aged women. She's going to get on with her life."

"That's right," Rhoda said from the doorway. She marched in, carrying her flowered carryall, and kissed Jane and Louise hello before falling into her usual spot on the sofa facing Jane, at the end near Louise and the fireplace.

Louise looked uncomfortable. "Sorry, Rhoda."

"Sorry? About what? What you said is exactly right, all of it. David is a pig, and I'm embarrassed I didn't see it sooner and divorce *him*. As it is, I'm grateful to know sooner than later. Let him have his little piece and see how long she interests him. And then . . ." She shrugged uncaringly.

Jane admired Rhoda's attitude. Rhoda really would be better off without David, and she was fortunate to see that so clearly. Rhoda was an attractive woman, trim and tallish, with lovely, gently waving variegated blond hair to her shoulders and a handsome face made striking by eyes as blue as a summer sky. Barely over forty, she'd have no trouble attracting a new man if she wanted to.

"So," Rhoda said, one brow lifting, "he was with her at Whipped Cream?"

Jane nodded. At that moment Ginny appeared in the doorway. Jane breathed a sigh of relief. Let Ginny tell the story. All eyes turned to her.

"What's going on?" Ginny asked. She sat down next to Jane on the sofa, placing her canvas bag on the floor at her feet.

"We were telling Rhoda about David and Lola today," Jane said uneasily.

Ginny looked horrified. "You were?" She looked at Rhoda.

"It's all right." Rhoda looked unflappable, as if she were waiting for the details of a movie Ginny had just seen. "Really."

Ginny looked at Jane, who nodded encouragingly.

"Well," Ginny said, "he put a present on her plate when she wasn't looking. It was a ring."

"I know that," Rhoda said. "What kind of ring?"

"A diamond."

"Big? Not so big? What?"

"Big."

"Hah!" Rhoda leaned back against the sofa, as if that settled everything. "The bastard. I'm going to take him for all he's worth."

"Attagirl," Ginny said.

"Room for one more?" came a deep, brisk voice from the doorway. Doris, thin and stooped, was already making her way slowly into the room. When she reached the chair facing Louise's—Doris's special chair—she looked around at the other women, and her dark eyes sparkled in her wrinkled face. "What are we dishing up tonight?"

"My divorce," Rhoda said.

Doris fell into her chair. "Divorce! Rhoda Kagan, what the blazes are you talking about?"

"David wants a divorce. He's marrying his hygienist."

"Good. Let him drill her for a while. Never liked him. Now I can change dentists."

"You never told me you didn't like him," Rhoda said, leaning forward a little.

"Why would I have told you? You were married to him. Now I can tell you."

"Why don't you like him?"

"Because every time I went for an appointment I saw how he looked at those pretty young girls at his office and I thought, 'Look all you like, mister, but if you're smart, you'll appreciate what you've got in Rhoda.' "

"Why, that's awfully sweet, Doris," Rhoda said.

Doris ignored her remark. She hoisted her huge macramé bag onto her lap and started fishing around in it. "Now you can find someone good enough for you," she muttered. "Where's Penny?"

"Watching Rebecca. Alan's got the flu," Louise said.

Doris nodded. "So we're all here, then."

"Yes," Louise said. "Ladies . . ."

With synchronicity so perfect it might have been choreographed, the five women opened their bags and drew out their knitting, busying themselves with orienting needles and arranging balls of yarn.

Jane's mother had taught her to knit when she was eight years old. She had knitted through high school, forsaken it through college and into her career and marriage, and taken it up again when she'd moved to Shady Hills and learned of the Defarge Club from Ginny, who had herself just joined.

Knitting was the most relaxing activity Jane engaged in, despite the fact that she was the fastest knitter in the club, her needles flying so fast they were nearly a blur. She seldom missed meetings, treasuring their therapeutic benefits and treasuring even more the friends she had made. Here, she and the other women were safe to be themselves, to speak their minds, to admit to weaknesses, without ever being judged. For this reason, the Defarge Club was extremely selective about the people it allowed in: One bad choice could spoil the whole atmosphere.

Jane turned to Ginny beside her on the sofa. Ginny had been working for the longest time on a sweater for Rob, a complicated ribbed two-color design the others had warned her against as being too advanced for her. But Ginny had insisted, eager to improve her skills, and as a result often needed help from the other, more advanced knitters.

"What is it you're having trouble with?" Jane asked her.

"It's this color change." Ginny held up a place in the sweater where a maroon stripe met a navy one. "I've got holes."

"That's easy," Jane said. "You're not twisting."

"Twisting?"

"You've got to bring your new color up *under* your old color so that the strands twist. That holds the colors together. Otherwise you get"—Jane picked up the area in question—"holes. You'll have to rip out all these rows."

"Oh, pooh," Ginny said, though good-naturedly.

Jane herself was making a sweater for Nick out of green-and-blue hand-dyed wool she'd bought at the Yarn Basket, the needlework shop on the green. Several times in the past the store's owner, Dara Nielsen, had made disparaging remarks about the Defarge Club to Jane— proving, in Jane's opinion, that Dara was jealous of any needlework event in Shady Hills that was not of her instigation. For this reason, none of the club's other members would buy from Dara, choosing instead to travel to Morristown or even New York City for their yarn. But Jane took a perverse pleasure in buying from Dara and making her jealous. Besides, Jane didn't have time to drive to Morristown for yarn, and when she was in New York she barely had time for her business appointments and lunches.

"That yarn is exquisite," Rhoda said to Jane.

"Thanks," Jane said. "Also very expensive."

"Cheaper in New York," Doris said, not for the first time. She was barely visible in her chair, enveloped by the fleecy white afghan she had nearly finished for her new granddaughter.

"Doris," Rhoda said gently, "wouldn't it be easier for you to buy from Dara, or at least in Morristown?"

"Why, because I'm old?"

"Well, no, it's just—well—"

"Get rid of ideas like that, Rhoda, especially if you want to start again in the man department. Being old doesn't stop me from much, believe me. Not much at all."

While the other women pondered this last remark, Ernie appeared with the coffee. He set down the tray on the table next to the coconut bread.

"Whatever's under there sure smells good," he said, eyeing the foil-covered plate.

"Have a slice, Ernie," Jane said. "You can even sit with us."

The others giggled.

"Wouldn't dream of it," Ernie said.

"Wouldn't dream of what," Doris said, "having a slice, or sitting with us?"

"Either," Ernie said with a laugh.

"Don't worry about him," Louise said. "He'll eat some later, in private, when no one's looking. It's his favorite way to eat."

Ernie, looking stricken, left the room.

"That was a bit harsh, Louise," Jane said.

"I'm angry at him," Louise said. "The doctor says he wouldn't have high blood pressure and this sugar problem if he'd lose weight, but he refuses to even try."

"Sarcasm won't make him do it," Doris said.

Jane looked at Louise. Her face had turned quite red, and her mouth was working silently, as if she couldn't decide how to respond.

"Well!" Ginny broke in cheerfully. "I think it's time to unveil Jane's offering. Your new nanny made this, right, Jane? Florence?"

"Right," Jane said, unwrapping the plate. Slices of the creamy white loaf overlapped each other from one side of the plate to the other.

Jane poured cups of coffee and passed them with plates of cake and forks and napkins.

"Goodness!" Doris exclaimed. "This girl is a keeper, Jane. Damn sight better than that slut you had before."

Everyone stopped and looked at her.

"Doris . . ." Rhoda reproached her.

"No," Jane said, looking at Doris with new interest, "it's all right, Rhoda. Doris, did you know anything about Marlene?"

Doris put down her plate. "Not Marlene, no. But that boy she was dating, Gilbert Dapero—I taught him." Doris had taught at Shady Hills High School for forty-five years until her retirement five years earlier at the age of sixty-seven.

"I don't get it," Ginny said. "You taught Gilbert in high school but you know that his girlfriend of the past few months is a slut?"

"Yes," Doris replied, "because his aunt is a friend of

mine. We help at the Senior Center together. Silvana Mariano—you know her?"

Ginny shook her head.

"Silvana's sister Anna was Gilbert's mother. Anna died a long time ago—a terrible fire in her house. Gilbert's little sister was also in the house and died. Gilbert was seven when it happened. Horrible tragedy."

"What about the husband?" Jane asked.

"Never any husband," Doris said. "Silvana, Anna's only sister, was the only one who could take Gilbert. She did the best she could, but he gave her a terrible time. Police always finding him taking drugs or breaking into stores. A bad boy—period. In his junior year of high school he dropped out. A year later he left Silvana's house. She doesn't like the boy, but she watches over him as best she can, in honor of her sister's memory."

"And Silvana told you Gil was dating Marlene?" Jane asked.

Doris nodded. "She said Gil told her Marlene kept after him till he'd have her."

"Why didn't you tell me?"

"I thought you probably knew. And if you didn't, all the better."

"Why is that?"

"I told you. He's a bad boy. He was in my class two years in a row. Worst boy I ever taught—when he came to school. Most kids, they do pranks, kid stuff. But not this boy. When he was sixteen he raped a fourteen-year-old girl from Boonton. Just when it looked as if Gilbert would be sent away, the girl retracted the story, said it was dark and she wasn't sure it was him."

Doris chuckled ruefully. "Handsome boy, though, handsomest boy I ever taught. All the girls had crushes on him, from fat homely Helen Wichowski to beautiful Noreen Tyler. But Gil wasn't interested in high-school girls. Silvana told me that when he was seventeen he was already dating women in their thirties and forties."

"A gigolo," Louise said.

"You might say that," Doris said. "They liked him because he was handsome and dangerous and probably one hell of a lay."

"Doris!" they all exclaimed.

Doris shrugged. "He always looked older than his age, too."

"Okay," Rhoda said, "so these older women liked him. But what did he see in *them?*"

"Money, of course," Doris replied. "He was always after money—from women, drugs, robberies, any way he could get it."

"Why was he always after money?" Ginny asked.

"Some people just are," Doris said. "It isn't that Silvana was so poor. She had a lovely home up in the hills and a big expensive car. Silvana's husband was an executive at Johnson & Johnson. Gilbert didn't want for anything." She shook her head. "Some people are just always after money."

"I heard he once killed a man over some money in Newark," Jane said.

"So you *do* know about him," Doris said.

"Only a few choice bits."

"Never heard that one," Doris said, "but I'd believe it in a minute." She fixed Jane with a piercing gaze. "Shame on you, Jane, for letting Marlene get involved with a boy like that."

"Doris," Louise broke in, "that's hardly fair."

"No, no," Jane said, "Doris is right. I am ashamed. I disliked the girl intensely and therefore took no interest in what she did on her own time."

"I hear you're taking an interest in her now," Doris said.

"Who told you that?"

"Silvana. She said Gilbert was asking her about you."

"About *me*? Why?"

"Gilbert said you were asking around town about Marlene, asking if anyone knew where she'd gone."

"That's right."

"He told Silvana that he and Marlene broke up just before Marlene left town."

Jane nodded. "So he told me."

"You don't believe him?"

"I don't know what I believe," Jane said.

"Pray he's telling the truth," Doris said, raising one eyebrow meaningfully, and took another bite of coconut bread. Then she returned her attention to her knitting.

The room was uncomfortably quiet, the clicking of knitting needles the only sound.

Thirty-two

Jane was the last to leave.

"I hope you didn't let Doris upset you," Louise said, handing Jane her coat. "She has such a big mouth."

"Not at all." Jane slipped on her gloves. "Doris was right—though it's hard to have the truth thrown in your face."

Louise pecked her on the cheek. "Now you be careful driving home. We'll see you in a couple of weeks."

"Definitely. Tell Ernie good-bye and thanks."

"Will do," Louise said, and gently closed the door.

The night had turned bitingly cold, though there was no wind. The sky was clear, a three-quarter moon riding among a trillion stars. Beautiful, Jane thought as she got into her car. She drove around the circular drive and down the lawn toward the road.

A deep fatigue overcame her and she yawned mightily. The clock said 11:45. As soon as she got home she'd have a quick shower and crawl into bed.

She passed between the posts and turned left onto Plunkett Lane. It was nearly pitch-black in the woods, despite the moon, and Jane switched on her high beams. The harsh light gave the trees a ghastly surreal quality, as if they had been frozen in action. Slowly she navigated the road's twists and curves.

She slammed on the brake. A car blocked the way. It sat diagonally across the road, its rear to the right, its front to the left. It was an old white Monte Carlo, not a car she recognized. She wondered whether it might belong to Ginny or Rhoda or Doris. Rhoda would never drive a car like that, but Ginny or Doris might. Either of them might have borrowed this car. Jane gave the horn a little toot, but the car didn't move, and no one got out. She beeped again twice, louder this time.

Whoever it was must have broken down here. Had the car hit a tree? Jane couldn't tell. If it had, the driver might have been hurt. She might be at the wheel, in need of help.

Jane unbuckled her seat belt and got out. As she approached the driver's door of the Monte Carlo, she realized there was no one inside. The driver must have gotten out and gone for help. Perhaps she'd run out of gas. But if she'd gone for help, Jane reasoned as she walked back to her car, she would have gone to the inn, yet Jane had seen no one on the road. Unless the driver didn't know about the inn and had walked in the other direction. But she must have known about the inn, because her car was pointing back toward town, which meant she'd passed the inn on her way here.

But where had she been coming from? The only thing

at the end of Plunkett Lane was smelly old Hadley Pond. It didn't make sense.

Whoever the car belonged to, Jane couldn't get past it. She could never turn around on this narrow road, and she couldn't very well back up all the way to the inn. Should she walk? Wait for whoever owned the car to come back?

A hand clamped on her shoulder.

She screamed and spun around.

Gil Dapero stood only inches from her. He wore jeans and a black windbreaker zipped to the neck. On his face was the faintest smile.

"You wanted to see me?" he said.

Her heart pounded painfully. She spun around and yanked at the car door, but his hand was on it, holding it closed. When she tried to pull harder, he leaned against it.

She turned to run, but immediately he clamped his hand tight around her wrist and held her there.

"Let go of me."

"Not till we have a little talk."

"I have nothing to talk to you about."

He slammed his other hand against the car door, making her jump. "Yes you do!" he yelled in her face. "The cops have been all over me because of you, and I don't appreciate it. Just what is your problem, lady? Why'd you tell them I hurt Marlene?"

"I didn't tell them that," she said, her voice low.

"What *did* you tell them?"

"That you and Marlene were—involved."

"WERE! WERE! You sure you made that clear? Somehow I don't think so." His face was so close to hers she could smell his breath, not unpleasant but sweet. His black brows came together as he scrutinized her face. "Why do I get the idea you got it in for me, bitch? I tell you it's over between Marlene and me, and you tell the cops to go after me."

"I do know it's over," Jane said, bringing herself up straighter, "and I know why."

"Oh yeah?"

"I know about the tape of Marlene. I know how you felt about it."

He laughed in her face. "Then you know she was a pervert."

"No," she said. "I don't equate lesbianism with perversion."

"She said she wasn't really a lesbo," he said, shaking his head. "She said she only made it with that old broad to get enough money out of her so we could run off together. She said she knew how important money was to me. She had the money part right, but she chose the wrong way to get it.

"She begged me not to dump her. She told me she could get a lot more. I kept telling her no, but she wouldn't take no for an answer. She couldn't get it through her stupid head that I wasn't interested in no dyke, that no matter how much money she got, it wouldn't matter. She promised she'd be back with so much money I'd have to forgive her."

"But she never came back."

"Now you're getting it." He smiled, bringing his face close to hers again. He looked her up and down appraisingly. "You're not bad—you know that? A little old, but not bad. Nice eyes. Pretty brown hair . . ."

"Auburn."

"Mm. But you don't really do it for me."

"No?" Now she brought her face close to his, as if she were going to kiss him. "What does it for you, Gilbert?" she asked huskily. "Bullying girls? Cutting people with beer bottles? Killing people in Newark?"

She brought her knee up hard into his balls.

"Ah, jeez!" he cried, and doubled over.

She yanked open the car door, threw herself in, pulled the door shut, and slammed down the lock. Then she quickly reached over and locked the other doors. She fumbled in her coat pocket for her keys, and as she did she saw Gil straighten and stagger toward her. She turned the key in the ignition and the engine roared to life. Putting the car in reverse, she rested her arm on the back of the passenger seat and stepped on the gas. The car shot backward and, faster than Jane would have thought possible, she negotiated the road's turns. At the same time she used her forearm to lean on the horn, letting out a loud blare.

Trees shot out at her, but she maneuvered between them somehow, at the same time casting glances out the front windshield to see if Gil was in pursuit. So far he wasn't.

Suddenly from behind her on the road came the beams of another car's headlights. The driver beeped twice quickly and Jane saw that it was Louise. Jane stopped, jumped out, and ran to Louise's window.

"Let me in!" she shouted.

Louise, looking scared, nodded quickly and leaned over to unlock the passenger door. Jane ran around, got in, and locked it again.

"What happened?" Louise asked. "I heard the horn and knew something was wrong. Are you all right?"

"It's that Gil—he was waiting for me," Jane gasped. "He tried to scare me."

"Why?"

"He thinks I put the police onto him. Quick, Louise, we have to get back to your house. He's dangerous."

"Okay," Louise said fretfully and backed up the short distance that remained to the inn's entrance. She overshot it, shifted into drive, and raced up the lawn to the house. They hopped out and ran inside, locking the door.

"What's going on?" A sleepy-eyed disheveled Ernie stood at the upstairs landing in a red-plaid bathrobe. "Jane, are you all right? What happened? Was that you honking the horn?"

"Yes," Louise told him. "A man tried to scare her."

"What man?" he asked, alarmed.

"A man named Gil Dapero, who was involved with my nanny," Jane said.

Ernie looked confused.

"It's a long story," Louise said. "Go back to bed, dear. Jane's fine."

He hesitated at the banister, then nodded reluctantly and padded back down the hall.

"Oh, Louise, it was horrible," Jane said. "He blocked the road with his car and must have been hiding in the woods, because when I was getting back into my car he surprised me from behind and—" She broke off, remembering what Gil had done to Vernon.

"And all because he thinks you put the police onto him?"

"You heard what Doris said about him. Someone like that can't get far enough away from the police."

"Well," Louise said briskly, "that's who we're calling." She marched to the phone on the foyer table and dialed 911.

Jane grabbed the phone from her and hung it up. "No!"

"Jane, what's the matter with you? A dangerous man attacks you in the woods, and you don't want to call the police?"

"No—because he *is* dangerous. If the police go after him again, he'll come after me again. Then he'll come after Nick and Florence. I can't take that chance—at least not until after we find out what happened to Marlene."

"But what if he attacks you again? Next time you might not get away."

"He won't do it again. He said what he wanted to say."

"Which was what?"

"That he had nothing to do with Marlene leaving, and I'd better leave him alone."

"Do you believe him?"

"I don't know."

"Well, you're staying here tonight. Goodness knows we have room. Take your pick!"

"That's sweet of you, Louise, but I have to get back. I'll be fine."

"But what if he's out there? Let me at least drive you home."

Jane considered this. "All right. Thanks. But only if Ernie comes, too. That way he'll be with you on the way home."

"Good idea. Be right back." Louise hurried upstairs and reappeared a few moments later with Ernie, now dressed in jeans and a sweater.

"He's not quite awake yet," Louise said. "Come on, Ernie, we're taking Jane home."

"I appreciate this," Jane said, leading the way outside to the porch. "When we get to my car, I'll pull it over to the side of the road so we can get past it. In the morning I'll have Florence give me a lift over here to pick it up."

They piled into Louise's car, Louise at the wheel, Ernie and Jane in back, and rolled down the drive and out onto Plunkett Lane. Jane half expected Gil to jump out of the trees onto the windshield, but neither he nor his car was anywhere in sight.

Thirty-three

When Jane arrived at the office the following morning, Daniel hadn't come in yet, an unusual occurrence. She hung up her coat, opened the blinds to the grim gray day, and watered the philodendron that trailed down from the top of the bookcase in the outer office. Then she went to her desk and called Holly Griffin at Corsair.

"Well, hi, Jane. I was beginning to think you didn't want to sell me this book."

Jane had never liked Holly much, and Holly's passive-aggressive sarcasm was one of the reasons why.

"No, Holly, that's not it," Jane said, aware that her fatigue was evident in her voice. "It's been real busy here."

"Well, that's good to hear! Selling lots of books? Nothing I haven't seen, I hope."

Jane decided not to answer that. "I'm so pleased you're as excited about Carol Freund as I am."

"Carol, yes. She's very interesting."

"Interesting? Daniel told me you said you loved her work."

"I do like it, yes."

Jane rolled her eyes. This kind of feigned nonchalance was typical at this juncture. She had no patience for it today.

"Holly, why don't you cut it out and just admit you love the book? If you're worried it'll make me hold you up for more money, stop worrying—I intend to hold you up for a lot of money anyway."

"Now, wait a minute, Jane. I haven't said I want to buy the book."

"Oh. Then what are we talking about? Send it back."

Holly laughed, not a pleasant sound. "Oh, Jane, come on. Why are we playing games?"

"I don't know, Holly. Why are we?"

"*I'm* not. I do like Carol Freund's novel very much, and yes, I do want to talk to you about the possibility of our publishing it, but as for your holding us up for a lot of money, I'm afraid that's just out of the question."

"Send it back."

"Jane, wait a minute! Let's talk here. What are you looking for?"

"A hundred."

"*Thousand?*"

"You catch on fast. And that's for North American rights only. The book is already on submission with my subagents in Europe. Big buzz," she lied.

"Jane, have you lost your mind? This is a quiet first novel. If we're lucky we'll sell ten thousand copies."

"Send it back. You're definitely not the right house for it."

"Ja-a-a-ane, come on now. What are you doing?" Holly's tone was conciliatory.

Jane took a deep breath. "I told you, Holly, cut it out. I just don't have time. The book is fantastic and you know it as well as I do. I want a hundred thousand dollars for it, and that's hard/soft," she said, referring to a deal in which the publisher bought both hardcover and paperback rights at the same time. "That's a bargain."

"I can offer you fifty."

"Send it back."

"Sixty."

"I'm hanging up, Holly."

"All right! I can go to a hundred." There was a long pause. "Can I have two books for a hundred each?"

"No. You can have the first book for a hundred and the second book for two hundred."

"You're out of your mind!"

"Then one book it is. We can talk about the price of the second book later—assuming you get it."

"What do you mean, assuming I get it? It'll be my option book."

"Option, floption. Treat her right, publish her right, she's yours. Make a mistake, and we'll get out of the option and you know it."

"Jane, I've never heard you talk like this. Is something wrong? Are you angry about something?"

"Yes, something is wrong, and I am angry about something, but it's got nothing to do with you, Holly."

"Oh, good. Now where were we?"

"One book or two?"

"I'll have to ask Jack," Holly said, referring to her editor in chief. "He only authorized me to go to a hundred on the one book."

"Then why the hell didn't you just offer it to me instead of playing these stupid games?"

"You know why, Jane. If I could have had it for fifty, I'd have done so."

" 'I'd have done so,' " Jane mimicked her quietly.

From the outer office came the sounds of Daniel coming in the back door. He passed Jane's doorway and gave a tentative little wave.

"So do we have a deal?" Holly asked.

"I don't know. I have to run it past my client."

"Oh, right. Okay, speak with her and get back to me. By the way, where does she live? You said in your letter that she's a former schoolteacher, but you don't say where she lives."

"Northampton, Mass. A very nice woman." *Who doesn't deserve an editor like you.* "I'll call her and get back to you. Oh, and Holly—?"

"Yes?"

"If you get this book, when you speak to Carol, try to sound a little more excited about it than you have with me."

"Jane, I told you—"

"Bye, Holly." Jane hung up. "Jerk." Then she jumped up and began dancing in place beside her chair. "Yes! Yes!"

This was the biggest deal she'd made in a long time— not since making Roger's last deal, in fact. And this was a first novel—an amazing debut. Holly was excited, Jane could tell. This book was going to be big. She couldn't wait to call Carol.

She remembered that Daniel had come in. "Good morning," she called cheerily.

" 'Morning," he replied. He sounded different than usual, subdued.

She went out to see him. He was at his desk, sorting through some papers. When he looked up, his expression was glum.

She sat down in the chair facing his desk. "You and Laura stay out too late last night?" she joked.

"No." He didn't even smile.

Something must be wrong between them. Perhaps they'd had an argument last night, or even broken up. Jane realized she had better tread carefully. "Anything I can help with?"

Abruptly he put down his papers and met her gaze. "Jane, I'm leaving."

She stared at him, befuddled. "Leaving? Leaving where?"

"Here. This agency."

Comprehension hit her like a fist. She felt dizzy. She had never imagined that Daniel would leave the agency. They were friends. Like family. She had such plans for him. She would teach him all she could, as Kenneth had taught her, and when he was ready she would make him her partner. . . . But it was too soon; he hadn't given her a chance. She felt her world coming down around her.

"Why?" she breathed.

"Jane, I didn't tell you—I couldn't tell you—I was approached by Silver and Payne—"

"Silver and Payne!" she screamed. "You're going to Silver and Payne—that horrible place that treated Kenneth and me like dirt, that place that screwed Kenneth out of thousands and thousands of dollars in commissions? That place where that monster Beryl Patrice sneaks flasks of vodka into a stall in the ladies' room and comes out like Ms. Hyde?"

He just looked at her. "Well . . . yes."

"Oh boy." She looked away, studied the carpet. "This is too much. Why? How? When?"

"Beryl called me. She'd heard about me. They'd lost an agent, and she wanted me to fill the spot."

She looked at him shrewdly. "*How* did she hear about you?"

He hesitated, then said, "It must have been from Roger."

"Roger? What's he got to do with this?"

"He's signed with them. With Beryl."

She glared at him in horror. "Beryl Patrice—Silver and Payne—took *Roger?*"

He nodded.

"I can't believe it," she said. "I just can't believe it. It's surreal. And you're going there to be an agent."

He said nothing.

"Have you already accepted?"

"Yes. Jane, please try to understand. This was an offer I just couldn't turn down. It's—well, it's a lot more than I make here. Not that I've resented what you've paid me, but Laura and I, well, we want to get married and we'd like to buy a house someday soon, and to get a down payment . . ."

She put up her hand. "Say no more. I understand." She forced her mouth into a smile. "You're very dear to me, and I want what's best for you. You don't have to explain."

"That's what Laura said you'd say."

"But you could have told me," she reproached him.

"I'm sorry."

"So you knew Roger had signed with them, and you didn't tell me."

He looked down, ashamed.

"When are you leaving?"

"I thought two weeks would be fair."

"Fine. Fine." She knew she shouldn't say what she was thinking, but she couldn't help it. "Your timing is frigging perfect."

"What do you mean?"

"I just sold Carol Freund for a hundred, maybe even three hundred thousand dollars, so maybe things aren't as slow here as you think."

"Jane!" he protested. "I never said I thought things were slow here. I love it here. This has nothing to do with you or this agency. I—it wasn't me—"

"It was Laura. I understand. And she's right. You and I will still be friends. At least, I hope we will. And I do want what's best for you. It's just that this isn't it."

"The money . . ."

"Money is nice, Daniel, if you don't have to pay too high a price for it."

He sat thoughtfully for a moment. "What you said about timing. Is there anything else? Something wrong?"

"Oh, no," she said lightly, "other than that I still haven't found Marlene, and that last night a man attacked me."

"Attacked you! Who?"

"Gil Dapero. I was on my way home from Ernie and Louise's. He must have followed me earlier, known my car."

"What did he do to you?"

"Terrified me, mostly." She laughed, remembering. "I guess I was the one who attacked him. And I got away, obviously."

"What did the police say?"

"Didn't call 'em."

"Why not?"

"Because the reason he came after me in the first place was that he thought I'd sent the police to make his life a misery. That man is out of control. I can call the police and go to court and get restraining orders, but he'll ignore all that and come after me or Nick or Florence. No"— she shook her head vehemently—"no police."

She rose.

"Jane—" he said, clearly wanting to talk more, make things right between them. But she ignored him, walked into her office, and closed the door.

She sat at her desk and gazed down at the notes she'd made while talking to Holly. She picked up her pen and circled the numbers, doodled triangles and stars around them. She should call Carol Freund, but she couldn't yet, not now. Carol deserved an excited delivery of Jane's news.

In two weeks she'd be alone here. More alone than she'd been since Kenneth's death. She could hire a real secretary, someone without ambitions to be an agent. Or she could hire another Daniel, a brilliant, warm, funny, wonderful young man with the best judgment in books of anyone she knew. Sure, that was it. She'd place an ad and wait for the line to start forming.

"Damn it!" she said, throwing down her pen, and gazed out the window into the darkness of the woods behind the building. She shifted her gaze to one of the photos on her credenza. It was of her and Kenneth with four-year-old Nick between them, taken in Cape May. They'd rented a sailboat and Jane had worried about Nick, but Kenneth had insisted he'd be all right and bundled the poor little thing in an enormous orange life jacket. They were all wearing them in the picture, and they were smiling, laughing really, and Kenneth had his hand on Jane's shoulder—she could almost feel it there now—and Jane had her arm tight around Nick's middle.

So happy then. "Oh, Kenneth," she murmured, and her shoulders slumped. "How would you handle it?" And she burst into tears.

Thirty-four

At twelve-thirty Daniel had appeared in Jane's doorway and asked if she'd like to join him for lunch. She knew he wanted to talk more about his leaving, wanted to smooth things over between them, but she couldn't yet, it was too raw.

Now she gazed down at the dense print of a book contract, unable to concentrate. After twenty minutes she gave up and shoved the contract aside. Idly she embellished the doodles she'd made on her Holly Griffin notes.

She heard the front door open. Good, Daniel was back. She'd put him out of his misery, see if he wanted to talk now.

"Daniel," she said, emerging into the outer office, and stopped short.

Roger stood in the middle of the room, dapper in a navy overcoat. For a moment they just stared at each other.

He broke the silence. "Hello, Jane." His tone was formal.

"Roger," she greeted him, equally cool.

"I've come to say good-bye. I'm leaving Shady Hills. I've given up the bungalow, in case you know anyone who might like it."

"Oh, good, I'll get out my list."

He made a pained expression. "Please, Jane, let's be civil."

She put her hands on her hips. "Oh, I can do you one better than that. What do you say we just don't talk to each other at all? But then you wouldn't be able to say whatever it is you came to say, because you sure as hell didn't come here to say good-bye."

He shifted uncomfortably. "No, you're right, Jane. That isn't the only reason I'm here. I wanted to talk to you about Marlene."

"Marlene!"

"Yes. Have you heard from her?"

She shook her head, watching him closely.

"That's a shame," he said, "because I've been giving what happened between me and Marlene a lot of thought. Specifically, the money I lent her. And I've come to the realization that if Marlene is unwilling to pay it back, you're liable. She was, after all, in your employ—your responsibility, as you yourself put it."

Jane gaped at him, the way one might regard a creature from another planet. Then, before she herself was even aware of it, she was laughing hysterically.

Roger looked alarmed. "I fail to see the humor in this."

"Do you? I—" she said, the laughter rocking her. "I

think it's marvelously funny. Why don't you go to the police, see if they can help you out?"

His mouth set firmly in annoyance. "I couldn't do that, Jane, and you know it."

"Why not consider it Marlene's payment for services rendered?"

"I'm serious, Jane. As Marlene's employer, you owe me that money."

"Sue me for it."

"You know I couldn't—wouldn't do that, either. I want you to just think about what I've said. I want to work this out amicably between us. But I want that money."

Abruptly she grew serious, the laughter vanishing. "Listen, you pompous old fool. The only person who owes you that money is Marlene, whose location is a mystery to me. If you find her, you can take it up with her." She put her hands back on her hips, defying him to argue further.

He regarded her for a moment, sizing her up. Then he turned to leave. As he did, the door opened and Daniel entered.

Roger's face brightened. "Ah, the young prodigy. I understand you've accepted a job—"

But he couldn't finish because Daniel, his face the very picture of loathing, drew back his fist and drove it straight into Roger's nose.

"Ah! Ah!" Roger cried, his hands covering his face. Blood seeped out from between his fingers.

"Daniel!" Jane cried, horrified.

Daniel gave no response, continuing to watch Roger with contempt.

"What the hell did you do that for, you crazy fool!" Roger cried. "You've broken my nose! After all I did for you! Well, we'll see about that." Moaning, he stumbled out of the office, leaving in his wake a trail of red droplets on the carpet.

Daniel went behind his desk. He looked more agitated than Jane had ever seen him. Methodically he began sorting through some files, clearly trying to compose himself.

"I'm sorry, Jane," he said at last, without looking up. "I shouldn't have done that."

She smiled, though not understanding. "Anybody who punches Roger Haines in the nose is a friend of mine— just on general principles. But why did you do that, Daniel?"

"He . . . he told Beryl Patrice some not-very-nice things about you."

"Oh, really? For instance? Never mind," she added quickly. "I don't want to know . . . do I?"

"No," he said, looking at her soberly, "you don't."

She felt a warm rush of affection for him. She went to him and kissed him on the cheek. "My hero."

He looked away, busily shuffling and sorting.

Jane, smiling, quietly returned to her office.

Thirty-five

Jane closed her briefcase with a weary sigh. It had been a difficult day. After the Roger incident, she and Daniel had spoken to each other only when absolutely necessary, and even then their exchanges had been brief. Yet Jane yearned to say more to him and knew he felt the same way.

She had expected him to leave on the dot of five, but when she emerged from her office he was still at his desk, reading a manuscript.

"Well, good night," she said, smiling, trying to keep her tone normal and pleasant.

He smiled back gratefully. "Good night, Jane."

Through the window in the back door she could see the trees bending in the wind, and she buttoned her coat and put on her gloves before going out. But though it was windy, it was not especially cold, and the air felt good against her face. She breathed deeply, savoring the peaty autumn smells of fallen leaves and earth.

Her car was the only one in the lot. When she'd arrived at work this morning the lot had been nearly full, and she'd had to park in the back corner. Her shoes clacked hollowly on the pavement as she crossed to the car, half-lost in the shadow of the woods.

She got in and threw her briefcase on the passenger seat. Taking up her purse, she rummaged around for her keys.

Two arms loomed up from behind her, brought something down around her throat, and jerked it tight. She gasped for air but couldn't draw a breath. Panicking, she grabbed the thing at her neck and felt the rough surface of a rope. It cut into her skin. She reached back to grab whoever held it, but her hands met only air. The rope held tight, and no matter how hard she struggled to grab and loosen it, it was only pulled tighter.

Again and again she tried to draw air, but none could flow through her restricted throat. Her heart beat hard and fast. Strange strobing shapes swam before her eyes.

So this, she thought, *is what it's like to die.* But she couldn't die, not at the hands of this maniac, whoever it was. She had to take care of Nick, whom she loved more dearly than anything else in her world. A great rage blossomed inside her, and with renewed strength she pulled at the rope around her neck.

And then, as abruptly as it had appeared, the rope was removed. Somewhere in the back of her consciousness she heard the slamming of a car door. She slumped against the wheel, gasping in great gulps of cold air. She leaned on the horn, and its blare pierced the night. . . .

Thirty-six

"Jane!" Her door was pulled open. She sat up, still breathing hard. Daniel leaned into the car. "What happened?"

"Someone—someone tried to strangle me," she managed to say, and put a hand to her throat. When she brought her hand away her fingers were red with blood.

"Come on," he said, "let's get you inside."

He helped her out of the car, grabbed her briefcase and purse, and walked with her back into the office. She slumped into the chair near his desk and waited while he called the police.

"They're on their way," he said, hanging up.

"How—how did you know?" she asked.

"I happened to look out the back window and saw your car still there. I saw you struggling; then I saw the back door open. And then you beeped the horn."

"Whoever it was changed his mind," she said. "But why?"

"I can tell you that. Another car pulled into the parking

lot. I saw it pass. Whoever it was didn't stay—he drove on into the next lot—but it was enough to scare your strangler away."

"Oh, Daniel," she said in a low voice. "Don't you see what this means?"

He was at the storage closet, pulling out the first-aid kit. He carried it to his desk, opened it, and found some gauze. "Here, hold this to your neck." He thought for a moment. "Maybe I should have called the ambulance. . . ."

"Oh no," she said, waving the idea away. "I'm fine. Just shaken. Daniel," she repeated, *do you understand what this means?*"

"No, what?" he said, glancing out the front window.

"It means someone thinks I know what happened to Marlene."

"And do you?"

"That's just it!" she said, slamming down her fist on her knee in frustration. "I know most of what happened—I've got most of the pieces—but they don't fit together."

"So you don't know."

"No," she said, shoulders drooping, "I don't." She laughed ruefully. "If I'm going to die, I deserve to know the whole story."

"Jane, don't be ridiculous. You're not going to die."

"Oh, but that's not necessarily true. Unless I figure out what happened to Marlene . . ."

There was a knock on the front door. They looked out the window and saw a patrol car at the curb, lights flashing.

Daniel opened the door. A tall man Jane recognized as Detective Greenberg entered. He wore a black coat over his dark suit. With him was a shorter, heavily built man in a blue patrolman's uniform and a black leather jacket.

"Mrs. Stuart," Greenberg greeted her, nodding.

"Hello, Detective Greenberg. I'd like you to meet Daniel Willoughby."

They shook hands.

Greenberg said, "This is Officer Raymond."

Raymond nodded to Jane and Daniel.

"Now," Greenberg said, "Mr. Willoughby said you were attacked?"

"Yes, in my car just now. I went out to the parking lot to go home, and as I was about to start the engine, someone hiding in the backseat tried to strangle me with a rope." She lifted the gauze to show them the bloody mark.

Greenberg winced. "How'd you get free?"

"Whoever it was suddenly stopped. Daniel says another car had driven into the lot."

Greenberg turned an appraising eye on Daniel. "You saw the car?"

"Yes. And I saw Jane struggling, and then someone jumping out the back door."

"And going where?"

"Into the woods, I suppose. No one crossed the lot."

"Did either of you get a look at this person?"

Jane and Daniel both shook their heads.

"You saw nothing, Mrs. Stuart? A hand? An arm? Did you feel anything? Even a sleeve?"

"No. I tried to grab behind me but there was nothing

there. I mean, whoever it was must have been leaning back out of my reach. I'll tell you this: whoever it was was strong."

Greenberg shook his head. "You'd be surprised, Mrs. Stuart. It doesn't take as much strength as you'd think to strangle someone. It's all in the angles."

"I see. I'll be sure to tell that to my mystery writers."

Greenberg gave a small polite smile. "No idea, then, who it could have been?"

"Oh, I know exactly who it was."

The three men turned sharply to her, waiting.

"Yes?" Greenberg said.

"It has to be the same person who killed my nanny, Marlene. I'm sure she's dead now. I've been asking too many questions. . . . This person thinks I know his identity."

"I'm afraid that's impossible, Mrs. Stuart."

She frowned. "Why?"

"Because we arrested Marlene Benson's murderer at two o'clock this afternoon."

"*What?*"

He nodded. "I may as well tell you now. You'll hear about it soon enough. It's Vernon List."

Jane stared at him in shock.

"We did a thorough search of his car. We found a pair of ladies' panties stuffed under the backseat. We also found something else."

"Something else?" Daniel said.

Officer Raymond looked down at the floor.

Greenberg said, "A finger."

"A finger!" Jane cried.

Greenberg nodded. "A woman's finger. It was in the glove compartment."

"How horrible," Jane whispered.

"Yes, it is. But at least now we'll be able to get to the bottom of what happened to this girl. Eventually we'll get List to tell us what he did with the body."

Jane stared at the floor, lost in troubled thought. "Tell me, Detective Greenberg. What made you search Vernon List's car in the first place?"

Greenberg hesitated, looking uncomfortable. Then he said, "We had an anonymous tip. Which raises an important question. Who else knew that List killed Marlene? A very troubling question."

Jane nodded in agreement, still gazing down at the carpet.

"Mrs. Stuart," Greenberg said, "I imagine you want to go home and get some rest. Why don't you come see me tomorrow morning at the station and give a statement. You, too, Mr. Willoughby."

"All right," Daniel said. "But I have a question."

"Yes?" Greenberg looked annoyed.

"If you arrested the person who killed Marlene, then who tried to strangle Jane?"

"Obviously," Greenberg said, "the attack on Mrs. Stuart was unrelated to Marlene's murder."

"Oh," Daniel said, though he still looked troubled as he showed the two men out. He turned to Jane.

She was shaking her head slowly, still staring at the floor. "Wrong, Daniel, very wrong. They haven't got it. Haven't got *him*, I should say."

"What do you mean?"

"Vernon would never have killed Marlene."

"Jane, what are you saying? He was obsessed with her. She led him on, then dropped him like a piece of garbage. He would have hated her for that. He went into a rage. He killed her, then chopped off her finger as a memento, a trophy of his obsession."

She gave him a funny look. "I think you've been reading too many of Rosemary Davis's books. No, my dear, I've met Mr. List, and I'm telling you he's not capable of murder."

"Then who is? Gil Dapero?"

"Maybe. If the rumors about him are true, yes. But maybe not." She rose laboriously. "Can you give me a ride home? I'm a little shaky."

"Of course."

"Where's your car?"

"In the municipal lot. You know I never park in back."

"Smart boy."

She grabbed her briefcase and purse and followed him out the front door. She waited behind him on the sidewalk while he locked up. Then he turned and walked with her across Center Street toward the municipal lot across Packer Road.

"You may want to reconsider going to Silver and Payne," Jane said, shooting him a mischievous glance. "I'll bet exciting things like this don't happen there."

He looked at her, a deeply pained look in his eyes, and she wished she could take back her words.

Thirty-seven

"Missus, what is that on your neck!" Florence clutched at her own neck, her eyes wide.

"Oh, just a little blood," Jane said, cursing herself for forgetting to cover it up.

"But how?"

"I—fell and scraped myself on the corner of my desk."

Florence looked doubtful. "I'll get some first-aid cream and bandages."

"No, no, thank you, Florence. I'm fine. It's nothing. Where's Nick?"

"In his room with a boy from school—Aaron. I hope it's okay. I arranged the play date with his mother, and he stayed for dinner."

Wonderful Florence. "Mind! I'm delighted. Any dinner left?"

"Plenty, plenty. You sit and I'll bring you some."

Gratefully Jane dropped her coat on a chair in the corner of the dining room and sat down at the table. The sounds of Florence preparing Jane's dinner came from the kitchen.

A woman's finger ... Jane shivered at the gruesome image. And in the glove compartment! Someone had a sense of humor, albeit a dark one.

Suddenly Winky appeared in the kitchen doorway, a crazed look on her face. Like a shot she raced through the dining room, into the living room, and out into the foyer, where she darted up the stairs, her feet thumping frantically.

Florence came in with Jane's plate. "The cat does not like Aaron," she said with a laugh. "We figured out that it's because Aaron has a dog, and Winky smells it on him."

"Poor Winky—that's definitely it," Jane said, starting in on baked chicken, mashed potatoes, and string beans. "Thank you, Florence. This looks marvelous."

"My pleasure," Florence said. "Missus, do you mind if I go upstairs now? The kitchen is clean except for your plate, and I am getting a little tired. Aaron's mother is coming for him any minute. I'll get the door when she gets here."

"That will be fine," Jane said. "Thanks again."

Florence left the room. Jane heard her start up the foyer stairs. "Ah!" Florence shrieked, as suddenly there were more frantic footsteps. "You crazy cat, you almost pushed me down the stairs!"

Winky reappeared in the dining room, but this time she leaped straight to the top of the hutch, where she stood precariously among the photographs.

"Winky! You come down from there right now," Jane commanded.

Winky just stared down at her. Then she began picking her way gingerly around the photographs. Jane got up from her chair. "Winky, you get down from there. You're going to—"

Before Jane could finish, Winky brushed against one of the photographs, pushing it over the edge. It hit the floor with a crunch of broken glass.

"Oh, damn!" Jane said, and reached angrily for Winky, but she jumped down from the end of the hutch farthest from Jane and scampered into the kitchen.

Jane knelt to pick up the fallen photograph. She turned it over. It was her and Kenneth's wedding photo. Cracks radiated from the center of the glass like a spiderweb.

"Ohhh," Jane groaned in irritation. Fortunately, the photo itself appeared undamaged. Jane would buy a new frame for it tomorrow. She propped the frame carefully on the dining room table and returned to her dinner, hoping Aaron's mother came soon.

Gazing at the picture as she ate, Jane realized she hadn't looked closely at it in ages. She'd looked good in that dress—she'd give herself that. Really, it had been quite outrageous, tightly formfitting to the knees, where it flared in front and trailed behind in a ridiculously long train.

A train . . . She laughed at the idea. How frivolous. How . . . young! Yet that had been only ten years ago; she'd been twenty-eight. Not that young. But she'd wanted a wedding with all the trimmings, train and all. . . .

She froze.

She put down her fork and stared at the picture without seeing it.

Yes. It all made sense now. The pieces fit. Yes.

Now she knew everything.

Thirty-eight

She carried her plate to the kitchen, returned to the dining room, and put on her coat. Then she went upstairs to Florence's room and knocked on the door. Florence opened it. "Yes, missus?"

"Florence, I have to go out for a little while. Can you keep an eye on things?"

"Of course. I will leave my door open so I will hear Aaron's mother when she comes."

"Thanks." Jane stopped at Nick's room and peeked in. Nick and Aaron, a pleasant-looking sandy-haired boy, sat on the floor playing Clue.

"Hi, Mom."

"Hello, dear. Hello, Aaron."

The boy looked up and smiled. "Hello, Mrs. Stuart."

"I have to go out," Jane said. "I'll be back in a little while."

"Where are you going?" Nick asked.

"Just out."

She left the house by the front door. The wind had lessened, but it was colder now. The moon rode high in the sky, casting a pale glow over the small front yard within the holly hedge. Jane walked down the path and out to the road, turning right to follow it down the hill.

The roads here in the hills had no sidewalks. Jane kept to the grassy verge lest a car should appear around any of the road's sharp turns. Her hands shoved deep in her pockets, she continued downward, along the way glancing at her neighbors' houses with their warmly lighted windows.

Suddenly headlights lit up the road just ahead of Jane and a car appeared, coming up the hill. Jane pressed back into the trees so she wouldn't be seen. She caught a glimpse of the car's driver and thought it was a woman but couldn't be certain.

When the car was gone she resumed her downhill walk. The houses disappeared, and there was only woods now, a wilder part of the neighborhood that had never been developed. From the dense undergrowth to Jane's immediate right came a rustling sound, and she jumped. Just an animal. She kept walking.

Finally she reached the road's lowest point, just before its intersection with Grange Road. She peered into the woods to her right. By her calculations, somewhere in there lay what she was looking for.

She began making her way into the woods. The trees were not especially dense, but the undergrowth was thick—prickly tangled bushes that caught at her shoes and stockings, causing her to lift her feet high as she walked. She was grateful for the moon, illuminating her way.

The woods seemed to go on forever. Her legs were growing tired. She began to doubt her calculations, to wonder if she had veered off in the wrong direction without realizing it. But she pressed on, knowing she could always turn around if she had to.

Then all at once the woods opened up and she found herself standing at the edge of a vast clearing. She gaped, barely able to believe her eyes.

Before her lay a veritable dump, a repository of piled-up refuse. There were heaps of what looked like crumbled pieces of Sheetrock. There were rocks. Tires, dozens of them, tumbled together like a giant's toys. Lumber of assorted sizes and shapes. An upside-down baby carriage, one of its wheels bent sharply in half. A sofa with its springs bursting out. A card table with two rusty legs outthrust. A gashed green-and-white-striped patio umbrella. A jumble of rusted pipes. A massive old uphol-stered armchair lying on its side—perhaps Roger had managed to throw it over the cliff after all. She realized he'd never finished his story.

It was a sea of garbage, most of it lying at the base of the cliff to Jane's left—Mr. O'Rourke's cliff—which rose at an angle of perhaps forty-five degrees for about thirty feet. At the top she could make out the cliff's edge, a dim jagged line in the moonlight.

When Jane had heard Roger's story, when she had met the obnoxious Mr. O'Rourke, she had given no thought to what it must look like down here. Indeed, if someone had described this place to her, she would have thought that person was lying. Never, in a village as tightly regulated as Shady Hills, could such a place exist.

But here it was in front of her, a grim netherworld not meant to be seen. She recalled her brief conversation with Mr. O'Rourke. He had said he intended to clear this place for his luxury homes. Was that possible? Had he seen it? But of course he had.

Anyway, that was his problem. Jane hadn't come here to worry about him.

Once more she gazed up at the top of the cliff. Then she imagined a line of descent, probably a roll-and-tumble down the cliff's face of earth and gnarled low growth. Keeping her gaze trained on the spot she had fixed on at the cliff's base, she worked her way slowly through and around the refuse, which close up emitted a strong rotting odor even in the October cold.

Her shoes and legs and the bottom of her coat were filthy by the time she reached her destination. Carefully, she scrutinized the area. Just to her right lay a television, a huge ancient console of dark carved Mediterranean wood. Behind it a computer monitor with a smashed screen lay still attached to its processor by a cord, reminding Jane of an umbilical.

There were a lot of building scraps here—Sheetrock, powdered plaster, tangled wire, pieces of plywood and two-by-fours. How recently had these items been thrown over the cliff? That was important. Perhaps very recently, Jane thought, and resigned herself to ruining her gloves as she began lifting wood and jagged shards of plaster to peer underneath.

Her search was soon rewarded, but as it turned out

she hadn't needed to lift anything to find what she sought. For rising from the scraps like some bizarre signpost was a human arm, sticking straight up as if planted at the elbow. The hand, relaxed in death, was beautiful in its way, though not perfect. Its index finger had been roughly severed, leaving a white spur of bone surrounded by blackened crusted blood.

Jane fought down a rising wave of nausea and tried not to look at the arm even as she tugged at a triangular piece of plywood in an effort to uncover the body the arm belonged to. The plywood wouldn't budge, and she realized that one of its corners lay beneath a large rock. With a great effort Jane pushed the rock away, sending it rolling down the side of the junk heap. Then she returned to the plywood, which now lifted quite easily, revealing a shoulder and torso in a plaster-whitened sweater. The head was concealed by another piece of plywood, this one large and square. Jane lifted its edge and looked beneath it.

Marlene's teeth were drawn back in a hideous grimace that looked almost like a smile. Plaster dust filled her nostrils and coated her open eyes.

That beautiful face . . .

Poor Marlene. Poor Ivy. Tears came to Jane's eyes. Gently she lowered the plywood back into place.

A crunching sound came from the far side of the mound. Jane looked up sharply, her breath catching in her throat.

Not six feet away, at the foot of the cliff, a figure stood in the shadow of the trees.

"Happy now?"

Thirty-nine

Helen stepped from the darkness into the moonlight, her face its usual blank.

"I was just about to go see you," Jane said.

"Really? Why?"

"To ask you a question before I went to the police. I know *how* you killed Marlene. What I want to know is why."

Helen shrugged. "Because she found a way to keep Gil. Money. Lots of it. Money's all Gil cares about."

"And you couldn't let her have him?"

Helen's expression grew intense, as if she were willing Jane to understand. "Of course I couldn't. I love him. I've loved him since I was ten years old, since we were in grade school. Can you understand that, loving someone that way?"

Yes, Jane thought, *I can understand that. Love did exist before you were born.* She nodded.

"He's the most exciting man I've ever known. But you've met him, seen what he's like, seen what he *looks* like. And look at me. Do you think he'd ever be interested? Of course not. Not without money. Till now he's barely noticed me. But I have the money now."

"Marlene's money."

"Yes."

"She was your friend."

"My friend! She knew I wanted Gil; she knew I loved him. Marlene, the most beautiful girl anyone had ever seen, the girl who could have had any man she wanted. And who did she decide she wanted? Gil! My 'best friend' took the man I wanted, picked him like an apple off a tree, *and then told me everything that happened between them.*"

Helen snorted, screwing up her face in contempt. "She wasn't my friend. She was a sick, sadistic girl who manipulated people to get what she wanted. The only reason she buddied up to me in the first place was because she wanted Gil and knew that I knew him better than anybody. Hell, I've been obsessed with him for half my life. Marlene figured I could advise her on the best ways to get and keep Gil. She told me so."

"And did she know you loved Gil?"

"Hell, yes! That's what I mean by sadistic. She got off on it big-time. She knew he'd never be interested in me. So she said she'd tell me what he was like—you know, as a lover—so I could enjoy it vic—vic—"

"Vicariously. I'm surprised she knew the word."

"She was smarter than you think."

"And you stayed friends with her, even though she'd taken the man you wanted?"

Helen looked close to tears. "I *wanted* to hear those things she told me. I *liked* hearing what he was like in bed, what his body looked like, what he did to her. It was the closest I'd ever get to him ... unless I could find a way to get a lot of money."

"And you believed that if you got a lot of money, he'd want you?"

"Yes," Helen said simply. "At least for a while. You don't know Gil. He hates it here. He wants to get away. He'll tell anyone that. I knew if I could get enough money to get us away from here, he'd go with me."

"But even if you'd found a way to get the money," Jane said, "he was with Marlene."

Helen nodded. "I stayed up nights trying to think of ways to get them to break up. I thought about telling Gil some of the things Marlene had told me, about all the guys she slept with back in Detroit, how she'd used every drug there was—what a total bitch she really was. But nothing she'd done was as bad as the things Gil had done. And he knew what she was."

"But then they did break up," Jane said.

"Yes." Helen's eyes widened. "It was like a miracle."

"Did you know why they broke up?"

"No. And I didn't care." Helen's face darkened. "But then, that Monday morning, she called me at the store. She was all excited. She said she had enough money to get Gil to take her back. She wanted my advice on the best way to handle him, what to say."

Helen looked close to tears. "I drove to your house. Marlene was all fidgety and excited. She wanted to get out and take a walk while we talked. So we walked around the neighborhood. It was so quiet, no one around. She showed me the money, right there in her purse."

She put her hand to her forehead. "I'd never seen so much money. I knew it was enough to get Gil back, no matter what he said about never wanting to see her again. I was so upset I could barely talk. I—I couldn't let it happen."

Helen glanced upward. "We got to the cliff. Suddenly I knew what to do. It was so simple! Marlene was so happy she was laughing—you know how she laughed, with her head thrown back, all that hair flying. She was practically jumping up and down. I pretended to be excited, too. I laughed and jumped up and down with her, and at the same time I moved toward the edge of the cliff so she'd move with me. When I had her at the edge I grabbed her purse. She gave me this angry look, angry and surprised. And then I pushed her, right over the edge." She let out a hearty laugh. "She screamed all the way down. I was surprised no one heard anything, but like I said, there was nobody around."

She smiled slyly. "Now I had the money—and a key to your house. I walked back and parked my car in your garage. Then I let myself into the house and carried out all of Marlene's things. I stuffed everything into my trunk."

"So it was you," Jane said.

Helen nodded. "I drove back to the store. I'd done it.

I'd gotten rid of Marlene, I had enough money to get Gil, and I was going to get away with it." She gave Jane a fiercely resentful look. "Then you started snooping around. And every time you came to see me I could tell you were getting closer to finding out what really happened. I had to do something. So I decided to frame Vernon. The little creep was the likeliest suspect anyway."

Poor, hapless, besotted Vernon, Jane thought.

Helen continued. "I came down here this morning and found Marlene's body. I brought along a pair of pruning shears from my mother's gardening shed. I cut off Marlene's finger. Then I drove to Harmon's in Boonton, where Vernon works, and when no one was looking I put the finger in his car. I also took a pair of Marlene's panties from my trunk and shoved them under Vernon's backseat. Then I went to a pay phone, so I couldn't be traced, and called the Shady Hills police. I told them Vernon had the hots for Marlene and they should check him out."

Helen grinned proudly. "To make extra sure they thought Vernon did it, I drove to his house and got into his garage. I found a piece of rope. That's what I used when I attacked you. I was going to plant that in Vernon's car, too." She laughed. "I wasn't really going to kill you. I just wanted to scare you, make you stop nosing around. Anyway, that other car pulled into the parking lot, so I figured I'd better get out of there.

"Later I realized I'd better come down here and make sure Marlene's body was all covered, because if anybody found it, my framing of Vernon might not stick. So here I am. And here you are, still nosing around." She regarded Jane thoughtfully, the way one might look at a particularly stubborn stain on a shirt.

"Your timing was off," Jane said. "When you attacked me, the police had already arrested Vernon."

"Yeah, I know. Who knew the cops would get their act together and search Vernon's car so fast?" Helen shrugged. "Doesn't matter. They've got Vernon, and they'll make it stick. . . . How'd you finally figure it all out?"

"My train . . ." Jane said.

"Your what?"

"My cat knocked over my wedding picture. I was looking at the train on my wedding gown and *train* got me thinking. Then I remembered. You told me you'd driven Marlene to the train station on Monday and seen her off. *But no trains ran that day because of the derailment.*" How, she wondered, could she have missed it for so long?

"Just the same," she said, "you were seen visiting Marlene that morning. I knew someone other than Marlene had cleaned out her room, because something had been left behind that Marlene would never have forgotten."

"Oh, really? And what was that?"

"None of your business. You also let our cat out while you were moving Marlene's things to the garage. We're all very careful about not letting the cat out. Even Marlene was good about that."

There was no more to say. She would go to see Detective Greenberg, tell him everything. She cast a sorrowful glance at the mound of debris in which Marlene's body lay—poor Marlene, whose deadly sin had been to want the wrong man. "God help you," Jane said softly to Helen. Then she turned to start back through the woods.

"Stop," Helen said, and there was a faint metallic click.

Jane stopped and looked over her shoulder. Helen, her face a pasty blank, held a gun straight out before her, its muzzle aimed directly at the center of Jane's back.

Forty

"You didn't really think I was finished with you, did you?" Helen said, amused.

Once or twice in her life Jane, who knew nothing about guns and had never seen a real one before, had wondered what it would feel like to have one aimed at her. Now that it was actually happening, she felt surprisingly unafraid.

"We keep it at the store in case of a robbery," Helen explained proudly. "Now that's what I call a convenience store!" She laughed, then abruptly stopped, her face returning to its grim expressionlessness. "But I'm not going to use this. Not if I can help it. I'm going to get rid of you the same way I got rid of Marlene. It's a fool-proof method. But I will shoot you if I have to. Walk."

Jane led the way back through the woods, Helen crunching along behind her. As they cleared the trees, Jane saw Helen's old gray car parked at the side of the road.

"Get in," Helen said, and kept the gun trained on Jane

as she herself got behind the wheel. She started the car, one hand on the wheel, the other holding the gun on Jane, and drove up Lilac Way, past Jane's house. She turned left onto Magnolia Lane and followed it, past Roger's bungalow, until she reached Hawthorne Place, Mr. O'Rourke's cul-de-sac. She parked at the side farthest from the cliff's edge, close against the trees. Reaching across Jane's lap, she opened the glove compartment and took out a large flashlight.

"Get out."

Jane got out of the car and waited while Helen came around.

"Let's go," Helen said. "You know where we're going."

Jane marched toward the cliff's edge. Her mind raced— she had to think fast. She considered screaming but rejected that idea for fear Helen would panic and shoot her. She thought of Nick as an orphan and prayed she would think of something before it was too late.

Slowly, so as not to spook Helen, she turned to face her. "Helen, please. Think about what you've done, what you're doing. You're ill. You need help."

Helen threw back her head and laughed. "Aw, shut the hell up!" she said, and suddenly gave Jane a hard shove in the center of her chest.

Jane, thrown off-balance, flew backwards into nothingness. "Aaaiiiihhhh!" she screamed as she sailed through the air, and then the ground came up and hit her so hard it knocked the wind out of her and something cracked in her leg and she was rolling, down the rocky slope over rocks and bumpy earth and roots and branches.

Somehow she got her hand around one of the roots and gripped it tight, the rest of her body skidding downward. But still she held on and, scrambling with her feet, found a foothold among the rocks.

She was alive. Not dead like Marlene. Alive.

Carefully she glanced upward. She estimated that she was approximately fifteen feet from the top of the cliff, about halfway down. She couldn't see Helen. Praying that Helen believed that, like Marlene, she had fallen all the way to the bottom, Jane remained perfectly still, waiting for the sound of Helen's car starting.

But instead she heard the much deeper rumble of what sounded like a truck, and then headlights illuminated the top of the cliff. In the next instant Helen clambered over the edge and crouched on a ledge about five feet from the top.

What was going on?

Jane could see the flashlight in Helen's left hand, the gun in her right. Helen looked down, switched on the flashlight, and shone it on the debris at the bottom. Then she began slowly scanning the slope with the flashlight's powerful beam.

Jane froze. The beam passed over her—then quickly returned. Jane looked up at Helen and their eyes met. Helen leveled the gun at her. Jane knew that if she screamed for help to whoever had arrived at the top, Helen would shoot her.

The engine of whatever had arrived at the top continued to rumble. Agonizing pain shot continuously up Jane's right leg into her thigh. Her leg was no doubt broken. Her left foot rested on a narrow spur of rock that barely provided room for the toe of her shoe. She realized she needed to gain a better foothold because she wouldn't be able to perch like this much longer. Ever so carefully, she pivoted her foot, trying to dig deeper into the soil of the cliff face. The rock she was standing on came loose and fell away. Frantically, she dug at the soil for another toehold, but she only caused more rocks and dirt to crumble and fall, leaving her foot dangling.

Her hands burned, raw from clutching the rough roots. She couldn't stay here like this much longer. Falling was inevitable. Perhaps if she could control the fall ... She glanced back at Helen, who was still watching her, still training the gun on her. Jane knew her only chance of surviving was to move, and the only place to move was down.

She let go.

She slid down the slope, desperately trying to grab at the roots and branches and spurs of rock, but the weight of her own body pulled her swiftly down. She hit a bush which thrust her sideways and then she was rolling, grunting with each jolt, each sharp bump, the pain in her leg like fire.

Finally she reached the bottom and came to a sudden jolting stop against the mound of debris. She heard a scrabbling sound and, turning her head slightly, saw Helen sliding down the cliffside. Helen had more luck than Jane and reached the bottom without rolling. But when she turned toward Jane she no longer had the flashlight—she must have lost it coming down.

Jane knew she had better move. Fighting the searing pain in her leg, she managed to stand. Then she began limping toward the woods and the road beyond, hoping Helen wouldn't shoot as long as there was someone at the top.

Jane glanced back. Helen was chasing her, gaining quickly. When Helen was about ten feet behind Jane, a sharp cracking sound came from the trees. Both women stopped and stared into the shadows.

Faintly Jane could make out the silhouette of a person standing among the trees, absolutely still.

"Who's there?" Helen demanded in a raspy whisper.

Whoever it was made no response.

Helen shifted the gun to the dark figure and stepped closer, squinting. "Say who you are or I'll shoot you."

A dark extension seemed to grow from the silhouette. From the extension's tip a yellow burst of light appeared, and there was a loud popping sound.

Behind Jane, Helen made a strange grunting noise. Jane turned to her. In the center of Helen's forehead was a round black hole the size of a quarter. Helen teetered, fell backward, and lay still.

The figure stepped from the shadows.

It was Dorothy Peyton, the plain blond actress from the play.

Jane nodded. She'd had all of it right.

"Hello, Marlene," she said. "We've missed you."

Forty-one

"Nosy bitch." She spit out the words, her expression one of utter loathing—far more emotion, Jane reflected, than she'd exhibited in *Subways*. "And you're smart, aren't you? Figured it out."

Jane simply nodded.

Marlene shrugged. "We only meant it as a game, a prank. We thought of it on the plane from Detroit. All of a sudden we realized that each of us wanted to do what the other would be doing. I would be working for you as a nanny, but I wanted to be an actress and live in New York. Zena would be studying fashion design in New York, but she wanted an easy, partying life in a quiet town."

Marlene giggled. "So we traded places. We agreed to call each other at least once a week so we could each be convincing when we spoke to our parents. Of course, we had to work it out so our parents never called *us*. So Zena told her parents she had this roommate who worked nights and slept during the day and couldn't be disturbed. Zena would call them. My mother and I agreed you were rich enough to pay for my calls to her."

Jane had to smile at that. "You thought I was rich?"

"Of course. You're an agent, aren't you? . . . So how'd you figure it out?"

"First, that whole elaborate story about the roommate just didn't ring true," Jane said. "Second, the fact that Zena wouldn't give her parents her address, either, supposedly because their checks would be stolen from her mail. Highly suspect.

"Third, the fact that Zena often didn't answer when I called her Marlene.

"Fourth, I remembered that you had planned to study acting at college, before you decided not to go.

"Fifth, Helen threw a birthday party for 'Marlene' in September. But that was Zena's real birthday. I'd completely forgotten that you were born in March.

"Finally, when I realized that Zena's parents had stopped hearing from her at the same time 'Marlene' had disappeared from Shady Hills, it all made sense."

"For a while it worked beautifully," Marlene said. "Zena found herself a boyfriend—Gil—and I moved in with Trevor. He's helping me build my career, giving me acting lessons."

Then you need a new teacher, Jane thought.

"But then Zena stopped calling me," Marlene said. "I knew she wasn't calling her parents, either, because they kept writing to the post-office box, telling her to call them. That's why I called your house and asked for Marlene.

"Then you came to the theater and left that note. Now

I knew she wasn't here. I would have called my mother to get her and you off my back, but I didn't know what to tell her yet. Finally, I realized I'd better come out here myself and find out what was going on. I borrowed Trev's car."

"And his gun?"

Shaking her head, Marlene held up the gun and studied it. "This is mine. I've had it since I was sixteen. You need one in the part of Detroit where I hung out."

"If your mother only knew . . ." Jane said.

"There's a lot my mother doesn't know. Anyway, I drove past your house, and as I was coming down the hill, I saw you walking."

"How did you know it was me?"

"My mother has pictures of you in our living room. Her 'old friend,' " Marlene added sarcastically. "I parked up the hill and followed you down here. I couldn't figure out what you were doing, so I watched from the trees here. I saw you looking around. I saw . . . Zena. I saw the whole thing with Helen. Now I knew what happened to Zena. My beautiful friend who loved danger. And got in way over her head. Got herself murdered.

"I was just going to leave quietly. But then I accidentally stepped on a stick and gave myself away. I knew that if I didn't kill Helen, she'd kill me. So I killed her. And now I have to kill you, Jane. I can't let you run to the cops and tell them what I've done. I've got too much going for me. I have a whole new wonderful life now. I don't want my old life anymore. No one will figure out what happened to Marlene and Zena. And Dorothy Peyton will live happily ever after."

She leveled her gun at Jane's chest.

"Somebody down there?" a man's voice bellowed down from the top of the cliff.

Both women jumped.

"Keep quiet," Marlene ordered in a low voice.

Jane kept quiet, but she took a step back, then another, to make sure Marlene noticed. Marlene did notice, her brows knitting in a fierce frown of warning, and she took several steps toward Jane. She stopped at the edge of the mound of refuse, not four feet from Zena's chalky white upraised arm.

Just where Jane wanted her.

"Guess not," came the man's voice again. "Okay, let's do it and get outta here."

God forgive me, Jane thought.

From the top of the cliff came a loud groan of metal machinery. Marlene looked up, puzzled. There was a low rumbling sound, like the start of an avalanche. Then, as both women looked up, from over the cliff's edge poured what must have been a ton of rocks, dirt, wood, and plaster.

Realization suddenly dawning, Marlene screamed and covered her head with her arms.

It was her head that got hit first, smashed in by a watermelon-sized block of concrete. She crumpled straight down and was instantly buried by the rest of the debris that came crushing down on her with a sickening roar and a cloud of plaster dust.

Now from the top of the cliff came the hollower sound of the dump truck's hydraulics lowering the empty hopper back into place. Doors slammed. The rumble of the truck's engine faded to silence.

Jane realized she was crying uncontrollably. She felt her face contort, felt tears running down her cheeks. She took one last look at the smoldering mountain of waste. Then, crying out at the burning spear of pain that shot up her leg and thigh, she turned and took her first slow limping step toward the road.

Forty-two

It was the following Monday. Jane sat at her desk, forcing herself to make some sense of the chaos, to at least organize the long-neglected mountain of work into rough piles.

Not that her time was really her own now. The police would have many more questions. Ivy was still in town, and would stay until the police were finished with Marlene's body and Ivy could arrange for the funeral. The Harmons were here, waiting for Zena's body to be released. Jane imagined Helen's mother was waiting for Helen's body, too.

Jane wondered if Helen had hidden the money she'd taken from Marlene, wondered if Helen's mother would find it. Jane hadn't told the police about the money. Not that she cared about protecting Roger, but she had promised Audrey. And a promise is a promise. As far as the police knew, Helen had simply killed Marlene because Marlene had taken the man Helen wanted.

The reporters loved that story, called it juicy. Evil in a deceptively peaceful village, and all that. One TV reporter called it delicious. Hardly the word Jane would have used. Jane had talked to the reporters, would talk to more. Why not? The publicity might get her some new business.

One reporter, from a local newspaper, had asked, "How did you finally put the whole puzzle together?" Jane had explained that it had been her cat knocking down her wedding picture that had done the trick. The reporter had titled his story "Cat Solves Swapped Nanny Murder."

Jane had to laugh at that. Let Winky have the credit. She deserved it.

From the outer office Jane heard a knock on the front door, then the sounds of Daniel speaking to someone and the door closing again. Jane grabbed her crutches and hobbled out to see what was going on.

Daniel was sitting down at his desk. He looked up. "A reporter. I told him we're busy and to come back later."

Nervy, Jane thought, *for someone who's leaving in a week and a half.* But she said nothing, only smiled faintly and nodded. It wasn't worth arguing about.

"Jane," he said. "This manuscript, the one you didn't think was worth taking on. Would you mind terribly if I did take it on—after asking her to revise, of course."

Extremely nervy, she thought. "You mean take it with you to Silver and Payne?" She shrugged indifferently. "Do as you like. I don't want it."

"But *we'd* be representing it."

She frowned, confused. "What are you talking about? *You'd* be representing it—at Silver and Payne."

"Jane," he said, smiling now, "this is my cute way of telling you I'm not leaving . . . if you'll let me stay."

She stared at him. Finally she said, "You're not going to Silver and Payne?"

"No. We both knew it wasn't right for me. I belong here."

She nodded, staring hard at the floor, fighting down the lump in her throat.

"Jane, why are you crying?"

"I'm not." She crutch-walked back into her office and sat at her desk. Now the tears began to flow in earnest. She covered her face with her hands and soon found she was laughing, laughing in exultation.

She took her hands away and wiped her eyes. Then she turned to the photo of her and Kenneth and Nick in Cape May and smiled.

With new vigor, she attacked the pile of work on her desk.

There was so much to do.

Please read on
for an exciting sneak peek at
Evan Marshall's
newest Jane Stuart and Winky mystery
HANGING HANNAH
now on sale wherever hardcover mysteries are sold!

One

"Jane, can you help me with these rocks?" Ginny scrambled around the long picnic table, placing rocks from the supply of them in her arms at each corner of the table and at intervals along the sides. "This wind is fierce!"

She was right—the wind was strong, and without the rocks the tablecloth would have blown away. But it was a glorious day nonetheless, a perfect Sunday afternoon in May. The sun shone brightly in a cloudless china blue sky, birds sang in the woods surrounding the inn's backyard, and the air carried that scent of honeysuckle Jane had picked up leaving the Defarge Club meeting Tuesday night.

Suddenly the wind rose, flapping the edges of the canvas awning that shaded the patio. The tablecloth lifted at the edges, as if it would fly away.

"You know," Jane said, grabbing some rocks from Ginny and placing them between the ones already there, "they make special clips to hold tablecloths down. They have them at Kmart. This rock thing is what my *mother* did."

"I like the old-fashioned way," Ginny said defensively, though she was smiling as if she knew Jane was right.

"Me too," Louise chimed in, emerging from the inn with a tray of brightly colored napkins and plastic cups, plates, and forks. "It's more fun this way. Like ants at a picnic."

Jane shrugged. She gazed far across the lawn at Nick and his friends, who were playing a game Nick had made up called *Star Wars* tag. Nick shouted, "Obi!" and tore across the lawn, squealing with laughter. The dozen or so other boys and girls bolted after him.

"Aren't they sweet?" Ginny was watching them wistfully. Jane and Louise exchanged a silent, sympathetic look.

Louise worked her way around the table, setting down plates. "I'll leave the napkins in a pile over here," she said.

"Yes, under a rock," Ginny said, and plunked one down on the pile.

The door of the inn opened again and Doris appeared, barely visible behind a stack of pizza boxes.

"Doris!" Jane ran to her. "Let me help you with those." She relieved the older woman of half the boxes and set them down at one end of the table.

"Such a fuss," Doris said in her deep brisk voice, and set her boxes on top of Jane's. Doris, who was seventy-two, hated being treated like an old person. She put her hands on her hips and surveyed the table. "Now what?"

"Nothing, really, until the pizza comes," Louise said. "The children are having a wonderful time. How about some lemonade for us?"

"Sounds good to me," Ginny said.

"Me too," Doris said, sitting on a bench of the picnic table.

Ernie rounded the corner of the inn. "Did I hear 'lemonade'?" he asked brightly.

Louise's smile vanished. "I'll get it, dear." She was all business now. "And I'd better make sure the cake is ready. Twelve candles, right, Jane? Ten years, one for good luck, and one to grow on—that's how we've always done it."

"That sounds perfect," Jane said, and felt a rush of warmth for Louise, truly a good friend. Jane wondered why Louise seemed troubled about Ernie. Perhaps they were in the midst of some squabble.

Ernie dropped his ample form into an Adirondack chair near the door and smiled at the children, who were now piling all over Nick and screaming, "Darth! Darth!"

"I want to be a kid again," Ernie said dreamily. "Things were so simple then."

"Hello, all!" Penny appeared around from around the side of the inn, carrying an enormous box wrapped in vivid Looney Tunes paper. She set the box at the corner of the patio.

"Penny," Jane said, "what on earth—?"

"You said Nick liked *Star Wars*. This is Boba Fett's spaceship, or whatever it's called."

"That's much too extravagant," Jane said.

"Like I said," Ernie called from across the patio, "things were simpler when I was a kid."

They all smiled.

"Penny," Jane said, "where are Alan and Rebecca?"

Penny looked down at the patio, her hair falling to each side of her face. "Alan . . . had some chores to do. He's sorry he couldn't make it."

Ginny and Jane exchanged a knowing look. Poor Penny was constantly making excuses for Alan.

"Then he's watching Rebecca?" Ginny asked.

"No, she's in the car. I'm going to get her now." Penny turned and walked back around the inn toward the front drive.

Ginny shrugged and came over to Jane. "Do I *really* want to get married and have children?"

"Yes, Ginny, you do. Not all men are like Alan."

"I guess you're right," Ginny said.

At that moment Nick ran up to Jane. His face was red and sweaty, and he was breathing hard. His shorts were covered with grass stains. "Mom, I'm hungry. Are we eating soon?" He eyed the stack of pizza boxes.

"Soon, honey. It would be rude to eat before everyone's here."

"Who's not here?"

"Daniel and Laura. And also Rhoda. I'm sure they'll be here any minute."

"I know!" Ginny said. "Let's have the scavenger hunt now."

"But that takes a long time," Nick whined, "and we're hungry."

"We can call a time-out when Daniel and Laura and Rhoda get here," Ginny said.

Nick thought for a moment. "Okay. How does this scavenger hunt work?"

Ginny grabbed her bag from the edge of the patio and

peered into it, finally bringing out several stacks of cards held together with rubber bands. "First we separate into teams. I just happen to have a list of who's on what team." From her bag she whipped out a list of the children's names grouped into teams of four.

"So efficient!" Jane commented.

"It's the waitress in me." Ginny winked. "Kids!" she hollered. "Over here, please!"

She met them in the middle of the lawn and began explaining the scavenger hunt. How sweet their faces were as they listened in rapt attention, Jane thought.

"Coming through!"

Jane turned. Rhoda rounded the corner of the inn, arms full of cardboard boxes. "Hi, all," she said brightly. "My arms are numb. I'd better get this ice cream into the freezer. Where's Louise?"

Ernie got up. "She's inside, Rhoda. I'll stick that in the freezer for you. Thanks," he said, relieving her of the boxes, and he disappeared inside.

Rhoda, looking smashing in a culotte set, came over to Jane. "Hi, hon. Read any good books lately?"

Jane smiled. "No." She looked Rhoda up and down. "Pretty snazzy for a kids' party."

"I," Rhoda announced proudly, "have a date."

Penny, who had been fussing with the napkin pile, stopped and stared at Rhoda.

Doris sat up straight. "Way to go, girl."

"Yes, Rhoda, how wonderful," Jane said. "May I ask who?"

"You may," Rhoda said, beaming. "His name is Adam and I met him at an antique store in Chester."

"He works in a store?" Doris asked flatly.

"No, Doris," Rhoda said, rolling her eyes, "he was *looking*, like me." She smiled and wiggled her perfectly tweezed brows meaningfully. "He's terrific. This isn't our first date."

"Way to *go*," Doris repeated.

Somehow even Ginny in the middle of the lawn heard this, and suddenly turned toward Rhoda with a bright smile. "That's fantastic, Rhoda!" She turned back to the kids. "Now everybody got it? Ready . . . set . . . GO!"

"Thanks," Rhoda said to everyone, looking quite pleased with herself. "I'm meeting him for a movie and dinner later."

"Wonderful," Jane murmured. To her own surprise, she felt a pang of envy. Rhoda's divorce wasn't even final and she was already snagging terrific men in antique shops. Jane wondered if maybe she ought to develop an interest in that area.

"What's wonderful?" Daniel, dapper in a blue-and-white seersucker jacket over navy slacks and polo shirt, appeared bearing a small wrapped gift under his arm.

"My date," Rhoda said, coming up to Daniel and planting a kiss on his cheek. "Good to see you." She looked him up and down. "Damn, you're cute. If you're ever available, don't you forget old Rhoda!"

Jane looked at the easily embarrassed Daniel to see if this had flustered him, but he took Rhoda's comment with good grace.

"Where's Laura—your *fiancée*?" Jane asked, shooting a pointed look at Rhoda, who gave her a mischievous grin.

"She went in the front," Daniel said. "Needed to use the ladies'. Now," he said, producing a small camera from his jacket pocket, "before I forget, let's get shots of us for that convention you got us roped into."

"Wonderful think-of-everything Daniel," Jane said. "I forgot all about it."

"I knew that," Daniel said cheerfully, looking around. "How about right over here, in front of Louise's azaleas?"

"Sounds good to me," Jane said, feeling a flutter of nervousness in her stomach at the thought of the RAT convention and wishing he hadn't brought it up. She positioned herself in front of the vivid mass of fuchsia flowers while Daniel took her picture; then they traded places and she took his.

"Good, that's done," Jane said. "Thank you, Daniel."

At that moment Ernie emerged from inn. He looked preoccupied, and suddenly put on a smile as he stepped out onto the patio.

Behind him came Laura, smiling innocently. "Hello, hello." She looked summer stylish in a short lavender dress and a matching wide-brimmed hat that sat at a perfect angle on her light brown hair and complemented her pretty heart-shaped face.

"Love it," Rhoda said, eyeing the hat.

"Thanks," Laura said. "I thought it might be too—"

But before she could finish, the wind picked up her hat and carried it high into the air. "Oh, my!" she cried.

Daniel darted off to fetch it, but before he had reached the middle of the lawn he stopped short because a long shrill cry tore the air, and as it did a flurry of small black birds rose from the edge of the woods into the sky.

For the briefest moment Jane, in the confusion, thought the piercing shriek came from the birds. Then she realized, with a sharp intake of breath and a painful pounding of her heart, that the high-pitched sound was the terrified scream of a child.

And that that child was Nick.

Two

"Nicholas!" Jane cried.

She ran across the grass toward the source of his scream, the other adults close behind her. She realized now that the children had been in the woods, presumably gathering items for their scavenger hunt. Jane could see neither Ginny nor any of the children through the trees, but as Jane neared them, she could hear children crying.

She was the first to enter the woods, by means of a path that bored into the shadows between two wide oak trunks. She had walked only a few feet when she nearly collided with Ginny, who stood on the path with her back toward Jane and was calling desperately to the children, whom Jane could see just beyond her.

"Kids, quickly! Come out, follow me!" Ginny, oblivious of Jane and the others behind her, moved quickly among the children, roughly shepherding them toward the path that led out of the woods. Jane spotted Nick. His face was sickly white and tears ran down his cheeks. Ginny grabbed his shoulder and pushed him after the other children. At that moment Nick saw Jane and ran to her, hugging her hard.

Jane felt someone bump her from behind and turned her head. It was Ernie, who was looking past her with a look of alarm.

"Ginny, what on earth is going on?" he demanded.

Ginny, having gotten all of the children headed out of the woods, spun around to look at him. Jane had never seen her like this. Her face was white, almost green, and she looked as if she was trying hard not to pass out. She said nothing, instead pointing with her eyes to something deeper in the woods.

"Oh, good Lord . . ." Doris whispered.

They could see only feet, grimy feet in sandals, dangling about a foot and a half off the ground. Foliage obstructed the rest, and Jane, followed by the others, moved slowly around.

Jane's hands flew to her face. "My God." It was a young woman, thin, in a simple pale blue cotton dress sprinkled with tiny white flowers. She hung by the neck from a noose at the end of a rope that had been thrown over a heavy branch; from the branch the rope extended straight and tight at a downward angle to where it was tied to the base of another tree's trunk.

"Who is she?" Penny said softly.

Jane studied the woman. She didn't think it was anyone she knew but it was impossible to know for sure because even in the dappled shade of the trees it was clear that the woman's face was covered with garish makeup, almost like a clown: a red circle of blush, like old-fashioned rouge, on each cheek; scarlet lipstick applied so sloppily that it extended well past her lips to create a weird oval red mouth; deep blue eye shadow on her eyelids, which were, mercifully, closed. Her hair was an ordinary brown and shoulder length; it hung straight and limp—as if, it occurred to Jane, she'd had a bad haircut. Jane squinted, studying the woman's face harder. Could she be faintly smiling? It seemed so, but this, too, was impossible to say for sure because of the lipstick. If not for the unnatural angle of her head, she might have been peacefully asleep, so relaxed was her face, so gently closed were her eyes. But that was how death often looked, Jane told herself. That was what death was—a kind of sleep.

The wind rose, rustling the leaves on the trees, playing with the girl's hair. Goose bumps rose on Jane's arms, and she shivered.

"Does anybody know her?" Ernie asked softly, and Jane jumped at the sound of his voice.

No one answered.

"Come on, let's get away from her," Louise said, taking control, and like automatons everyone turned and started back along the path.

Nick held Jane's hand tightly. She realized now that she should have shepherded him out of the woods with the other children, that she'd allowed him to study the poor hanging woman along with the grown-ups.

"Mom?" Nick was crying. "Who is she?"

"I don't know, darling," was all Jane could say, wrapping her arm tightly around his shoulder. "I don't know."

ABOUT THE AUTHOR

Like his sleuth, Jane Stuart, Evan Marshall heads his own literary agency. He lives and works in Pine Brook, New Jersey, where he is at work on his third Jane Stuart mystery (to be published in 2001). He enjoys hearing from readers and can be reached at *evanmarshall@thenovelist.com*.